MONSTER AMONG THE ROSES

A Beauty and the Beast Story

LINDA KAGE

Monster Among the Roses

Contact Information: linda@lindakage.com

Publishing History
Linda Kage, July 2017
ISBN-13: 978-1546573678
ISBN-10: 1546573674

Credits
Cover Artist: Kage Covers
Editor: Stephanie Parent
Proofreader: Judy and Shelley

chapter ONE

I nervously twisted my ball cap between my hands, the frayed bill skimming across my calloused knuckles with each pass. The room where I waited was bigger than my entire apartment, and the seat on which I gingerly perched myself probably cost more than everything I owned.

It smelled rich in here. Like money. Like the walls had been papered in fresh, crisp hundred-dollar bills straight from the bank. I glanced between my knees to my shoes, hoping I hadn't knocked any dirt onto the opaque marble floor, only to discover a small clump of dried mud did rest by my right sneaker. Shit. I quickly kicked it under the chair to hide the evidence just as the door beside me opened.

A gray-headed woman in a blue pantsuit—the same one I'd spoken to, announcing myself when I'd arrived twenty minutes earlier—peered out. "Mr. Nash is ready to meet with you."

Feeling caught in the act, I stopped messing with the dirt clod and jerked to my feet, my face flushing hotly. I started to slide my hat back on to hide what must be a nasty case of hat hair, only to wonder if it would appear more respectful to keep a hat off when meeting a man such as Henry Nash. After hesitating a good five seconds, unsure of what to do, I pulled the hat on. This was who I was. Putting on airs felt deceitful.

Nodding to the secretary to let her know I was ready, I followed her inside the lion's den, only to slow to an intimidated stop just inside the doorway. If I'd been daunted by the opulence of the waiting room, the interior of Henry Nash's office blew me away. Huge mural-sized paintings would've given the museum effect if the slate-gray chairs in front of a colossal black granite and silver desk hadn't screamed corporate office. I was afraid to move and track more mud across the floor. Hell, *breathing* in this place felt taboo.

I didn't belong here. What had I been thinking to schedule a meeting with *the* Henry Nash? He was going to laugh me from his museum office before I could even start begging.

The massive chair behind the desk revolved to face me just as the man planted in it hung up the phone on which he'd been talking. Then he stood.

"Ah, Mr. Hollander." Rounding his desk, he strode toward me where I stood petrified in the doorway. "It's nice to finally meet you. Your mother's said only good things."

The mention of my mom caused the ball of dread in my throat to harden and cut off my air.

"How is she?" he asked as he held out a hand for me to shake. The question was pleasant and polite. The look in his eyes was kind and interested. The entire way he'd come to me, not made me approach him, was just—I wanted to shake my head, confused.

I'd built this man up in my mind as a rich, heartless beast who ate baby kittens for breakfast and flambéed the weak and needy for dinner. He stomped on dreams and mocked the poor, gaining power with each tear he forced to fall. The overdue notices that littered our mail with increasing regularity, demanding money, only seemed to enhance my impression of him.

But here he stood, a normal mortal with a slight paunch to the gut and thinning hair on top, and…and he *smiled* at me as if he were genuinely pleased to meet me.

Flustered, I didn't know what to say. What to do.

"She…uh…she's…" Quickly, I reached out to shake with him. His skin was warm, dry—human—and his grip was sincere. "She's not well," I blurted.

Damn, I'd hoped to work into that topic subtly.

"Oh?" Mr. Nash tipped his head to the side, concern marring his eyebrows.

"Yeah, she…" I ripped my hat off and began to fidget with it again.

"Here." Mr. Nash stretched out a hand, inviting me further into the office. "Let's sit and discuss it. Miss Givens…" He nodded to the secretary, and she left the room, shutting me inside the grandiose office alone…with the one man who could destroy my mother.

Palms sweating, I wiped them on my thighs and followed him to a chair placed in front of his desk. Instead of moving back around behind the table, he sat in the other seat next to mine. It didn't put me at ease, as I think was his intent; I only felt closer to the chopping block now.

"Tell me about Margaret."

At the mention of Mom's name, I blew out a long, steadying breath. I was here for her, here to beg and accept anything Henry Nash wanted of me. For my mother, I could do this.

"Well," I started slowly, swiping my tongue over dry lips. "As you know, she fell and broke her hip about three months ago."

"*Did* she?" Mr. Nash lifted his eyebrows, the soul of ignorance and surprise, maybe even worry.

His shock confused me. "Yeah…" I said slowly, trying to discern if he was lying and really knew or if he honestly hadn't a clue. "Didn't she mention it when she asked for the loan extension?"

The older man opened his mouth, only to shut it. He seemed to deliberate something before speaking again. "I'm sorry, but your mother never asked me for a loan extension."

I stared at him.

What? Of course, Mom had asked. She'd *told* me she'd been denied. She'd told me…what the hell had she told me? My brain sputtered, trying to remember her exact words.

I was sure she'd gone to Nash Corporation and asked for some leniency. She'd sworn that she'd tried everything. Wouldn't everything logically include asking for a loan extension? That was why I was here. If Henry Nash wouldn't listen to my poor, broken mother, maybe I could get him to listen to me, maybe I'd have more to bargain with than she'd had.

But if Mom hadn't even talked to him—

I shook my head, denying the possibility. Of course, she'd asked for an extension. Anyone in her position would. "Maybe she asked one of your people and it just never got back to you," I allowed.

Except the man before me squinted in doubt. "All requests for loan extensions are passed through me, Mr. Hollander. I make those final decisions."

My shoulders collapsed. Well, this changed things. This…

I needed to regroup and figure out what to do.

Except no, honestly, it didn't change much at all…maybe just the way I viewed the man before me.

Mr. Nash cleared his throat discreetly. "If I may, I know your mother's been behind on her payments. Very behind. And I *am* aware the people who come to me for a loan usually do so after they've been declined help from the bank. Lending your mother money to start her bakery was a risk. I was aware of this from the beginning and made my own allowances to prepare for any worst-case scenario. So, if Margaret has fallen on hard times and needs some leeway, I'm perfectly willing to—"

"You don't understand," I blurted harshly, causing Mr. Nash to pull back and blink at me. Running my hands over my face, I clenched my teeth and tried to quell the rising panic. After taking a moment to calm myself, I quietly confessed, "It's worse than that. We had to close the bakery." And we were about to be evicted from our apartment if we didn't pay our back rent, and the medical bills kept coming, and the utilities never stopped, and—

And it was enough to make me feel as if I couldn't breathe every time I thought about it.

"It's gone way past needing an extension." I hated to expose this. I felt like a failure every time I thought it. Saying it aloud, to Henry Nash, might possibly be the most humiliating moment of my life. "At the state we're in, I don't see how we could ever pay you back."

"Oh." Mr. Nash calmly clasped his hands together as he studied me. His intent gaze seemed to bore through my skull as if he were searching for all my innermost thoughts. Then he murmured, "You looked like a man on a mission when you came into my office, Mr. Hollander. It makes me think you have an idea about how you want to resolve this problem."

I gave a slight nod. "I do."

He nodded back to me. "Then I think I'd be very interested to hear it."

"A trade," I said, without thinking.

Mr. Nash lifted his eyebrows. "A trade? What kind of trade?"

"My mother's debt," I said, pausing before I added, "For me."

With a squint, the other man slowly began to shake his head. "I'm afraid I don't understand."

"I swear, I'll be at your service, do whatever you want me to do, for the rest of my life, if...if you wipe away her debts." I said it this way in the hopes he'd take care of *all* her debt, not just the one she owed him.

"At my service," he repeated, cocking his head to the side as if trying to understand what I really meant. "In what way?"

I shrugged. "Any way you want. I'll do anything." When he simply blinked at me, I more emphatically added, "*Anything*."

I wasn't stupid. I knew men as powerful and rich as Henry Nash had to have gotten to this point by doing a little bit of dirty work. I was fully prepared to be one of his dirty men, deliver illegal supplies, break kneecaps, help him cover up his dark deeds, whatever he required of me. It made me feel sick and slimy every time my mind wandered in that direction, but to save Mom, I would cope.

He repeated, "Anything?" as if an idea had started to brew in his head.

I nodded and eagerly sat forward. "If you would help my mother, I'd give you my life."

I could tell my passion impressed him. His raised eyebrows yet considering gaze said as much. But he kept the rest of his thoughts close. Drawing his clasped hands up to his chin, he measured me pensively.

"Tell me this, son. If I clear your mother's debt in exchange for your servitude, how do you foresee her taking care of herself after that? I mean, with no bakery to bring money in, a broken hip to prevent her from seeking work elsewhere, and a son who will no longer be there to help—as he will then belong to me—what do you think will happen to her?"

I gulped, not quite able to ask the bold, daring thing I really wanted to ask.

But Mr. Nash must've read the plea on my face. "Oh, I see. You don't want me to just help her out of her debt to me. You're actually asking for more financial assistance. I'm assuming you want me to set her up for the rest of her life, then?"

I couldn't speak. My voice box had frozen over with fear, anxiety, and hope. So I merely nodded humbly before I bowed my head, bracing to be forcibly removed from his office for my brazen request.

He drew in a deep breath, and for the longest time that was the only sound he made. He waited until I looked up before he exhaled. "You must think very highly of your ability to serve, Mr. Hollander."

"I…" I flushed. Honestly, I didn't think I was worth the lavish chair I sat on. But my pride was the first thing to go when it was my mother's future on the line.

"I'll do anything," I whispered.

Mr. Nash ran his gaze over me, from head to toe. It was such a personal scrutiny I almost felt violated. A new thought struck. Oh hell, what if his idea of service meant something more…carnal? I gulped, wondering if maybe there were a few things I wouldn't do after all.

Then the old man made it worse by asking, "How old are you…Shaw's your given name, isn't it?"

My skin crawled and my stomach churned. "What?"

He made an amused sound. "I inquired about your age."

"I…I'm twenty-eight," I confessed, hoping maybe I was too old for his taste.

But then I thought about all twenty-eight of those years—all that time I'd had to make something of myself—and a swell of shame consumed me. So many people I'd attended school with had gone on to become successful and accomplished. I felt as if I was still drowning under bills and trying to keep my mother from losing everything.

"Do you not have employment elsewhere?"

More humiliation coated me. Ducking my head, I cleared my throat and admitted, "The, uh, the factory where I worked went out of business about six months ago."

I'd been approached by other factory owners almost immediately; word had gotten around I was an honest, dependable, and hard worker. But Mom had already been having trouble at her shop. She'd been forced to let go of all her employees and the bank had just foreclosed on her house, so I'd moved her into my one-bedroom apartment, sold my truck to pay off one of her loans, and tried to salvage her business.

"I started helping my mother at the bakery, but…" I shook my head.

By the time I'd become involved, there was no saving it. Mom never should've been allowed to run her own business. Always the bleeding heart and more concerned with helping others than making a profit, she'd only accumulated more debt instead of paying any off. She'd never charged what she should to customers, oftentimes giving away her food for free to people in need. Then she'd trusted the wrong people, er, person, her own daughter to be exact.

"You have other siblings, though, isn't that correct? Five if I remember. Could they not—"

"No," I damn-near snapped before flushing hard from embarrassment. But mentioning my older brothers and sisters lately was a prickly point for me. None of them were willing to help. Justin had flat-out refused, coolly stating Mom shouldn't have gotten herself into such a mess in the first place. Alice never answered her phone, avoiding us at all costs. Mom and I had both lost contact with Bryce and Becky. No idea where they even were. And Victoria was a big reason why we were in this mess in the first place. She'd actually helped Mom start her shop, only to turn around and empty the bakery's bank account before taking off to parts unknown.

Clearing my throat, I glanced away before more quietly admitting, "They're not…*available* to help."

"I see," Mr. Nash murmured. I was beginning to hate it when he said that. Just what the hell did he really *see*?

Certain that whatever he saw in me couldn't be good, I blew out a silent breath of defeat. Coming here had been a fool's mission. No way would he help me. If I were him, *I* wouldn't help me.

Mr. Nash lowered his hands to the arm of the chair. "Well, I think we can work out a deal," he announced, sounding way too jovial. "How soon can you start?"

My mouth fell open, unable to quite believe what I'd just heard.

I wanted to ask, *start what*? What exactly did he have in mind for me? But I was afraid to hear the answer. So I said, "Anytime. Now. Whenever you want."

He chuckled and rose to his feet. "I like the enthusiasm, but I think tomorrow will be soon enough." Snagging a pen and notepad from his desk, he jotted something down. "Can you make it to this address in the morning by nine?"

A disorienting sense of surreal doom struck me. Was this really happening? Fortunate things never happened to me. There had to be a catch.

"I… Yeah, sure." To save my mother, I'd be wherever he needed me to be, whenever he asked.

He nodded in satisfaction. "Good. I'll draw up a contract tonight, agreeing that I'll help your mother through her financial situation in exchange for your services, and we can go over it when you arrive. Then you can get started."

He tore the top piece of paper from the pad and handed it to me to reveal he'd only listed a street address. A bead of sweat coursed down the center of my back. It was cold and made me shiver.

With no doubt in my mind I'd just sold my soul to the devil, I said, "Okay. I'll be there." And then I thanked him from the bottom of my ill-fated heart.

chapter TWO

What the…?

I stood at the end of the drive that led up to 24 Porterfield Lane and gaped. With another glance at the Post-it note in my sweaty hand containing Mr. Nash's heavy scrawl, I took in the numbers and letters before turning my attention back to the brick-covered mailbox that said *24 Porterfield Lane.*

Right address.

Shaking my head, I faced the gate. A metal sign hung from it, telling me I'd arrived at *Porter Hall Estate, Residence of Entrepreneur Henry Nash.*

Holy shit, this was his home. He'd brought me to his house. The place had to span at least fifteen acres just to make up the manicured front lawn. A row of evergreens concealed most of the building from the road, but a couple stories still peeked up above them. And from what I could see, the mansion was huge. I'm talking over ten-thousand-square-feet huge.

I shook my head and pressed the intercom button

located on the brick pillar part of the closed gate.

When a female voice flickered through the speaker, asking, "Can I help you?" I cleared my dry throat, growing more nervous by the second.

"I, uh...yeah. Shaw Hollander here to see Mr. Nash."

"Of course. Come on up."

Come on up? Were they sure? It didn't feel as if I should. This kind of place was so far above me, even standing this close to the property felt as if I was doing something wrong.

But one half of the wrought iron steel bars began to peel away from the other half, inviting me inside. My heart gave a wild jolt. What the hell was I doing? Why had I agreed to *anything*? How was I going to live with myself afterward if he...if he...?

God, I thought I might be sick to my stomach.

Ornamental pear trees lined the driveway and provided a nice shade for me to walk under, but my stomach continued to roll. A clammy sweat stuck to my brow and gathered under my pits. I hadn't realized 24 Porterfield Lane would be so far out of town and away from my rundown neighborhood. It had taken me an hour and a half to get here on foot, and now I probably stunk to high heaven.

Maybe that would turn Mr. Nash off, and I'd be saved from "servicing" him today. Or maybe he'd require me to bathe first. Fuck, what if he wanted to bathe *with* me?

I couldn't do this. I couldn't do this. I couldn't...damn it. I was going to do whatever I needed to do...I think. My mother's life depended on it.

Okay, fine. I had no idea what I was going to do. And that made me more uneasy, not only over what he'd require of me, but how I'd react to it.

Reaching the beginning of the lane, I cleared the pear trees, then more evergreens and—wow—beheld the beauty of the Nash homestead. Porter Hall. Never in my life had I been in a house so nice. I felt too filthy and poor to even stand here, looking at it. With another glance at the soggy note in my hand to make absolutely certain I was in the right place, I straightened my shoulders and marched toward the front door. Didn't matter if I was freaking out inside; I would face whatever I had to face.

It occurred to me that maybe I should've found a side entrance—more of a servant door—to knock on just as this one opened. A woman in her forties smiled out at me. "Mr. Hollander?"

I nodded. "Um, yeah. That's me."

She smiled reassuringly. "Come in. I'm Constance, the housekeeper. Mr. Nash is expecting you in his study, if you'll just follow me."

"Sure." After stepping inside, I peered up open-mouthed at the two-story foyer with a grand, curving staircase, a fountain in the center, and—

"This way," Constance called, jerking my attention from what I swear was a fish tank inlaid into the freaking floor around the base of the fountain.

Hurrying my pace, I almost ran into a naked baby with wings, posing on a pedestal and holding a bow and arrow, because I was still so busy gaping at the goldfish swimming underfoot.

Grateful I hadn't impaled myself on the statue's arrowhead, I decided to actually watch where I was going. I followed Constance down the hallway, past more statues, half a dozen paintings, and around two corners until she came to a closed door—a door shaped like an arched cathedral entrance with scrolling metal designs on the wood. It looked like a freaking castle door.

She knocked.

"Come in," I heard the muffled voice of Henry Nash inside.

Oh, God. Here we go.

Constance opened the door. "Mr. Hollander's here,

sir."

"Good, good. Right on time. Let him in."

Stepping aside, Constance waved me into the room, which turned out to be another office, but this one was more oak and carpet with a fireplace than the cold, marble and glass one he had in the Nash Corporation building in town. More paper and books and photos littered this workspace, and even Mr. Nash himself was more casually dressed. He wore khakis and a collared shirt that was nicer than anything I owned but still much less ostentatious than the suit and tie he'd been in yesterday.

"Looks like you found the place okay," he greeted, waving me forward toward a chair to sit in. He didn't rise to greet me but remained seated in front of the computer, intently studying something on the screen.

"Yeah. I, uh…sorry. I melted a little on the way over." Wincing, I spread my arms to show off how much sweat I'd collected.

He fluttered an unconcerned hand, paying my appearance no attention. "No worries. I'm sure you'll work up an even bigger sweat before the day's over."

I paused just before lowering myself into the chair, trying to picture what exactly he meant by that.

Noticing my frozen state and no-doubt panicked expression, he glanced up before his eyes grew. "Oh, hell. We never went into detail about what I wanted you to do, did we?"

I gave a small, silent shake of my head, dreading… This was the moment I'd learn—

"Well, with the rate of repairs we've been needing on this place lately, I had general handyman in mind for your official title. But today, I wanted you to work in the roses."

I blinked, sure I'd misheard him. But did he say handyman?

A handyman, as in someone who did house repairs?

Holy shit, so he didn't want me to perform any sexual favors for him?

My relief was so profound I almost passed out.

Mr. Nash kept watching me as if he expected a response. Hugging him probably wasn't appropriate, so I cleared my throat and squinted. "Did you say roses?"

A proud smile bloomed across his face before he began to type something on his keyboard. "Yes. They're my daughter's prized possession—aside from her library—so I want her garden to be in tip-top shape."

Daughter? He had a daughter? I glanced toward a wall full of photos across the room to see it appeared he had a daughter *and* a son, and a wife as well. I wasn't close enough to see details, but his children seemed to be in their teens and both had dark hair like him, while their mother was blonde.

"There's a supply shed out back where you can find all the tools I'm sure you'll need," Mr. Nash continued. "I'll show you where everything's kept in a minute, but first..." He stamped his finger down on a button on his keyboard, and sheets began to spit from his printer.

Pulling them free, he handed them to me. "Read this over and sign if you agree."

I took the contract from him slowly, worried I'd find something I didn't want to see, some hidden clause that really doomed my mother instead of helped her. Then I drew in a long breath and proceeded to read.

What I found was better than I could've possibly believed. It was as if I'd drafted the agreement myself, detailing everything I'd ever hoped for. He would provide well for Mom, and even my terms of employment sounded fair and legitimate. He wanted me here eight hours a day, six days a week, but allowed for vacations and holidays and sick leave. It sounded like any regular, valid job.

It was so...well, it was too good to be true.

There had to be a catch. Somewhere.

I looked up, hoping to glean the trap from his expression. But he merely watched me from inscrutable blue eyes.

"I, uh…" My gaze strayed back to the document in my shaking hands. "This all sounds great, actually."

I swear, a relieved breath escaped him. His shoulders relaxed. But that was the only tell he gave away. Then he nodded and held up a pen.

My attention returning to the words, I tried to find something that ensnared me, that hurt my mom, but I couldn't. So I held my breath, reached for the pen, and I signed my life away.

No floor dropped open casting me into a dungeon, and no bars crashed down from above caging me in. Nothing dramatic happened at all.

Which only set my nerves more on edge.

Why was this going so smoothly?

"Well…" Mr. Nash took the contract from me and signed it himself, a bit too eagerly if you asked me. Then he glanced up and flashed a congenial smile. "Now that that's out of the way, let me show you around."

He stood and started toward the door, already chattering something about roses. "Some of them are rather rare, I believe. They require a little extra care. Isobel—my daughter—could tell you all their names, I'm sure; she's become quite the expert. And I think she has some books in the shed to help with any question you may have."

I nodded. Rose-care books would be awesome since I knew next to nothing about roses. Or flowers. Or any plant in general. I'd killed a cactus once.

We exited the office and took a short hallway until we reached the back of the house, where we entered what seemed to be a salon or sitting room of some sort with one wall made entirely of glass, facing the backyard.

"One entrance into the conservatory where the roses are is through those doors right there."

I blinked at a set of French doors that led into what looked like a glass-domed corridor that connected to a greenhouse shaped like a massive gazebo.

"Wow," I breathed, stepping closer and needing to see more.

Drawn to all the beauty, I reached for one of the French doors to enter the conservatory, but Mr. Nash waved me in a different direction. "The supply shed's out back, this way."

I followed him, but not before taking one more look into the rose garden. There were some climbing rose vines, some bushes, and rows of long-stem, varying from white to pink to blood red, yellow, and lavender, peach, and purple. I swear I even saw a black rose. Just looking at them filled me with a sense of magic.

I'd never been a flower person before, and I didn't have the first clue how to take care of them, but suddenly, I was excited about entering that garden.

"These doors will be unlocked during your work hours so you'll be able to come and go as you please." Pulling open a sliding glass door that led directly outside onto a bricked patio, Mr. Nash started toward a row of pruned hedges that opened up into what looked like a maze.

Once we entered it, however, it was basically a straight shot—with one turn—that led to the shed he'd mentioned. A keypad of numbers kept the door locked. Mr. Nash quickly tapped in the code before swinging it open and stepping inside to turn on the light. I followed hesitantly, only to blink in awe. If I were a gardener, this was exactly the kind of dream shed I would want. All the hoes and rakes and…just, the whole place was neatly organized and top of the line. And yes, thank you, God, there was even a small shelf of books about roses.

"Well, I'll let you to it. Lunch is at noon." Already backing out of the shed to leave me to my duties, Mr. Nash waved me goodbye and disappeared.

I gaped at the empty doorway where he'd last stood and shook my head, a little lost. The man wasn't much for detailed instructions, was he?

Amazed they had all this gardening stuff and no full-time gardener, I ran my fingertips across the hanging handles of shovels of all shapes and sizes, then moved toward the books.

Books I could do. I used my library card well and had learned over the years that if I could just check out the right book, I could usually fix most problems in my apartment. Feeling a little more optimistic about my future, I pulled down *Roses for Dummies* and got to learning.

It seemed the roses had already been picked, purchased and planted, so I skipped ahead to the watering, mulching, fertilizing and pruning chapters. As I read, I gathered supplies I thought I might need: watering can, clippers, miniature shovels and a small bag of potting mixture. Then I piled everything into a convenient little rolling cart I found sitting against one wall and wheeled it from the shed.

Back outside in the broad daylight, I squinted. There were three different openings to the hedge path from here. I couldn't remember which one we'd taken to get back to the house, or which one I should take now to reach the conservatory.

Great. I was lost. Shading my hand over my eyes, I decided the far right should take me in the general direction I wanted to go. So I went that way, only to end up at the edge of the house, but not where I'd started, and not close enough to the rose garden to get me inside.

Strangely enough, however, a boy played outside, using sidewalk chalk to color a picture of...what the hell was he drawing? Maybe some kind of dying animal with blood gushing from its side and an arrow sticking out of its back.

It didn't look right, whatever it was.

I shook my head and jerked my gaze from the disturbingly morbid sketch. "Hey, kid."

The boy jumped and looked up, hopping to his feet and backing away from me as if *I* were the scary one.

No idea who he was; he looked too young to be Mr. Nash's son from the photos I'd seen, plus he had white blond hair, the complete opposite shade of the young man in all the pictures in Mr. Nash's office. But he was here, so he'd have to do.

Wanting to appear as nonthreatening as possible, I smiled and waved. "Hey. Sorry for bothering you, but do you know how to get to the rose garden?"

That must've been the wrong question to ask. His face drained of color. "No," he said, shaking his head. "You can't go there."

What? "Why not?"

"A monster lives in there. Half her face is melted off. She eats the thorns from the roses so she can spit them at people, stabbing them in the neck to slice their throats open until they bleed out and *die.*"

O…kay.

Somehow, I'd stumbled across one of the children of the corn. Nice.

Lifting my eyebrows, I drew my own step in reverse. Time to retreat. "Dude, that's gruesome."

Please don't kill me. Please don't kill me. Please don't kill me.

He gave a serious nod. "It's true. My mom'll tell you she's real too."

"Oh yeah?" Relieved he wasn't claiming he'd sprouted from Satan's cabbage patch but instead actually had a mother, I glanced around for this wise, all-knowing parent of his. Maybe *she* could tell me how to get to the conservatory. "Who's your mom?"

"The cook," he said, puffing up his chest as if that were the most important title in the house. "She's worked here for fifteen years. She knows everything about this place there is to know. So...don't go into the roses. You won't come out alive. Lewis, the groundskeeper, doesn't even go in there."

Aha! So this place *did* have a gardener. I knew it.

I took a second to ponder why I was being sent to garden then, when Mr. Nash already paid someone to maintain the place. But if Lewis refused to go into the roses, as the kid had said, maybe it was rumored to be haunted or something, and that was where I came in. Then again, why wouldn't Mr. Nash just hire a new groundskeeper who wasn't so scared and superstitious? Then I stopped pondering the whys. It wasn't my place to question strange, rich people and their strange, oddball orders. I was just here to do what I was told and save my mom.

Nodding gravely to the boy, I said, "Thanks for the warning, kid. But I think I'll take my chances. Which way?"

He looked at me as if he'd never see me again because I was headed forth to my death, then he lifted his hand and quietly pointed toward another opening in the path of bushes.

"Thanks." I nodded and got out of there before some of his creepiness started rubbing off.

Fortunately, he'd steered me in the right direction. I landed right at the outdoor entrance into the glass gazebo. Propping the door open, I carted my supplies inside and then paused to breathe deeply.

But fuck me, it smelled good in here. You didn't have to be a flower enthusiast for this garden to amaze you. It was like the holy shrine of roses. A hallowed kind of reverence filled my chest. Haunted or not, I liked it. It felt peaceful and yet revitalizing.

Suddenly intimidated because I didn't want to mess anything up in such a perfect place, my hands shook as I flipped back to the pages about rose care. The more I skimmed, however, the more confused I became.

These roses didn't need a lick of my attention. They were all in excellent condition as if someone already tended to them. Maybe the creepy kid had been wrong, and Lewis, the groundskeeper, came in here hourly to care for them.

Still… What the hell?

I frowned and slid my finger along the silken petals of a blood red rose. Perfectly pruned, weeded, and watered. It was as flawless as a flower could get.

But I couldn't go tell Mr. Nash they didn't need anything, could I? What if he fired me for lack of work to do, or because he thought I was lazy and lying about the roses not needing care?

I looked around again, searching for anything to water, or clip, or re-soil. It was crazy how every single flower seemed to be thriving.

Maybe this was some kind of test, and Mr. Nash wanted me to fail. What if he'd never intended for me to work for him, and the contract I'd signed to save my mom was being burned in the fireplace in his office as I stood here like a dumbass with nothing to weed?

Confused and worried, and growing a little angry, I scowled at a wall full of pink vine roses growing to my right. But they were honestly too pretty to be glared at, so my mood settled.

I bet Mom would love them. She was a fan of pink. And flowers. Plus, these were the good-smelling kind. I'd be a good son if I brought home such a flower to her. And it seemed as if they grew in abundance, not as if they were one of the rare breeds Mr. Nash had spoken of. So I reached for a bloom to pluck it from the vine without even thinking beyond how much it'd make my mother smile.

Behind me, a voice growled, "What the hell do you think you're doing?"

Jumping half out of my skin because I'd been certain no one had been in here with me, I whirled around only to gasp, "*Shit!*"

The creepy cook's son hadn't been lying.

In front of me stood an irate woman with half her face melted off.

chapter THREE

Had to be a burn wound, I decided. One half of her was perfectly fine, beautiful even. I doubted anyone would be aware she had the scars if they saw her from the good side. The other half was full of puckered and stretched skin that looked as if it had been heated to liquefy and then cooled again all wrong. It wrinkled down her neck, then was briefly covered by her short-sleeved shirt, only to continue down to the end of her arm and over the back of her hand. I wondered if it extended lower, but pants and shoes concealed the rest of her.

She appeared to be around my age, maybe a year or two younger, with a full head of dark hair, super-blue eyes and the longest eyelashes I'd ever seen. Except the look in those exceptionally lovely eyes was anything but friendly.

"I asked you a question," she reminded me, her tone truculent. Couldn't say I blamed her; I had been gawking pretty rudely. But she'd shocked the crap out of me, popping up out of nowhere. Seriously, where had she come from? "What're you doing in my garden?"

"Your…?"

Oh! This must be Mr. Nash's daughter. What had he called her? Elizabeth? No. Izz…Isobel! That was it. But all the pictures I'd seen in his office showed a younger girl. I hadn't gotten close enough to pick out details or even remember if this was her face, but I didn't recall any of the photos showcasing a scarred child. Which meant the scarring must've happened after her teen years…and maybe Mr. Nash hadn't updated his pictorial collection since then.

It would be a shame if he'd been too disgusted by her wounds to hang any more pictures of her after she'd gained them. I'd just started to think I might like Mr. Nash; I didn't want a reason to be disappointed in him. And him suddenly growing disinterested in his daughter merely because she'd been hurt would kill my respect dead.

"Hello? Are you deaf?" she hissed.

"What? No! I…" Damn, what had she been asking me, again? Roses! Why was I in *her* rose garden? I frowned, confused. "I was told to come in here."

She snorted. "Not likely. Get out." Her long, silken hair was pulled up into a ponytail, boldly showing off her wounds, but she shifted to the side, hiding them from me.

When she pointed toward the exit that led back into the house, I glanced that way before turning back to her. "I…but I can't go," I started, not sure what else to say. I didn't *want* to piss off Mr. Nash's daughter and get myself fired. But I didn't want to disobey Mr. Nash either, because coming in here and fiddling with her stupid flowers was the only job he'd given me.

Isobel narrowed her eyes and stepped closer. "What do you mean, you *can't*? Your legs seem to work just fine to me."

God, there was something alluring about her that made me draw in a sharp breath when she stepped right up into my face like that. She was a head shorter than me and slight of frame, but her challenging demeanor, showing me how little she feared me, made her personality big and vibrant, almost as if she had to puff herself up deliberately to hide everything small and insecure inside her. She had a delicate bravery about her. Plus, she smelled good, like her roses.

"I can't leave," I told her, trying not to like her nearness but failing. "Didn't you hear me? I was *told* to come in here."

"By whom?"

I tugged my hat off only to jam it back onto my head, refusing to reveal my nerves as I answered, "Mr. Nash."

She arched an eyebrow. "Mr. Nash as in *Henry* Nash?"

"Yeah. Yes, of course. Who else?"

"Well, that's impossible." She leaned toward me as if trying to intimidate me. "He knows I'm the only one who touches these flowers. He would never send someone else in here to do so. This is *my* garden."

I leaned in toward her as well, unwilling to be the first to back down. "Well, that's exactly what he did, so I don't know what else to tell you."

"You're lying."

I laughed and lifted my hands as an incredulous snort escaped me. "Why would I lie about this?"

She didn't have a ready answer, but her scowl sure was immediate. It pinched with annoyance before she sniffed. "Let's just see what my father has to say about this."

"Fine. Whatever. Great." I shrugged, actually relieved to get Mr. Nash's interference on the situation.

She scowled even harder from my lack of fear. Then she whirled away and stormed toward the entrance of the house.

I followed, hoping to learn what the hell was going

on myself.

She moved quickly; I nearly had to jog to keep up with her. She sharply rounded corners and flounced over hardwood floors, each footstep clanging out her anger, before she flung open the door to Mr. Nash's office without knocking.

"Who the hell is the idiot in my rose garden?" she demanded without preamble.

"Idiot?" I squawked, chasing her inside. There was no call to be labeling me an idiot. "You're the one who started yelling at me for doing what I was *told* to do."

Isobel crossed her arms tightly over her chest, shifted again to hide her bad side from me, and then proceeded to ignore me as her father lifted his face from whatever he was reading on his computer.

He glanced back and forth between us with raised eyebrows. "I see you two have met."

"*Met?*" Isobel repeated the word as if it were some kind of sacrilegious act.

"Yeah," I muttered, crossing my arms over my chest as well, glaring her way. "Shaw Hollander. So *nice* to meet you." Then I nearly pissed myself when I realized how disrespectful I'd just been to Mr. Nash's *daughter*. Right in front of him.

Damn, he was going to kick me off his property in about five seconds flat, wasn't he?

None too keen about my greeting, Isobel narrowed her eyes my way before whirling back to her dad. "Who *is* he?"

Instead of growing angry with me, Mr. Nash actually looked amused. His eyes crinkled and flittered with mirth as his lips tightened, trying to hide a smile, which made me think, holy shit, maybe he wasn't going to fire me after all.

"He just told you, sweetheart. His name's Shaw Hollander. I hired him this morning to be our new handyman."

"Handyman?" She stared at her dad as if he'd lost his mind. Then she shook her head. "Why? We don't need some fumbling, inept *louse*," and yeah, she just had to fling her hand in my direction when she said louse, "screwing up things when we can just hire a *professional* whenever we need something fixed."

When Mr. Nash opened his mouth—hopefully to object on my behalf—she rushed to add, "And besides, how does handyman equate to him plucking *roses* from my garden?"

Her father paused to send me a sidelong glance. I flushed, unable to lie and claim I hadn't been half a second from scoring a flower for my mom. He blinked at me before turning back to his daughter. "The fact of the matter is I *want* a handyman, so we're keeping the handyman. And I only *suggested* he help with your roses as a way to relieve you from all the work you put into them. You slave away hour after hour every day, darling. I thought you'd like a break every once in a—"

"Well, I don't!" she snapped. "I don't want anyone else messing in my garden. Especially *him*."

Hey. What was that supposed to mean? *Especially* me? I hadn't done anything wrong, except try to steal a single rose I was sure she wouldn't even miss, and I bet anyone would've done that. She didn't have to go making me feel like a worthless scumbag because of it.

I glared at her, mentally concocting half a dozen nasty comebacks, like sarcastically apologizing for being too lowborn for her lofty rose garden's standards, but I kept my mouth shut.

She growled, "Keep him out," and spun away to storm from the office.

Well. Goodbye to you too, princess.

God, what a bitch.

Except I felt bad for thinking that as soon as it entered my brain. I didn't know anything about her or what her life had been like. I could only imagine the pain and suffering she'd gone through to gain those scars. And the cook's son had called her a monster. What if he'd called her that to her face, or other people had? Maybe she had a perfectly good reason to attack first. Maybe she was just that used to *being* attacked. Her mood really did scream defense mechanism. It made me feel even guiltier about labeling her bitchy when honestly she was probably just in self-protect mode.

"She seemed particularly passionate about you, didn't she?" Mr. Nash murmured, almost more to himself than to me. And what was more surprising was that he seemed *pleased* about Isobel's "passionate" dislike of me, like maybe something was going exactly according to his plan.

That made my suspicions rise. I squinted at him. "You *knew* she wouldn't want me in her garden."

Mr. Nash glanced over before smiling brightly. "Of course."

Shaking my head, I had to ask, "Then why did you send me in there?"

With a sigh, the older man settled back, deeper into his chair, as if his explanation was too long and complicated to answer sitting upright. But all he said was, "Because I knew you two would run into each other if you went in."

Huh? "I don't understand."

He nodded as if sympathizing with my confusion. "You know, back in the regency era, affluent spinsters and widows paid nice young women to come sit with them and be their companions."

Okay. That explained…well, nothing.

"But if you try anything like that *these* days," he added with an irritated sniff, "it's *barbaric* and you're accused of buying someone friends."

When I squinted, totally lost, Henry gave a small growl. "My Izzy hasn't left the property except for doctor's appointments and the rare special occasion in eight years. *Eight* years. She's turned herself into a hermit because of those damn *scars*, and I hate it. It's no way to live. She says she's not lonely, but I know my child. And she's lonely. I've tried to bring in young women her age to keep her company, but she…"

He shook his head, looking vaguely ashamed.

My ultimate purpose here finally began to sink in. But it seemed preposterous, so I shook my head, even as I said, "Sir, if you brought me here to befriend you daughter, why didn't you just say so from the beginning?"

And why did he seem so pleased that my first encounter with her had ended disastrously? I'd done the very opposite of befriend her.

"Because that's not why you're here," he answered, actually answering nothing. "Izzy was right; a paid companion wouldn't ensure genuine friendship for her. And that's what she needs—someone who actually *likes* her. If she had anything less, it would only leave her feeling more hollow. So I don't *want* you to befriend her."

Damn, I was back to being confused again. "You don't?"

"Of course not. I'm not stupid. No matter how much he might wish it, a father can't *force* anyone to love his child, or even like her." His expression took on a melancholy despondency. "But I *can* provide her with…I don't know, entertainment, maybe. Which made me think maybe you could…"

I shook my head, not at all sure what *I* could do to entertain Isobel Nash. "You thought I could what?"

His shoulders slumped. "I'm not sure, entirely, just…break up the monotony of her day. Give her contact with someone other than family. Interrupt her routine, annoy her, make her mad, make her smile, make her laugh, make her shout, I don't care, just…just make her feel again. Take away her loneliness and be genuine about it." After a pause for thought, he lifted a finger. "The only thing I forbid you to do is hurt her. If you hurt her, you're gone. No exceptions."

I nodded. No way would I ever do anything to hurt Henry Nash's daughter. But I was still trying to figure out what exactly I was supposed to do to "entertain" her.

"If nothing else…" Henry reached for the coffee cup sitting on his desk to take a deliberate sip. Then he flushed and shrugged ruefully. "Well, you're a good-looking kid. Maybe she'll enjoy just watching you work. She's already given away how pleasing she finds your appearance."

My mouth gaped open, stupidly, not remembering that moment at all. "She did?"

Mr. Nash grinned. "Of course. When she said 'especially him,' the way she did, she outed herself. Your handsomeness made her feel insecure."

I shook my head, not gleaning that perspective from her comment at all. Glancing at her father as if he'd lost his marbles, I murmured, "I'm not so sure that's what she meant by that."

"But it was," Nash argued cheerfully. "I know my Izzy, and you intimidated her." I started to shake my head again, but he pointed at me. "You did. You're a pretty person who didn't seem bothered by her scars."

"I wasn't," I assured him.

"Exactly. And that's why I need you. You're just the thing I want throwing a wrench into her gears and forcing her from her comfort zone. Since her scars don't adversely affect you, I know you won't make her feel like a freak, yet you won't back down from any challenge she issues, and she'll keep coming back for more because she's attracted to you."

Beginning to maybe believe his claim that Isobel thought I looked good, a rush of endorphins took control of me, whooshing through my bloodstream and suddenly making me feel very alive. I remembered how close she'd gotten in the rose garden and how good she'd smelled. The urge to kiss that sassy red mouth of hers to shut her up properly had been strong. It was starting to stir again.

In fact—

I paused, realizing what this whole thing actually meant. Dear God, I'd been hired to be a piece of meaningless pretty for a lonely mutilated woman.

I cleared my throat, not sure what to make of that. Then again, I'd come here earlier, worrying Mr. Nash might want to make me *his* sex slave, so technically this was a lot more relieving. A hell of a lot more relieving, since I was actually attracted to Isobel in return, and he wasn't asking me to do anything sexual. But then…that part also made me more uncomfortable. What if I crossed a line I knew I shouldn't? Nothing in Mr. Nash's manner suggested he wanted me to actually make an advance toward her. But it would be too easy to fall into flirt mode now that I knew my purpose was to pay attention to her.

Except, nope, I wasn't going to think about that right now. My mother's safety and security depended on this, so I'd behave.

I would.

"Okay, so, uh…how do you want me to do this, exactly?"

Mr. Nash shrugged again, no help whatsoever. "We're calling you a handyman, so go do something… handy."

Something handy. Wow, that was specific. Seeing the look on my face, Henry snuffled out his impatience. "I'm sure you can find something to clean or fix around this old place."

Old? He was calling this immaculate piece of state-of-the-art architecture *old*?

I came from a totally different world than this guy.

He fluttered out a hand as if to shoo me along. "Just go where Izzy is and start fixing or cleaning…or organizing whatever is around her."

My mouth fell open. He really didn't plan on being any more helpful than that, did he?

"How do I know where she's going to be?"

This place was huge, and apparently *Izzy* had exiled me from her precious rose garden.

"Oh, that's the easy part." Mr. Nash seemed entertained to inform me. "My girl's religiously predictable. If she's not in her garden, she'll either be in the library reading, the theater watching a movie, or in the kitchen."

chapter FOUR

So there I was, lost in a mansion I totally didn't belong in.

I wondered if all millionaires—or was Henry Nash a billionaire?—let broke, unknown guys like me wander through their homes unescorted? It would be too easy for me to pickpocket something and resell it. I mean, a single painting, or clock, or statue could pay for months' worth of rent or groceries.

Not that I would ever do that, but I had to wonder what everything I passed must've cost. It was crazy how much unnecessary crap rich people collected. Yet the place still looked frightfully bare, the complete opposite of my cramped apartment where all of Mom's bakery shit sat piled into every nook and cranny we could possibly fit it into.

Maybe that's why Isobel felt so lonely. There was simply too much empty space here. Each footstep echoed, and echoes seemed like such lonely things. The hallway itself must practically tap out the rhythm of seclusion right through her chest whenever she walked down it.

Not that clutter filled loneliness, per se. Sometimes I lay squished on my sofa sleeper at night, feeling as if no one else in the world could ever really reach me, or understand me. Which must mean my theory that big houses brought out loneliness was all wrong. Rich or poor, crowded or spacious, we were all in danger of falling into isolation.

But seriously, where *was* everyone? Isobel had fled to who-knew-where, the creepy cook's son was long gone from the patio outside, and Constance, the housekeeper, had disappeared without a trace. Even if I could find his office again, I refused to return to Mr. Nash and ask where the library, kitchen or *theater* was—*God, really? They had a theater?* I'd already interrupted him enough. I didn't want to risk termination by bothering him again.

So I continued to meander down large, echoing halls and into rooms, filling my gut with jealous injustice.

It wasn't fair that some people had so much, while others—

Muted conversation echoed down the next hall I entered. I paused, cocking my head to determine its origin. When I decided it was straight ahead, I hurried my pace.

"…Just saying. The guy's utterly gorgeous," Constance was spouting to some woman as I entered what was—yes!—the kitchen, an industrial-sized kitchen with a ridiculous amount of cabinets and counter space, but a kitchen nonetheless. The other woman stirred something on one of the three stovetops while the creepy kid from outside sat at the table, watching some video on an iPad, probably a documentary on the goriest torture devices ever invented.

"Like ten out of ten on the hotness scale," Constance ranted. "He looks like Robbie Amell, I kid you not. No way did Mr. Nash suddenly hire some no one from nowhere for his *handyman* skills. I think he's been brought here to—"

Before Constance could finish her assumption, the cook turned from the stove, only to catch sight of me standing in the doorway. She gasped, cutting off whatever reason Constance had for my presence.

While the cook clutched her hands to her cheeks, Constance whirled around, her eyes going big with guilt. "Oh, God."

I gave an uncomfortable wave, wishing I could back out of the room and flee but needing their help navigating this damn house.

Wincing, I said, "Sorry. I didn't mean to interrupt. I was just trying to get the lay of the land. And…this must be the kitchen," I added lamely as I spread my arms to encompass the room around me.

"Hey, you made it out of the rose garden alive," Creepy Kid cheered as he lifted his face from the show he was watching. He smiled, revealing a gap in his top teeth.

"Kit, you've met this man before?" the cook asked, startled.

"We met outside," I answered for the boy. "He showed me how to get to the conservatory."

"This is Mr. Hollander," Constance told the cook, whose mouth fell open.

I gave another lame wave. "Or you can just call me Shaw."

"This is Mrs. Pan, the cook," Constance introduced before motioning to the boy. "And her son, Kit."

I smiled to both. "Nice to meet you."

The cook and her son stared at me as if I were an alien being who'd been beamed down through the ceiling.

Clearing my throat, I shifted a step in reverse. "So, uh, I was just curious if anyone knew how to get to the library."

"Yes, of course." Constance bounded forward. "I'll show you." She darted past me, her face flushing red.

I waved a goodbye to Mrs. Pan and Kit before hurrying after the housekeeper. "I hear there's a theater somewhere in here, too," I added, sidling in beside her.

She nodded. "On the second level, sure."

Mimicking her serious nod, I bobbed my own head. Second level. Good to know. "So am I really the first handyman Mr. Nash's ever hired?"

Constance began to cough and her face morphed into a purplish hue. I wasn't sure if she felt embarrassed for being caught talking about me, or if she was genuinely choking on something. It seemed pretty genuine to me.

I began to panic a little. "Are you okay?"

Her head jerked up and down. "Yes. Fine. Uh, sorry, there…there's the library, just there, straight ahead down that hall." She pointed, already backing away from me. And then she was shifting around and taking off in the opposite direction.

"Okay. Thank you," I called after her. Then I sighed and faced the end of the hall. I guessed I was on my own from here on out.

An ornate set of double doors, one of them propped open, stood before me, almost inviting me to come closer while at the same time warning me away. I went closer, but with each step, my pace grew slower until I was practically a sloth by the time I reached the library's entrance.

Holding my breath, I peered inside.

And there she was: Isobel Nash, Kit's monster among the roses.

I watched her from the doorway as she lay on a sofa, her stockinged feet kicked up on one end with her legs crossed at the ankles and head propped on the opposite armrest while she read from an e-reader.

I wondered if it were possible for someone to irritate you as much as they intrigued you because that's exactly what she did for me. I didn't like her, or at least I didn't want to like someone so testy and degrading, except I kind of craved more encounters with her. There was an exhilarating addictiveness about her presence. Maybe that made me messed up. I'd never thought of myself as masochistic before, but butting heads with her had been electric. She was a worthy opponent.

Then again, when she didn't know anyone was watching her, she didn't come across as such a harsh, heartless woman, and I still felt the pull. I wanted to get closer, peel away layers and learn more about her, see what made her *her*. So maybe it wasn't only her antagonistic side that drew me. Maybe it was just her.

I remembered what her father had told me about how isolated she'd become, except she didn't appear lonely or miserable at the moment. She seemed quite comfortable and content to bury herself in her story. I actually envied her that and could picture myself stretching out next to her or curling around her to read the words on her screen over her shoulder. Spending my days lazing on a sofa and reading would be a dream come true, especially with someone who smelled like roses tucked on a couch with me.

Not that I should let my mind wander into that territory. I was supposed to talk to her, just talk. Engage the mind, not the body.

Oh, but that body—

Down, boy.

Forcing myself back to the task at hand, I glanced around the room and decided I'd turn hermit too if I had this in my house, because finally, I'd found a room that didn't look bare.

The shelves were crammed with books, overflowing really. Many were stacked on the floor with no other place to go. The place was dim; the two floor-to-ceiling windows it housed didn't let much light in. And the dark walls with a limited amount of hanging lamps didn't brighten things either. If this were my library, I'd lighten the color of the walls, install some more overheads and then build more shelves for all the books.

But first, I'd clean the grimy windows.

It was strange; Porter Hall had a housekeeper, but

the windows still looked unwashed. Maybe Constance was too busy gossiping about people to get a good day's work in, or maybe this place was so big it was impossible to keep spotless. Or maybe I should just stop assuming shit, mind my own business, and get myself to work.

That's what I did. I backed from the room before Isobel could lower her e-reader and notice me spying, and I wandered around a bit more, opening odd doors until I found a supply closet, hosting a bucket, sponge, and all-purpose house cleaner, plus a stepladder.

Good enough for me.

When I returned to the room, supplies in tow, I didn't make a sound, just moseyed past the resting dragon—er, Isobel—as if I had every right to be there. All the while, my heart pounded so hard I was surprised she didn't hear the chaotic lub-dub as soon as I strolled by.

I made it to the window without being roasted to death by dragon fire. Then I set down the bucket of warm suds and opened the ladder. Didn't take me long to realize the ladder wouldn't be tall enough to help me reach the zenith of the window—God, the ceiling in this room was abnormally high for a one-story room—but it would be a start. I climbed to the top rung, bucket in hand, and pulled the soaked sponge out before slopping it across the glass.

By this point, there was no way she could've missed me in the room with her, but she'd yet to say anything, so I figured she'd decided to ignore me.

I figured wrong.

"What do you think you're *doing*?" she screeched suddenly, nearly making me upset my perch on the ladder because I jumped so hard.

But, damn, what a way to kill a guy: wait until he wasn't expecting you to talk, then jar him from his work with haughty demands.

Swearing under my breath, I steadied myself then

dipped the sponge back into the suds. "I'm washing the windows," I answered before finally glancing over my shoulder at her. "Sorry, was I bothering you?"

The question was so innocent and friendly it was hard to tell if she knew I wasn't sorry at all.

She blinked blankly before setting her e-reader down and climbing from the couch. "That's not how you wash a window. That's how you wash a *car*."

I lifted my brows before glancing at the window where soapy water streaked down the windowpane in little rivers. "There's a difference?"

Sniffing out her censure, she shook her head. "My God. Have you never washed a window before?"

With a shrug, I admitted, "Now that you mention it, no, I don't think I have. Unless a car window counts." Though I spoke the words pleasantly, the challenge in my glance made her eyes narrow when I added, "Have *you* washed a window before?"

Her eyes narrowed. "Come with me. And bring this…nonsense."

I had no idea what she had in mind for me, but remaining in her presence was my primary function, so I dutifully climbed off the ladder and refolded it before tucking it under my arm and lifting the soap bucket. When I faced her, ready to go wherever she wished, she blinked at me as if she hadn't actually expected me to follow her orders so readily.

To show her I hadn't yet turned into the meek, obedient servant she suspected, I gave her a mocking little half-bow and smirked. "As you wish."

Huffing irritably, she turned away and strode from the room. I followed, feeling a thrill from ticking her off. Trailing from a leisurely distance, I fell far enough behind that she paused once and turned, waiting for me to catch up. She glared at my pace when I refused to hurry, but I returned the look with a sunny smile, which only seemed to put her in a worse mood, making mine better.

God, this was fun.

I had no idea why it was so invigorating to rile her, but it really was. I bet it wasn't often the pampered princess came across someone who didn't break his neck trying to please her. Her shocked outrage over my indifferent attitude was like a small, personal victory.

We returned to the supply closet, where she made me put the bucket and sponge away. Then she handed me a bottle of Windex and roll of paper towels plus a squeegee, muttering, "Here. Use this instead. And that ladder too." She pointed to another wall, which finally brought my attention to another, larger ladder I hadn't noticed before.

"Ah," I cooed appreciatively. "Much better. Thank you." I sent her a true smile of gratitude before I realized what I was doing.

But the honest grin seemed to piss her off just fine, so I couldn't regret it.

I made my way back to the library, new supplies in hand, and this time I led the way. I knew she had to be following me, though, if for no other reason than to make sure I didn't fuck up again.

"Start high and work your way down," she instructed as soon as I opened the ladder.

I nearly laughed. Yep, she hadn't been able to keep herself from bossing me around.

"Whatever you say, princess," I answered, climbing the rungs.

The growl that rose from behind me made my heart swell with conquest. "My name is Isobel."

"Oh yeah?" Able to reach the top of the window, I sprayed the cleaner then wiped it away smoothly. A screeching sound to cut across the glass, letting me know I was doing my job well. Squeaky clean. "Your dad called you Izzy."

"Well, *you're* not my father."

I almost snorted, *Thank God.* I'd consider it a personal failure if I ended up with a daughter as snooty and rude as her. But what I said was, "Fair enough." I liked how *Isobel* sounded in my head better, anyway.

I must not have made any more cleaning mistakes because the critique queen stayed quiet. Pleased about finally doing my job right and meeting the high standards of the window-cleaning police behind me, I threw myself into my task until sweat collected on my brow and more trickled down the center of my back.

Just as I thought how much cooler it would feel to take my shirt off, I realized, hey, I probably *should* take my shirt off.

Mr. Nash had hired me to play man candy, after all, hadn't he? Maybe I should earn my keep. Besides, the sunlight coming in through the glass just kept growing warmer.

But mostly, if I wanted to be honest with myself, I was curious what Isobel would do. Would she be the uptight, prissy type and demand I put my clothes back on? Would she silently ogle the muscles in my back and ass as they stretched and shifted with each move? Would she like what she saw?

A rush of anticipation flowed through me, and before I could question myself, I tugged my shirt over my head, then tucked it into my back pocket.

She said nothing. I held my breath, eager to know if her silence meant something good or bad. One thing was certain: this suspense was killing me.

Unable to help myself, I glanced back as I moved down to a lower step.

But I never got my answer as to what Isobel thought of my bared torso. She was no longer in the library.

chapter FIVE

I didn't see Isobel again for the rest of the morning. She wasn't in the theater, which I found after washing the library windows, and I didn't spot her through the French doors that led into her garden. I meandered my way back to the kitchen just in time for lunch, but neither she nor Mr. Nash showed to eat.

So I sat down with Constance, Mrs. Pan, and Kit, wondering, "Where do the Nashes eat?"

"Mr. Nash has already taken a tray in his office," the cook replied.

I nodded and waited to hear what the rest of the family did or would do, but no one spoke again.

Just as I began to feel awkward from the brutal silence and bit into a homemade roll to combat the feeling, Constance said, "I noticed you were cleaning the windows in the library earlier."

I lifted my eyebrows and chewed before wiping my mouth. Mrs. Pan's rolls tasted good, almost as good as one of Mom's creations. Then I answered, "Yeah. Was that okay? I didn't steal your job from you, did I?"

"Oh, no." She swung out a hand, absolving me from

guilt. "Not at all. I don't often disturb Miss Nash's spaces, and besides…" She flushed before admitting, "I'm a bit afraid of heights. The windows in there go way too high for my taste."

I nodded, relieved I hadn't stepped on anyone's toes…except maybe Isobel's, but that was kind of why I was here, so she'd have to deal.

"Actually, I was wondering…" Constance started before she discreetly cleared her throat. "Since you seemed okay on a ladder, would you be willing to change a few lightbulbs in the foyer's chandelier? I usually hunt down Lewis to help, but if you're willing…"

After Mr. Nash's reluctance to assign me any specific task, I was surprised—and grateful—for a little direction. "Sure," I said, smiling my appreciation at the housekeeper. "I'd be happy to."

Constance's face bloomed with pleasure. "Great. Thank you."

I nodded just as Kit finally broke in, watching me closely. "How'd you escape the monster in the rose garden?"

"Kit!" Mrs. Pan chastised, her face going beet red with embarrassment. "Hush. We don't speak of Miss Nash that way."

I glanced between mother and son, wanting to defend Isobel and yet not wanting to alienate myself from my coworkers on my first day on the job by calling one of their kid's a rude little shit.

So I smiled tightly at the boy. "Turns out, there was no monster after all. She'd transformed into a beautiful princess who pardoned me from death by thorn."

The two women seemed pleased by my answer, while Kit wanted to hear more about the mysterious princess.

"How did she turn into a princess? What'd she look like? Why didn't she kill you?"

I shrugged, giving the kid a mysterious little grin.

"Apparently, I'm thorn resistant. And since, you know, the best way to defeat your enemy is to befriend them, she decided to be nice to me instead."

Mrs. Pan snorted her amusement into her hand, while Kit scowled at that answer before he demanded, "Is that really true?"

Laughing, I ruffled his hair. "I'm working on it, kid. I'm working on it."

While Kit appeared to grow more confused, the two ladies beamed their approval. "But, what—" He was cut off by the opening of the back door.

A small, whistling old man with a trimmed gray beard, wearing a straw hat, tan shorts and a dark shirt with a red bandana tied around his throat, entered the kitchen, rubbing his dirt-stained hands together. "Boy howdy, it's already getting hot out there." He moved toward the sink as if to wash his hands only to be waylaid by the pot simmering on the stove. "Well, I'll be, Mrs. Pan. Your food actually smells good enough to eat today."

"Get your dirty paws away from my stew, Lewis," Mrs. Pan scolded, making the man jerk his hand back. "And what do you mean *today*? You say my cooking smells good *every* day."

"Yeah, but…" He turned with a mischievous grin, as if he were about to say something else to make the cook scowl. I got the feeling he drew as much of a kick from pissing her off as I did from irritating Isobel. But then he saw me, and all teasing fled his expression. "Well…" he murmured in curious intrigue. "Who do we have here?"

"This is Shaw Hollander," Constance introduced me. "He's the new handyman Mr. Nash hired this morning."

Two shaggy gray eyebrows lifted. "Handyman, you say? Hmm." His gaze wandered over me before settling on my biceps. "He looks strong enough," he decided before addressing me directly. "How much weight do you think you can carry, kid?"

I blinked. "Excuse me?"

"Hey, I'm not as spry as I used to be," Lewis defended as if he were being confronted. "This old body can't carry around forty-pound bags of topsoil the way it used to. And they called you handy, so can you help me with some of the heavy lifting or not?"

"I..." Glancing at the other two employees of Henry Nash, I tried to come up with the appropriate answer. I was supposed to be here to connect with Isobel, but Constance and now Lewis seemed to need my assistance, and I'd already told the housekeeper I'd help her, so—feeling as if I couldn't say no, and not really *wanting* to turn down the old man anyway—I shrugged. "Sure. Whenever you need me."

Lewis gave a satisfied nod and commenced to wash his hands before spooning up his lunch. Meanwhile, Mrs. Pan tried to coax Kit into eating more of his meal. "You can't survive on rolls, honey. Take three more bites of the stew and make sure there's some carrot and meat in each spoonful."

As Kit groaned but complied with his mother's wishes, I glanced at the three employees around me: Constance, the housekeeper; Lewis, the groundskeeper; and Mrs. Pan, the cook.

"Are there any more employees who work here?" I asked, growing more curious about the dynamics of the household by the minute. I also wanted to know when and where the Nashes ate, and where Henry's wife and son were hiding away. I hadn't spotted either of them all day.

But one thing at a time. So I started with questions about the staff.

"It's just the three of us," Mrs. Pan announced cheerfully before adding, "And now you, of course."

She made it sound as if four made up a skeleton crew while I was still trying to wrap my head around the fact that anyone could ever need that many full-time employees to take care of their home.

"Oh, and Mrs. Givens shows up every couple of weeks to assess the place," Constance put in. "She's Mr. Nash's personal assistant, who mostly works from his office in the city, but ever since his wife died, he's had Mrs. Givens make the main household decisions."

I'm not sure why hearing that Mr. Nash was a widower took my breath, but learning Isobel had lost her mother on top of getting scarred knocked me for a loop. I blinked at Constance. "Mr. Nash's wife died?" I thought of the pictures in his office of the blonde woman with two dark-headed children.

"In the fire," Kit was quick to supply.

"Fire?" I repeated just as his mother shushed him, her face falling gray with sorrow.

But Kit wasn't so easily silenced. His eyes alive with eagerness, he gushed, "The fire that burned down the first house. But they rebuilt it, even bigger and better. I was only a baby at home with Mom when it happened, but my dad was here. He was the groundskeeper back then, and he tried to save Mrs. Nash." His gaze slashed to his mother before he finished, "Except he ended up dying with her."

Mrs. Pan made a choking sound of grief from the back of her throat and pressed a napkin to her mouth.

"All right, enough talk about that, now," Lewis said gently but firmly, setting a hand on the kid's shoulder. "It makes your mother sad."

Blinking cluelessly, Kit said, "But it was years ago."

About eight years ago if I had to guess. Mr. Nash had said Isobel had been isolating herself for eight years, and the fire her mother had perished in must've been the one to leave her scarred. Besides, Kit didn't look much older than eight, and if he'd been a baby at the time, well…it all added up to me.

Sympathy speared through me. It would be one

thing to recover from a wound of that magnitude, but to lose a parent in the middle of it… I shook my head, unable to even imagine what she must've gone through, when I remembered the dark-headed boy in the photos with the Nash family. Oh hell, maybe she'd lost a brother in the fire, too.

"What about Mr. Nash's son?" I asked, worried he'd perished as well. Exactly how much crushing sadness had been laid on Isobel's shoulders at once?

The three adults blinked at me as if I'd just asked the strangest question they'd ever heard. Finally, Constance said, "Ezra? What about him?"

"He didn't…?" I flushed, realizing this was quite the awkward question to pose. "In the fire, I mean."

"Oh! No," Mrs. Pan was quick to reassure me. "No, Ezra was away at college by then. He's still hearty and hale, living a few miles from here in his own house now."

I nodded, feeling suddenly silly for worrying about him, a complete stranger. But the idea of Isobel losing both a mother and sibling at the same time was more than I could bear.

"Mr. Nash was away on a business trip that weekend," Mrs. Pan added, not mentioning where Isobel had been.

Even though I already knew the answer, I had to confirm it. "And that's how the daughter—Isobel—got her…that is, I mean, that's how she became…?" I cleared my throat, trying to think up the most sensitive way to ask when a voice from behind me spoke.

"Yes, Mr. Hollander. *That's* how I became the monster I am today."

My stomach dropped at the sound of her voice before I twisted in my chair to find Isobel standing in the entrance of the kitchen, her hands fisted at her sides and blue eyes layered with icy disdain.

Earlier, she'd had her hair up in a ponytail, revealing her entire face, but now it fell down, one half working to cover the mutilated side while the other half lay tucked behind her ear to show off her good side. It filled me with a moment of regret, hoping she hadn't felt the need to hide her scars because of me.

Across from me, Kit gasped and dove under the table to hide, while the other three adults froze guiltily as if they thought they'd been caught doing something wrong.

Flushing because her narrowed eyes made me think I'd misspoke, I stuttered, "I…I…" Gritting my teeth over such nonsense, I scowled at Isobel and moodily muttered, "I was just curious." Seriously, how could asking a simple question be that wrong? Then, because she was still glaring at me and making me feel crappier for opening my mouth at all, I hissed, "It's smart to learn about the household you're supposed to be working for."

Yeah. That sounded good. If I was supposed to do a decent job here, I needed information.

But Isobel's glare turned into two thin slits of rage. "Rest assured, my personal life will *never* be any of your business. And if you simply can't control your curiosity, then ask me directly instead of gossiping about me behind my back."

I hadn't even been gossiping about her, but I felt ashamed as if I had. And the way she so easily drew the shame forward pissed me off. So, I sneered. "Fine. I will. Question number one: have you *always* been this bitter and rude, or did the accident *burn* your bad attitude into you?"

I'd just wanted to ask her something—anything—to show her I wasn't afraid to stand up to her, but as soon as the question left my mouth, I knew it was wrong. All wrong.

Dead silence filled the kitchen. Mrs. Pan, Constance, and Lewis gaped back and forth between us before the cook surged to her feet.

"Can I get you a bowl of stew, Miss Nash?" she

asked as she rushed toward the stove.

But Isobel waved a hand. "No, thank you, Mrs. Pan." Her gaze swerved my way before she added, "I've lost my appetite."

As suddenly as she'd appeared in the kitchen, she was gone.

My shoulders slumped and I ran a hand through my hair. "I'm a complete jackass, aren't I?"

Lewis choked out a sound before admitting, "Well, I've never seen anyone react to her the way you did, that's for sure."

"Is she gone?" a small muffled voice asked from under the table.

"Yes, dear," Mrs. Pan said gently. "She's left. You can come out now."

No one scolded him for treating Isobel like a freak by hiding from her. It itched at my craw that they let the kid get away with hurting her feelings. And it made me feel worse about hurting them myself. Mr. Nash would probably fire me if he knew what I'd just done.

Worried about that, but even more concerned about how my behavior had affected Isobel, I rose from the table and excused myself.

I tried to find her so I could issue a genuine apology. But she wasn't in the library. She wasn't in the theater and I couldn't spot her through any of the glass walls of the conservatory. So I found myself peering in at her flowers through the windows instead, wondering, *why roses?* Did she just like the peace and serenity that came with gardening? Flowers couldn't knock her ego down by hiding from her under a table or making her feel like less of a person.

Or was it a simpler reason, like maybe they just smelled good?

Or did it stem from something more psychological? Maybe she believed she'd become so hideous after the fire that she needed to make up for it to the world by creating something beautiful. Balance things out.

I hoped that wasn't the case. I hoped I hadn't made her feel ugly by arguing with her.

I hoped she'd become a hermit in this huge house because she was just that big of an introvert and didn't like people. I hoped the scars didn't rule any part of her life at all. I hoped I hadn't made everything worse.

When I trudged home that evening, it was nearly seven before I made it to my building. I felt bogged down and exhausted even though I hadn't done much more than climb a ladder to wash windows and change a few lightbulbs in a chandelier. My soul felt weary because I kept worrying about Isobel.

I didn't even know why I was so concerned; she'd been twenty times nastier to me than I'd been to her. Why should I care if the barbs I'd slung her way had actually hit the mark?

Because I'd meant to infuriate her and cause steam to rise from her collar. I'd wanted her face to flush with the lively rage I knew I could summon right before she fought back, belittling me in return. I'd wanted to taste the victory of another sparring match. Instead, nothing but acid had filled my tongue because it felt as if I'd hurt her. Truly, bone-deep hurt her.

Dragging, I pushed open the front door to my building, only to fall to an uneasy halt when I saw the woman sitting on the bottom step.

When she saw me, she sprang to her feet, her eyes brightening and blonde hair bouncing. "Hi, Shaw. Where you been all day? Your mom said you got a new job. Did you get something at the new factory in Dover? Do you like it?"

I let out an exhausted sigh, barely holding in the groan I really wanted to release. "Hey, Gloria."

I itched to brush past her and keep going up to my door, but her expression reminded me of an eager little puppy. I couldn't kick the puppy, even though I knew any kindness on my part would only encourage her into thinking she might finally stand a chance with me. So I made a production of checking my mail slot, delaying the moment I'd have to face her again.

Gloria was a dilemma I didn't know how to navigate. She was pretty, got along with my mother, adored the ground I walked on, cooked the best pumpkin pie I'd ever tasted, came from the same background as me and was only a year younger. On paper, we looked perfectly suited for each other, and I should probably thank my lucky stars I'd found such a gem.

In reality, she was clingy, nosey, annoying and I couldn't summon an iota of chemistry for her. So I usually felt like an ungrateful ass when she threw herself at me, so obviously letting me know I could have her any time I wanted, or whenever my mom tried to nudge me in her direction. But seriously, a clammy sweat broke out over my skin when I even considered getting my mouth close to hers. I couldn't do it. I just…I couldn't. Which made me feel worse, and then caused me to be extra nice and polite to her, which, yeah, in turn fed her hopes and dreams that I'd eventually develop some affection for her.

I didn't string her along. I swear, I didn't. I'd explained to her—and to my mother—on numerous occasions that we would never have a relationship. And they both nodded as if they completely understood, only to concoct some new trap to try to snare me into Gloria's clutches a week later.

The whole situation was a hot mess, and I would give anything to escape it.

Suddenly deciding I wasn't in the mood to put up with a Gloria encounter after all, I closed the empty mailbox door, gave her a stiff nod, and hedged around her to head upstairs. "Well, have a good night."

Not that she was deterred. She followed me up the steps. "So, what kind of stuff did Mr. Nash make you do?" Her voice lowered as she moved closer. "Was it illegal?"

I sighed, wondering why she'd asked me where I'd been and if my new job had been at another factory, when she'd obviously already gotten all the inside dirt from my mother. I really, really wished she and my mom weren't so close, though I felt bad as soon as that thought arose. Mom didn't have a lot of friends. It was sweet of Gloria to visit her, even though I suspected she only did it to get the scoop on me.

"No, it was nothing illegal," I answered, knowing she'd probably glean these very details off Mom sooner or later. "He just wanted me to be a handyman at his house."

Her nose wrinkled. "A handyman? That's all?" I guess it would've been more exciting for her if I'd been breaking kneecaps and handling illegal substances.

I shrugged, inordinately pleased to disappoint her. "That's all."

She nodded. "So you got to see his house? I bet that was fancy. What's the inside of Henry Nash's place look like?"

"Big," I answered, reaching my floor and pausing before darting past her, careful not to physically touch her, and hurrying toward my front door. "Well, I'm going to check on Mom now. Have a nice day, Gloria."

"Oh, she's fine. We had a lovely—"

I cut her off by slipping inside my apartment and closing the door as quickly as possible. The rest of her words went muffled and I shut my eyes as I rested my back against the door, feeling crappy for probably hurting yet another woman's feelings today. I was certainly on a roll, wasn't I?

"Shaw?" my mother's weak voice called. "Is that you, dear?"

My eyes flashed open, and I immediately pushed myself forward. "Yeah, Mom. It's me." I hurried into the only bedroom in our apartment to find it dark with a blanket hanging over the window to keep as much light out as possible, which meant she'd had another migraine.

Wincing because I hadn't been here to help her through it, I eased down next to the mattress beside her so I could stroke her thin, graying hair. "I just got home. Are you okay? Do you want me to get you some aspirin? Water?"

"No, no. I'm fine. Gloria took care of me." She made a vague motion with her hand. "I was worried that man would keep you all night."

I sent her a gentle smile. "Nah. He only worked me eight hours. It just took me a while to walk home."

"He was…the work was okay?" She sounded worried so I kissed her forehead and smiled again.

"The work was fine, Mom. He just wants me to fix odds and ends around his house. Nothing more."

She sniffed. "Nothing more *so far*. Rich, powerful men like that always have a hidden agenda."

I thought of Henry Nash's hidden agenda: Isobel and her angry, sad eyes and wounded soul. "Not this time," I lied. "I think he's on the up and up, and ulterior-motive free."

"Humph. We'll see about that."

I stroked the back of her hand and changed the subject. "Are you hungry? Do you want me to fix you something?"

"Aww, sweet baby, don't worry about me. I told you, Gloria took good care of me." With a wistful sigh, she added, "Such a lovely girl. I still don't understand why you won't even give her a chance."

I groaned. "Mom, we've been over this. Gloria and I have nothing in common."

"I know, I know," she lamented. "She doesn't like books the way you do. Or have such fanciful ideas."

And right on track, the guilt clouded me, for not being able to like Gloria like I should, for being a nonsensical dreamer who wanted…hell, I'm not even sure. Maybe *smart* and *accomplished* were the right words for what I wanted to be. I wished to be something that made me feel meaningful, anyway. I'd always thought it would be cool to be an archeologist or even work in a museum. I loved history, discovering new cultures and learning about hidden societies. Becoming a real-life Indiana Jones would probably be the biggest high of my life.

Both Gloria and my mom thought that dream was silly…their words. They didn't care so much about the past, or its cultures. They preferred to live in the present.

"It's more than that," I told my mother.

The few times I'd tried to open up to Gloria and talk about my passions and life goals, she'd either tried to convince me that wasn't really what I wanted to do, got too bored to listen, or changed the subject. The true problem was she didn't want me to be *me*. And what's more, she didn't seem to have her own dreams either, except to land me. I seriously didn't know what she wanted from life, what goals she had, what she feared or loved. I wasn't even sure if *she* knew. And that's what ultimately made me shy away from her. There was no connection there at all.

"I just want to see you happy and settled down." This time, Mom was the one who reached out to touch my face. "I want my baby boy to have the best."

"I do," I told her, clasping her hand more firmly to my cheek. "I have you." And I would take care of her until my last breath.

"Oh, you…" She smiled and patted my cheek before dropping her limp, exhausted hand. "You're the sweetest boy ever. I don't know what I'd do without you."

I kissed her forehead one more time, glad she'd dropped the subject of Gloria, and rose to my feet. "Well, you don't have to find out, because I'm not going anywhere. I'll always take care of you. Always."

And I would. To keep my mother safe and settled, I'd brave Isobel while resisting that powerful, undeniable draw I felt toward her. And I'd do it so well Henry Nash would praise the day he met me.

Everything was going to end up just fine.

chapter SIX

The next day was Sunday. I didn't work at Porter Hall on Sundays, so I spent a good portion of the afternoon at the library, studying up on roses. No idea why since I wasn't allowed to go near Isobel's garden again. But I learned as much as I could anyway, because she intrigued me, and roses seemed to intrigue her. Plus, I felt bad about the way things had left off between us the day before, which was why I arrived to work on Monday with a small packet of seeds in my pocket.

I had stopped by a garden store on the way over, planning to get something amazing for Isobel in the hopes she'd forgive me for hurting her feelings on Saturday. Since she'd made it impossible for me to apologize to her in person, I thought maybe a gift—an olive branch, as it were—would do the trick.

But I hadn't had much luck at the store. Most of the rosebushes they stocked were common, hearty brands. I'd wanted to get something rare, something special that stood out, like *she* stood out. When I asked the owner, she'd shaken her head before telling me all she had were a couple seeds for some midnight supreme rosebushes.

The catch was that no one who'd bought them before had ever been able to actually get them to grow. I thought that if anyone could coax a rose from its stubborn seed, it'd be Isobel, so I asked to purchase a few anyway. The owner'd had pity on me, certain I wouldn't have any more success than anyone before me, so she'd thoughtfully given me a discount.

When I reached Porter Hall, I rang the bell at the end of the drive, and the gate automatically opened before I could even tell anyone who I was. I walked around to the back where the bay of glassed entrances was unlocked, and I let myself inside.

No one was around, so I trudged to the library, which was empty. I waited a few minutes, except Isobel never showed, so I set the packet of rose seeds on the seat of her sofa with a note.

Dear Miss Nash,

I just wanted to apologize for my behavior on Saturday. I hope you will accept these seeds in peace offering. I was told they are for a rare midnight supreme rosebush that's supposed to bud into black roses with blue tips. No one else who's planted them has gotten them to grow, but I had a feeling you would be the exception to the rule. Good luck with your growing endeavors.

Regards, Shaw Hollander

I felt stupid for leaving such a cheesy note, but I stopped myself three times from going back to fetch it or even revise it, no matter how corny "growing endeavors" and "regards" suddenly sounded to me.

Lewis kept me busy most of the morning, doing some lifting, and carrying, and climbing for him before Constance came out to ask if I could help her move a statue she feared was leaving too big of an indent in the carpet.

The bronze sculpture of an eagle was heavy, but together we got it shifted to the other side of the hall. *Rich people,* was the only thing I could think as I stood back and stared at the ugly, gaudy thing after it was in its new place. They definitely had strange tastes.

Unable to help myself, I made my way back to the library to see if Isobel had seen her gift yet. She wasn't there, but the packet of rose seeds along with the note I'd written were both gone.

My heart jolted.

I stared at the empty divan for the longest time, wondering what this meant. She'd taken the seeds, so it couldn't be bad. Then again, she was still avoiding me after seeing them, so that couldn't be good. It probably meant I was most definitely not forgiven. I bet she'd torn the note up and thrown the seeds away.

That didn't deter me, though. I wanted to see her again, make sure she was okay, and it had nothing to do with her father's wish that I break up the monotony of her day. I hadn't been able to fall asleep the last two nights because she'd reined over so many of my thoughts. And then she'd been the first thing to enter my brain when I'd woken. I'd been antsy when I'd dressed, more ready to return to Porter Hall than I'd been for anything in a long time.

Her continued hiding frustrated me. I wandered around her empty library, hoping she might appear. She didn't. So I read the titles of her books, pausing at the ones I could tell were her favorites. Their spines were worn and the pages not so crisp and new. I supposed it was possible she'd bought them already used and well read, but a rich girl like her? Probably not.

I picked up one story, curious to know how many times she'd had to have read it to make it look this used. It wasn't a novel I'd read before, so I made a mental note to stop by the public library on the way home and see if I could check out a copy.

By the end of the day, after I hadn't spotted her once, I tried to convince myself it was for the best. She just needed some time and space before she was ready to return to our sparring matches.

Except Tuesday and Wednesday were a repeat of Monday. No sign of Isobel anywhere. I did finish *Dragonflight*, though, and had to check out the next book in the series because I enjoyed the first so much. She definitely had interesting taste in literature. When I returned to the public library for *Dragonquest*, I popped by their perpetual used book sale as I usually did to see if they had anything new. When I spotted an Anne McCaffrey book, not from the Pern series, I snagged it. It seemed old but was in pristine condition, not as if it had been read before, so I gave up two quarters to buy it.

When I returned to Porter Hall on Thursday, I carried the book with me and headed straight to Isobel's library. For once, I was actually happy to find she wasn't there.

Though there was no way to fit all her books onto her shelves, she had a decent organizational strategy going on. Authors and even similar genres were grouped together. So it didn't take me long to peruse her shelves and the floor around them to discover which Anne McCaffrey books she had. Thrilled to learn she didn't own the one I'd purchased—at least, not a physical copy—I left it on her sofa with another note.

Thought you might like this one. –Shaw

I felt tons better about that note, and yet still, it inspired nothing from its recipient. Isobel stayed hidden. The book disappeared from its spot on her sofa, however. When I returned to the library a couple hours later to find it gone, my frustration gave way to irritation.

Why the hell was she staying away from me but accepting my gifts? I was trying to make friends with her.

Even though Mr. Nash had told me that wasn't what he wanted, it *was* what *I* wanted. I wanted her to like me, damn it. I had no idea why, but something about her captivated me, and I wanted to do the same for her. It sucked to know I didn't affect her in the same way she affected me.

Disheartened, I helped Lewis outside for the rest of the day. I told myself not to check the library before I left. I wouldn't find anything there, but an ember of hope inside me refused to listen. I'd always sucked at giving up, even when I probably should have.

I stole into the library one last time for the day, bummed again.

On Saturday morning, though, I struck gold. Something sat on the sofa in exactly the same place I'd left my two gifts for Isobel.

Holding my breath, I drew closer to discover it was another dragon book: a mint-condition hardback copy of *Eragon* by Christopher Paolini. It had been popular when I'd been a teen, but I'd never read it.

I stared at it for the longest time, tempted to flip open the first page and get started right then, even as I wondered why it was lying here. No note had been left with it, but I couldn't help but think... Had Isobel perchance left it there for me to read? The assumption seemed reasonable, but I wasn't sure. If I borrowed it and took it home, would she accuse me of stealing it and have her father fire me?

It was also possible she'd been reading it herself and had just negligently left it there. But it sat in the *exact* same spot where I'd left my presents, and it shared the same genre as the book I'd left for her. Maybe she was just suggesting something for me to read. I could check it out from the library and not bother her copy. But what if she really did want me to take it, and I hurt her feelings if I didn't.

Damn, I swear I was stuck in a catch-22.

A note would've been so nice right about now.

Holding my breath, I picked up the story and took it with me. She didn't track me down all day at work, so I took that to mean she wanted me to read the story.

Not wanting to keep it too long, regardless, I was determined to finish it before Monday. Problem was it wasn't a short novel. I stayed up late both Saturday and Sunday evenings to finish it, making my mom ask me continually what book was so interesting that I couldn't pull my head from it. Thank goodness, it was easy and entertaining enough to take in, but I was dragging when I walked into work Monday morning, yet I was strangely energized too. My mind spun over all the different ways I could return the book. Should I lay it on the sofa where she'd left it? Wait until I saw her in person? Leave a review or a thank-you note?

Would she come out of hiding today?

I hoped so. I ached so.

I had no idea what I'd say to her if she did, but I looked forward to the opportunity, anyway.

The library was empty when I strolled in. My disappointment was profound, but I immediately saw that something else had been left on the couch. Heart kicking into gear as my blood raced with anticipation, I hurried forward, only to slow to a stop when I saw the novel I'd bought her from the public library's book sale sitting there again.

She had returned my gift. Thrown it right back in my face.

Maybe I shouldn't have taken *Eragon* after all if it had prompted her into giving this one back. Crestfallen, I began to reach for the paperback when I noticed a slip of paper tucked into the middle of the book and sticking out the top like a bookmark. Curious, I slipped it free, and my breath caught.

She'd written me a note.

I liked the Chronicles of Pern better.

I'm not sure why that caused me to laugh, but I threw my head back and shouted with glee. It was just…the words sounded so much like her: negative, haughty, and straight to the point. Plus, it meant she'd actually read the book.

In truth, it wouldn't have mattered what she'd written in her note; the fact that she'd taken the time to read the book and then write anything at all was what made my day. Isobel was communicating with me again. And she'd treated the book as if I'd lent it to her, which hadn't been my intent, but knowing that felt better than her purposely returning what she thought was a gift from me.

Feeling brighter and lighter, I took her note, crossed out her pessimistic words and decided I had to write something extra cheerful and positive, just to piss her off. So I flipped the sheet over and began to scribble:

Thank you for the loan of Eragon. Your generosity is inspiring and makes me wish I could be more like you. The book was amazing, by the way. I am already enjoying the Inheritance Cycle more than the Chronicles of Pern, so much so that I gotta know what happens next. Most Gratefully–Shaw

All that optimism would probably sour her mood like a tart lemon, which made mine even more buoyant. I hummed to myself as I left the library and found something to do. I managed to keep busy the rest of the morning, or rather Constance and Lewis kept me busy, and even Mrs. Pan had me opening jars for her or reaching up onto high shelves to fetch appliances. The staff seemed to appreciate my presence, even though anyone by the name of Nash, not so much. But that was okay; Isobel had written to me. Life was better than it'd been the day before.

I returned to the library later in the afternoon, only to find book two of the Inheritance series waiting on me in what had become our spot. No note sat with it, but a smile spread across my face, anyway. It wasn't an official sign of forgiveness, but she was interacting with me. My bones loosened at the joints, and I finally relaxed.

I whistled as I strolled home that evening.

It took me until Wednesday evening to finish *Eldest*. After I returned it to our spot Thursday morning, book three was waiting for me by the time I left work. But this one—*this one*!—had a note with it.

I think this was supposed to be the last book, but the author split the story in two (and then he's supposed to write a fifth, I believe). I was happy when he made this one into two. I didn't want the series to end yet.

Blinking, I read and re-read the words over and over again, unable to believe my eyes. But…but…Isobel had been…she'd been so positive. A sudden smile lit my face. Did this mean she'd forgiven me, was ready to talk to me again?

That night, I read until almost dawn. But I couldn't get all the way through *Brisingr*. When I hurried into work on Friday, Isobel still wasn't in the library, or anywhere else, but that was okay. Our couch communication was turning out to be the highlight of my day. I think it was just as thrilling to receive something from her in our spot as it would've been to talk face-to-face to her. So I jotted out a quick note:

I'm on page 458. I hope Murtagh is good. I like him.

When I returned at noon, a new piece of paper was waiting for me.

Want me to tell you?

I grinned and wrote out my answer directly under hers.

Good God, NO!

When I checked the library at the end of the day, she'd answered.

LOL. Okay, then. My lips are sealed.

A laugh. Holy shit. I'd gotten her to laugh. On paper, but still. I felt like I was the king of the world. I strolled out of the library with what felt like a manly strut and was almost all the way home before I realized I hadn't written anything back to her!

Oh, shit.

My step faltered and smile dropped. The urge to turn right back around and walk another hour back to her house to answer her mounted, but I'd be back in the morning. That would be soon enough, and besides, it'd give me all evening to think up the perfect reply.

I planned to go straight to the library on Saturday, except Mr. Nash was waiting for me in the salon when I entered through the back door. I was surprised to see him. I hadn't seen him since that first day. But then, he probably worked at his office in town most of the time, and since it was Saturday, he was probably off work.

"Can I have a word with you?" he clipped out, not sounding very pleased.

Startled by his tone, I nodded immediately. "Of course."

I followed him to his office, feeling like a scolded schoolboy being sent to the principal and not even sure why.

He stood at the door, holding it open as I passed him

to enter his office. Then he calmly closed it before turning to me and hissing, "What the hell is going on, Hollander? I swear she's become *more* of a hermit than she was before."

I blinked at him, stunned. But how the hell had he known she'd been avoiding me?

He lifted an eyebrow. "Constance says she stays out of sight while you're here."

Constance? That rat!

I'd had no idea someone would be giving him progress reports.

Cornered and attacked, I shook my head and stuttered, "I…I…are you sure it's *me* she's avoiding?"

He narrowed his eyes. "When was the last time you talked to her?"

It took me a second to answer. Would our notes be considered talking? They were definitely a form a communication, but they were a private correspondence, just between us. I didn't want her dad to know about them—it would ruin what they'd come to mean to me.

So I mumbled, "The first day I worked here," since that was the last time I'd actually seen her face and heard her voice. Then I winced a split second before he exploded because I knew how bad that sounded.

"*The first day*? It's been two full *weeks* since then. That is not acceptable, not acceptable at all. What did you *do* to her?"

"I...I don't know, sir," I lied, knowing exactly what I'd done to make her retreat. "I'm trying. I go everywhere you said she should be, and she's never there." I hung my head in shame and tried to brace myself against the possibility I was about to be let go. Strangely enough, my first thought was not about how my mother would cope, but that I might never see Isobel again.

She couldn't just blow into my life one day, stir everything around, and then never be heard from again. That wasn't right.

I risked a glance at Mr. Nash, only to find him as frustrated and upset as I was, for completely different reasons. "Well, something's got to be done about it," he huffed.

When he glanced at me, I knew that this "something" he spoke of had to be done by *me*. Except I didn't know what. I had thought the books and note exchanges had been progress, but since I refused to tell him about those, I had nothing.

Short of storming her bedroom and dragging her out by the hair, I had no control over where she might be at any given time. Maybe I could plant myself on her sofa in the library and wait there all day. I knew I could keep myself occupied with the rest of *Brisingr*. I could just wait until she snuck in since it was obvious she visited the room while I was working. I just had to be there at the right time. But would Mr. Nash be okay with me reading on the job, or would any of his staff mind such laziness?

There had to be something I could do inside the library to keep myself busy.

When an idea struck, I blurted, "Bookshelves."

Mr. Nash glanced curiously at his own shelves. "What about them?"

"No, in the library," I said, growing eager. "There's not enough shelf space for all the books in there. So what if I made more? I'd have to consult with her on designs, and wood types, and just…" With not much knowledge about the topic, I lamely added, "Just every step of the process. Right?"

The idea appealed to him. His eyes lit with hope and he nodded slowly before squinting. "You know how to build bookshelves?"

I knew how to cut wood and then nail it back together. The rest I could learn, after another trip to the public library. So I gave a vague nod, mumbling, "Mmm, hmm."

That was good enough for Mr. Nash. He clapped his

hands together, his grin blooming. "Perfect. You head to her library now and get started. I'll make sure Izzy knows she *has* to see you if she wants any say in how her library's renovated."

I nodded. "Sounds good."

And so it was decided; I would build bookshelves. Except…

Fuck me, what the hell had I just gotten myself into? I didn't have a clue how to really build bookshelves.

chapter SEVEN

Back in the library, paper and a pencil in hand, I began to draft.

I was scribbling my idea for the third wall when I heard her.

"Let me guess. You've never built a bookshelf in your life, have you?"

My heart gave a crazy, massive ka-pow before I could even lift my head. Then my breath caught in my throat. She wore her hair down, one half covering her scars, as well as long sleeves and thin black gloves. It was impossible to tell she'd ever been wounded. But not being able to see her scars wasn't why she looked so beautiful to me.

The fire was back inside her. She was ready to spar again. It made her sizzle with a sparkling vitality.

Sending her a crazy grin, because holy shit, there she was, in person, I chuckled. "What gave me away?"

She sighed heavily and wandered closer. "What exactly *have* you done to inspire my father to hire you as our handyman?"

"I have mastered the art of begging," I answered,

lifting my nose as if supremely proud of my ability.

Isobel quirked an eyebrow and slowed to a stop about five feet from the study table where I sat. "Pray tell, what does *that* mean?"

I stopped preening and sent her a rueful grin. "It means my mom owed him a debt…a very large debt. So I begged and pleaded until he agreed to let me try to work it off for her."

Rolling her eyes as if finding that news typical of her father, she sighed. "I always knew his kind, generous heart would get him into trouble."

Refusing to take her insult personally, I merely kept grinning. "Bet you won't be saying that once I make you the most amazing bookshelves ever."

She lifted an eyebrow, letting me know she highly doubted my abilities, but all she murmured was, "Hmm."

I laughed and waved her forward. "Take a seat. Listen to my ideas. Then tell me what you really want."

After a confused blink, she said, "What?"

"Let me know what you think about my ideas for your bookshelves." I swiveled the piece of paper upside down so it'd be right-side up for her. "I already have a few plans."

Successfully drawn in by the lure of bookshelves, she eased closer. Five feet became three. Then one. When she saw I really did have a ton of ideas, she silently pulled out the chair across from me and sat.

"Why are these shaded and these aren't?"

"The shaded ones are the shelves already there," I explained, growing eager to tell her the ideas stirring in my head. "The non-shaded ones are the ones I'd like to add."

Her finger slid over the three rows of shelves positioned above the shaded ones. "But…"

"The walls in here are so tall," I explained before she could ask. "Wouldn't it be awesome if the shelves went all the way to the ceiling, and we installed one of those rolling library ladders to reach them?"

Lips parting in awe, she turned toward the wall where I wanted to do just that. "That would be so cool," she breathed more to herself than to me, in a voice I'd never heard her use before, a voice I had a feeling was her real one, not some haughty tone she put on just to speak to me.

Then, suddenly, as if remembering herself, she cleared her throat and spun back to me, her cheeks tinged with pink.

A smile exploded across my face. "I know, right?" I tugged the sheet of paper closer to me so I could point out a few more ideas. "And the shelves you have now are fixed and permanent. But I'd like to install adjustable ones. You don't organize your books in alphabetical order, so it would be easy to economize space by grouping similar-sized books on each row to fit in more rows."

Her face shot up. "How do you know I don't organize alphabetically?"

The look I sent her was sly and knowing. Ignoring the question, I tapped my finger against the design. "I'll figure out what wood and styles the current shelves are and try to imitate them, unless you want something different."

Isobel stared at me a moment, obviously still stuck on the fact that I knew her library so well, before she shook her head and blinked. "I…the same style would be fine."

"Okay, then." I nodded. "I'll look for a matching stain finish while I'm at it. Did you want doors on any of the shelves to house some of your favorite or rarer books?"

"I…" She turned to study the wall. Then she nodded. "Yes, I think that would be lovely to have maybe one bookcase with doors. Thank you."

I'm absolutely positive her *thank you* came out completely by accident, maybe without her being aware she'd said it. It took everything inside me not to react in fear she'd realize what she'd just said and try to retract it.

I liked this side of her, this softer, human side. I liked it a lot. Maybe even more than her bitchy side.

"Great," I said, jotting down a note that she needed some doors as I tried to control the racing of my heart. "Is there anything in my plans you want to alter?"

She blinked at the scribbles I'd made, and I took a second to clear my throat. "Sorry, I'm not much of an artist. Hopefully you can still understand what I was trying to convey though."

"Yeah," she murmured vaguely, "I mean…" She looked up into my face. "Actually, this looks fine. If you can do it."

I gazed into her unnaturally blue eyes and felt something inside my chest unfurl. Why did she have to seem so soft, almost vulnerable, today? It tugged at something protective inside me.

"I'll figure it out," I assured her.

Her lips parted and she dragged her gaze away. "Well…we should probably…we should probably figure out some calculations." Popping out of her chair as if it had bitten her, she began to back away. "I'm going to go find a tape measure."

As she hurried from the room, I watched her go. What I wouldn't give to see what was going on in her head. Neither of us had mentioned the notes, or books, or seeds we'd been exchanging on the couch, and yet it seemed natural to pretend they had never happened.

When she returned, I was standing in front of the longest stretch of wall that would hold the most shelves, jotting down notes on a fresh piece of paper. "Looks like this wall can hold maybe seven shelves across and ten up," I said as she approached. "So that'll make a total of seventy shelves. And since we already have four across and seven on each bookcase, that would mean there are already…"

"Twenty-eight," Isobel informed me when it took me too long to calculate in my head.

I pointed my pen at her and winked. "Thank you. Twenty-eight. So we can add…forty-two more shelves for this wall alone. Wow. That'll give you over twice the space you already have."

A look of awe entered her expression as she stared at her shelves. In that moment, her thoughts were loud and beautiful. She was already thinking about how she'd rearrange her books with that much more room.

"Did you find a tape measure?" I asked.

She held one up.

"Sweet. Do you think you could measure the distance from here to here for me?" I stepped past her, brushing so close her rose scent clogged my nostrils. My body went into extreme focus, becoming all too aware of how near she lingered as she leaned forward to place the tape measure where I asked.

God, she smelled so good, I couldn't help myself. I tipped closer and—

No, I shouldn't be doing that, especially when her father was home and would probably walk in at any moment to assess our progress.

That thought helped kill the reaction I was having. I cleared my throat and wrote *width of each shelf* on the paper to distract myself. But the moment I glanced up, all I saw was her…from the back, lifting her arms to carefully measure. It brought up the back of her shirt, showing off a small slit of skin between the bottom of her shirt and the top of her pants. Pants which covered the most luscious, tightly rounded, perfectly curved ass ever.

"Thirty-five and three-eighths inches," she reported, making me jump and dart my attention back to the sheet of paper and clear my throat before writing down the information.

"Great. Thanks. And how thick is the wood?"

Oh, hell. I hadn't really just asked that, had I? If she

asked *which* wood, I was a dead man. I wouldn't be able to control myself.

"Looks like five-eighths of an inch," Isobel said, and I almost lost it.

Five-eighths of an inch? Um, no. It was definitely thicker than that, especially at the moment.

When I didn't respond soon enough, Isobel turned, blinking at me. "What's wrong?"

"What?" My eyes flashed open wide. Bookshelves! We were talking about bookshelves, here. Nothing else. Get your damn mind back in the game, Hollander, you fucking fifth-grade pervert.

Isobel tipped her head, studying me. "Are you okay?"

"What?" I asked again. I was acting completely unhinged. "I mean, yes. *Yes,*" I nearly hollered. "I'm good. Great. How the hell do you stay in such good shape?"

And oh my God, *what*? Had I really just asked her that? Why, why, why did some things just tumble out of my mouth?

I wanted to smack my hand to my forehead, then sink through the floor and die.

"Excuse me?" she asked, and for once she totally lacked any bitter, insulting, or haughty attitude when I actually deserved it most. She merely sounded utterly confused.

"I just..." My face on fire, I cleared my throat and motioned to her. "Sorry, I just noticed you seem to be really fit, and I wondered…" Damn, I didn't think I was making anything better. More awkward, but probably not better. "I just wondered what your secret was."

Because that ass. Holy damn, a guy could bounce a dime off that perfect, tight ass.

Not that I'd noticed. Of course not. That would be shameless, unbecoming behavior. And I was a decent guy.

"I run," she finally said.

"Really?" Holy shit, she wasn't going to ream me up one wall and down another for checking her out. Thank you, God. Clearing my throat again—man, I needed a drink of water or something, for all this throat clearing—I forced myself back to the conversation. "When do you run? I've never seen you—"

"Early in the morning," she cut in, thankfully stopping me from more uncontrollable jabbering. "Before you get here. There's a trail around the lake. When the sun comes up, it reflects off the surface of the water. Sometimes there are ducks or geese swimming in it."

"It sounds beautiful." And she looked beautiful while she described it.

Isobel shrugged and turned away. "It's peaceful."

I nodded. "I don't run, like ever…unless something's chasing me."

Grinning at the joke, I cleared my throat when she didn't laugh back.

God, I was such a dork.

"It's a good cardiovascular workout," she said, opening the tape measure to measure the height of the bookcases.

Again, I stupidly bobbed my head up and down. "I should try it then. You think I could run with you some morning?"

She whirled around to stare at me as if I'd lost my mind, the tape measure snapping back into its shell as if equally shocked by my question.

I flushed, feeling like a moron. "Sorry. That was a stupid question. Ignore me."

After a couple blinks, she returned to measuring. But every time she bent down to tuck the end of the tape measure into the very bottom of the bookcase, her hair would fall into her face. She'd try to spit it out, then wipe it away so she could see what she was doing, only for the tape measure to pull free of wherever she was securing it to.

"Here," I offered, stepping forward to assist, but she hissed, "Blast it," and yanked a hair tie from her pocket before pulling her long, silken dark locks back and securing everything out of her face.

I pulled to a stop, shocked she'd done that. Then a ball of warmth grew in me, realizing she felt comfortable enough around me to expose her scars. As if hearing my thoughts, she shot me a hard glance and narrowed her eyes, her expression daring me to say a single word.

With her glare, she let me see the skin that had been marred and distorted, but she also reopened her defiant, I-will-crush-you, snooty attitude. It was amazing, really. She hated people seeing her scars so much that she cloaked this self-protective anger around her as if bubble-wrapping her vulnerabilities. The only problem with that method was instead of hiding her tender spots, she actually brought more attention to them.

It was sad, and made me want to hug her until all the pain inside her went away.

"What?" she demanded, narrowing her eyes.

Smiling, I offered a thumbs-up. "Much better. Now that you're done fiddle-farting around with your hair, let's get some shit measured."

chapter EIGHT

We couldn't finish our measuring without the use of a ladder. So I returned to the supply room and dragged my window-washing ladder back to the library. Before I reached the entrance, however, I noticed some guy ahead of me approaching the door as well.

Frowning, I slowed to a stop.

Who was this?

He wasn't Mr. Nash or Lewis. He was younger, around my age with dark hair and mirrored sunglasses. When he stepped into the room, I hurried after him, because seriously, who the hell *was* he?

When he caught sight of Isobel with her back to him as she stood at the study table, studying our "blueprints," his face lit with a mischievous grin, and he snuck up behind her.

Not sure if I should alert her to his presence, I paused in the doorway to watch him say, "Boo," just before he tapped her on the back.

Isobel yelped and spun around. She appeared irritated until she focused on his face. Then she transformed, springing toward the stranger and flinging her arms around his neck with a happy laugh. My eyes narrowed as he picked her up and spun her in a circle.

Something solid and nasty plopped hard into the base of my stomach. It swirled and frothed as Isobel cheekily smacked the man's arm until he returned her to her feet and took a step back. They both continued to grin at each other.

She liked him—whoever he was—she really liked him. I'd never seen her show genuine affection for anyone before, and it didn't sit well with me, mainly because she'd never seemed to like *me* that well.

Ah, hell, I was jealous.

Mentally swatting that nasty realization away in my head, I studied the man, dissecting him. He looked rich, friendly, clean, and pretty much too fucking perfect to be true. I decided I didn't like him. All that shine had to be fake or hiding something ugly.

"When did you get here?" Isobel asked, her blue eyes glossy and bright with a special glow just for him, the lucky bastard.

He grinned, his teeth way too white, and way too straight. "Just now. I thought I'd come see you before I got stuck in some long, boring meeting with the old man." Then he sighed dramatically, making Isobel laugh.

Holy shit, she'd just laughed, truly honestly laughed. How in the world had this douche gotten her to laugh? It wasn't right. Totally wasn't fair.

I pretty much had to hate him now.

Who was he?

Was he her boyfriend?

Her dad made her out to be so lonely and solitary with no one to talk to, yet Mr. Perfect here seemed to be doing just fine making her smile and laugh.

My jealousy burned hotter.

As if feeling my glare beaded in on him, Prince Charming glanced my way, only for his glowing smile to pause with a hint of shock. Instantly, he turned back to

Isobel and grasped her shoulders.

"Don't freak out," he told her in a steady voice as if he'd just spotted a spider in her hair and needed her to remain calm so he could remove it, "but there's a guy in your library."

Immediately, Isobel spun toward me as if remembering I still existed.

Yeah, remember me? The man building your bookshelves.

Her cheeks looked flushed, but I wasn't sure if that was from embarrassment over forgetting about me or excitement from *his* arrival.

"Oh," she said, making me feel even smaller because she really *had* forgotten about me. "He's here to build bookshelves."

Sure, yeah, tell your boyfriend that's all I'm here for, I wanted to snarl, before it struck me that building her bookshelves really *was* the only reason I was in her library. I wasn't here because we were friends or because she actually wanted to spend time with me. I was only providing her with a service for her precious books.

Acid slithered around the jealousy bubbling in my stomach, while the pretty, shiny man perked to attention at the mention of bookshelves.

"Really?" he asked, intrigued. Slipping off his shades and tucking them into his front pocket, he strolled toward me and eyed the ladder I was so lamely holding. "What a good idea. I'd started to worry all those books you were collecting were going to start overflowing out into the hall one of these days and overtake the whole house."

"Hey." Isobel, who'd followed him to me like a faithful pet, drilled a reprimanding finger into his side. "If you're so worried about the number of books I collect, then why do you always bring me a new one every time you visit?"

With a grin in her direction, he winked. "Oh right,

thanks for reminding me… Here you go." He pulled a miniature book from his pocket and tossed it her way.

She fumbled a moment before catching it. Then she took in the cover and gasped. After she flipped it open to the title page, she gasped again. "Oh my God, this is a first edition fairy tale book. I've been looking for one of these forever. Where did you find it?"

"Oh…" After breathing on his knuckles, the man buffed them against his shoulder in accomplishment. "I have my sources."

"Thank you." Pressing the tiny book to her chest, Isobel sent him a look full of adoration and complete devotion.

I thought I might puke.

He nodded, looking similarly taken with her before returning his curious gaze to me.

"So…" When he said nothing more, merely examined me as if I were an artifact in a museum, I self-consciously stuck out a hand.

"Shaw Hollander." I meant to add *nice to meet you*, but that part stuck in my throat.

He nodded and shook with me. "Ezra Nash."

"Oh!" I blurted. "You're the brother."

Relief and a flood of understanding poured through me. In one brief fraction of time, I felt both foolish for being so irrationally jealous and yet so pleased he wasn't actually dating Isobel I almost laughed. Then the moment passed and a cold sweat shrouded me as I realized what this meant. I wouldn't have been so upset to learn she had a boyfriend if I hadn't been interested in the position myself.

And that thought scared me. I knew I'd always been interested in her—in that way—but my reaction had been so extreme.

She was supposed to be a job, just a job. Falling for her could only cause problems. I needed to keep my feelings in check. I needed to stop thinking of her like that, or looking at her like that, or—

"The brother," Ezra Nash repeated on a grin. "That sounds so ominous, but yeah, I'm…*the brother.*"

"The annoying brother," Isobel snickered, which prompted Ezra to reach over without even looking her way and pinch her in the side.

She shrieked and slapped his hand, causing him to grin wider at me.

I stared between the siblings in awe, intrigued by their comfortable, teasing relationship and once again struck by how glad I was to learn they were only brother and sister.

Completely revising my opinion of him, I decided I liked him after all. I liked him a lot. He could make Isobel smile and laugh, and he wasn't dating her, so he was aces in my book.

"When did Dad hire a carpenter?" he asked, making me gulp because the glint in his eyes showed suspicion, as if he already knew why Henry Nash had truly brought me into his home.

"Two weeks ago," Isobel answered, sticking her thumbnail between her teeth as she studied a section of wall near us. "And he's our new general, overall handyman, not just a carpenter."

A little pocket of warmth grew inside me at her words. She knew I was by no means a carpenter in any sense of the word, but she still let her brother believe I could actually make these shelves with no trouble. The urge to touch her—just a simple touch, maybe on the arm, to show my gratitude—mounted.

Ah, shit. Yep, I was definitely into her, as into her as a guy could get. This was bad. This was so bad.

Fortunately, she pointed to the wall, tearing my attention from my doomed fate. "How close to the window are you going to make the shelves?"

I glanced over, taking in the space before answering, "As close as you want me to get."

She beamed, not a full smile, but something warm and pleased enough to slice through me with greediness, wanting more of it, craving her pleasure like a plant thirsty for water and sunshine.

"Not too close," she said. "I don't want to block out any more light than necessary. It's already dark enough in here as it is."

"Actually…" I lifted a finger, glad she'd mentioned the lighting. "I was thinking we could maybe lighten the walls and add some drop-down lamps or something to help with that."

Isobel glanced around the room, her eyes wide as she considered my idea. After a moment, she nodded. "Yeah," she said slowly. "Yes, I think that will work well."

Again, I glowed from the inside, soaking in her good mood.

"Sounds like you two are going to overhaul the entire room," Ezra put in.

"Well, it needs it," Isobel told him.

I nodded. "Libraries should be bright, wonderful spaces since they hold so many bright, wonderful worlds and adventures."

After a startled blink, Isobel sent me a soft smile. "Exactly."

And yep, I blossomed under her radiant stare. My chest expanded with air, making me feel like a helium balloon, and I swear I would've floated right off the floor if my feet hadn't been tethering me down.

"Hmm," her brother murmured, glancing speculatively between the two of us. "Well, I best get to my meeting with Dad." He clasped his hands together and took a step in reverse as if he felt like three of us were too many for the moment and he was the odd man out.

Isobel swung to him, flushing as if she'd been caught doing something wrong. "Is your coworker still giving you trouble?"

Ezra shuddered, and an expression of absolute disgust cloaked his face. "You mean the wicked witch?" His tone turning snide and stiff, he rolled his eyes insolently. "That woman lives to make my life a living hell. I swear she tries to nix every goddamn thing I suggest. I have to fight tooth and nail to get anything. It's completely ridiculous. And uncalled for."

Isobel sent me a cringe as if she regretted asking before saying to her brother, "I'll take that as a yes."

"And yet yes is so mild an answer for the indigestion that woman gives me." His face started to turn red as if merely mentioning her made his blood pressure rise unnaturally.

"Maybe you should talk to Dad about it," Isobel suggested. "I bet he'll have some good suggestions on how to deal with her."

"If it's not how to hide a body, then it's not going to be a good enough suggestion," Ezra mumbled moodily even as he bent to press a kiss to the good side of Isobel's cheek. But his lips barely grazed her skin before he straightened in surprise. "Hey." His gaze shot to me, then returned to her. "You have your hair pulled up."

Isobel flushed and sent me a quick, guilty glance before tucking a stray piece that had come undone from her ponytail behind her ear. Then she shifted to the side, hiding her scars from us. "Yeah. So?"

"So..." Ezra drawled. "You always keep it down and covering your...your face."

The urge to step in and defend her was strong. Except her brother had done nothing whatsoever to attack. He'd just made her uncomfortable by so boldly pointing out she wasn't hiding her scars. And I didn't like her being uncomfortable.

"He's just *staff*," she muttered defensively, making me feel less than human, as if being part of the *staff* made me a nobody. *Staff* didn't have thoughts or feelings or a brain. *Staff* didn't count.

Ezra glanced toward me as if he could smell the insult oozing off me. With a small clearing of his throat, he announced, "All right then. I'm going to go talk to Dad now," and he booked it out of there.

Isobel remained frozen, purposely avoiding looking in my direction. So I turned away to set up the ladder by the wall. Then I found the tape measure on the table and grabbed it before climbing. Once I reached the ceiling, I blindly lifted the tape measure toward the wall, not recording a damn inch.

"So, that was your brother, huh?"

"Yes." She sounded distant and stiff as if she'd been the one who'd just been insulted. Or maybe she felt guilty for hurting my feelings and didn't know how to apologize. I had no idea.

I nodded, grinding my teeth. "He seemed nice."

"He is."

Okay, I guess the one and two word answers meant she didn't feel like talking to the *staff*. Message received.

But then she said, "He just got a job in the fashion industry this last year."

I turned to her, surprised she'd voluntarily offered information to me. "Oh yeah?" I asked, more interested in the fact she was finally talking to me, opening up—about her brother, but still…opening up.

She nodded, rigidly, as if this talking rationally stuff was all too new and foreign to her. "Yeah. My dad did this merger with a clothing company that was struggling and instead of selling it off again, he decided to put Ezra in charge of the half he'd bought to, you know, give him some life experience on how to administrate and run a real company."

"And he's doing okay with it?" I asked, eager to hear more of her voice in that tone. When she wasn't mad, or condescending, or bitter, she sounded softer. Feminine. Sweet.

Captivated, I watched her face as she shrugged.

"Yeah, I guess. Dad seems pleased anyway. I mean, he—Ezra—struggles a lot to get along with the co-CEO of the original half of the company. I guess she's a real witch. But I can still tell he gets a thrill out of the rest of his job. He likes it, and I think it suits him."

I smiled. "Well, good. That's pretty cool." Then a thought struck me. "Did you ever want to be a CEO or run a multimillion-dollar company?"

"Me?" Her lips parted and lashes fluttered for a second before she jerked her head back and forth. "N-no. Not at all. That was never my dream."

"What was your dream then?"

Shadows and ghosts filled her eyes, haunting her. Panicking because I'd put them there, I revised my question. "When you were five," I blurted. "What did you want to be when you were five?" Then I grinned and laughed at myself. "I wanted to be a mailman. Nothing gave me a bigger thrill than mail time. Mom always let me open the junk mail advertisements, and I'd pretend all day they were important documents that needed to be archived and organized."

Isobel gazed at me a moment before saying, "I was pretty typical for a five-year-old, I think. I wanted to be a princess."

I grinned at the idea of her running around in a dress full of tulle, a tiara and maybe a magic wand. She was probably the cutest little five-year-old princess ever.

"And when you were fifteen?" I asked.

"Fifteen?" she asked, lifting her eyebrows before drawing in a breath and thinking. Then she said, "I wanted to be a professional reader."

That one made me laugh, before nodding my approval. "I like it." Then a thought struck. "Do you now? Write reviews for all the books you read, I mean?"

She shrugged. "Not really. Nothing in a professional capacity, anyway."

"Oh." I didn't know why that depressed me. It

just…it was sad that none of her dreams had come true, and on top of that, she'd been hit with the fire, and her mom's death. How many other things had she missed out on doing? How many things was she avoiding because of her insecurities?

"How old were you when your mom died?"

Holy shit, where the hell had that question vomited from? I hadn't even really been thinking about it. It had seriously just popped out without any kind of prompting from my rational brain.

Isobel froze for a second before slowly saying, "I was seventeen."

A knot formed in my throat. What an awful age for a girl to lose her mother. About to finish high school and move on to adulthood. Everything in her life was already changing; she probably needed her mother most then, to help guide and advise her.

"So, you're twenty-five now?"

That question seemed to throw her. It boggled my mind too. I had no idea why I'd asked it, probably to help drag sad memories away. But she nodded.

I nodded too before mumbling, "I'm twenty-eight."

"Oh," she said.

She didn't seem to know what to do with that information, and I had no idea why I'd offered it. Feeling like a moron, I rushed to add, "I was three when my dad died."

She blinked. "Oh, I…" Her hand slowly moved to the base of her throat. "I didn't know."

I shrugged. "It was a car accident on his way home from work. His fault, so we had to help the insurance company pay a bunch of others who were injured that day. I guess we weren't that bad off—financially, anyway—until then. Not that I remember. I don't remember what our life was like before that…or anything about my dad."

"What do you think is worse," she murmured, watching me thoughtfully. "Having gotten to know your parent and missing her terribly after she's gone, or never remembering him at all, and always feeling like this huge hole of nothing is stuck in the middle of you?"

I stared at her, shocked. She'd just nailed what I'd always felt. I'd never mourned for my father properly because I hadn't remembered him the way my older siblings had. They'd always told me how lucky I'd been, that I didn't have to hurt as much as they did, but I'd still felt something. An ache I couldn't describe.

But the way she just said *huge hole of nothing* had labeled it perfectly. I *had* suffered, just as my siblings had, except in a different way.

"I don't know," I murmured. "They both kind of suck."

"Yeah," she agreed slowly. "They do."

Silence fell between us, but a good silence, a bonding kind of silence where for once we seemed to understand another soul and that other soul understood us in return.

"I usually start running at five every morning," Isobel said.

I jerked my attention to her. My heart began to hammer. "Five?"

She gave a single, abrupt nod, refusing to look my way.

Hope—hope like I'd never felt before—exploded inside me. "I'll be here."

chapter
NINE

It was early. It was way too fucking early for me.

I'd left the house at three thirty to get here by five, and I felt dead on my feet. After spending most of the weekend taking care of my mom, who'd caught the flu, reading up on carpentry, and finishing *Brisingr*, I'd already gotten to bed late on both Saturday and Sunday nights, but waking up at three in the fucking morning was what was going to lay me flat.

When I reached the gate at the end of the drive, I almost wept, ready to curl up on the ground and sleep for a couple decades. Except I'd told Isobel I'd run with her this morning.

Run.

Right.

I could barely make my feet keep walking.

Since about my third trip to Porter Hall, I'd stopped ringing the intercom at the gate to ask for permission to enter. There wasn't a fence around the property; it seemed bothersome and time-consuming to call someone to open the gate when I could just walk around it. And since I was beginning to feel as if I was actually welcome here, I walked around it now and trudged up the long lane.

I wore sweats and running shoes instead of my usual blue jeans and work boots, but I'd tucked my work clothes away in the book bag I carried as well as a change of T-shirts.

The sun hadn't risen yet, but it was thinking about it. Shapes and shadows were beginning to become distinct. When I reached the end of the drive, I could make out someone there, stretching and pulling her leg back so far that her toe was nearly touching the center of her spine.

"Isobel?" I asked, just to make certain it was her.

She yelped and dropped her foot, before gasping. "Oh. You're here." Then she glanced around me. "Wait, did you walk?"

"Yeah." I approached her, suddenly not so tired anymore. "Have you been waiting long? I'm not late, am I?"

"No…no. You're five minutes early, actually." I swear I heard embarrassment in her voice before she cleared her throat. "I decided to meet you out here in case you didn't know how to get to the running trail."

"Oh," I said before laughing. "You're right. I would've had no idea how to get back there."

She nodded. "Then follow me."

I did. We walked behind the house and under a couple large trees, past a few outbuildings and onto a narrow gravel path lined with trees. But she continued to walk, so I figured we hadn't reached the "trail" yet. I hadn't seen the lake she'd mentioned either.

Crickets chirped around us, an owl hooted overhead, and gravel crunched under our feet. For as warm as the days were, it was still chilly this early in the day. I swiped my hands up and down my arms, wishing for about the fiftieth time in the past hour and a half since I left home that I'd brought a jacket with me. Isobel was smart; she wore a long-sleeved running hoodie.

"How far do you walk to get here every day?" she asked, breaking the silence.

I shrugged. "Oh…not that far."

"Couldn't be that *close*," she argued. "Most of the houses out here, for a good five-mile stretch, belong to the…"

Rich, she didn't finish.

"I live near Pestle." Pestle had been the name of the shoe factory I'd worked at that had gone out of business. But it had been well-known enough for people to still call that part of town Pestle.

She made an audible gasp. "But that's in the middle of town. God almighty, Shaw, you must walk over an hour just to get here every day."

"Barely over an hour," I said, as my body clanged out of control over the fact she'd used my first name for the first time. I liked how she said Shaw. It sounded good on her tongue, coming from her mouth. Sweet. Genuine. Intimate.

Isobel stopped walking and turned to face me. "Why in the world would you want to run after walking over an hour to get here?"

I faltered, not sure how to answer that without lying *or* giving away the truth. "I just…yeah. I don't know."

A spot started to itch directly behind my ear. I ripped off my hat to scratch it, then slammed the hat back on, feeling even more exposed by Isobel's penetrating stare. So I cleared my throat and started walking up the path without her.

"I checked out all these books from the library this weekend about building bookcases, but the most useful tips I found were actually on Pinterest. And what do you think of this…a hidden passage bookshelf door?"

When she didn't answer soon enough, I rushed to argue my point, because seriously, nothing on earth could be cooler than a hidden passage bookshelf door. Right? "I don't know where that doorway on the south wall in the library leads, but that would be an awesome place to put a bookshelf door. Don't you think?"

"I…" Catching up to me, Isobel shook her head. "Yeah. Sure. That would be okay."

My abrupt change in subject might've thrown her or she just wasn't as enthused about the idea as I was, but her indifferent answer made me rush to add, "Of course, we don't have to do it if you don't want to."

"No, I do. The idea sounds fun."

"But…?" I pressed, my stomach churning with unease. It was pathetic how much I wanted her to love all my ideas.

She merely shook her head. "No buts. I like the idea. I'm just worried about how difficult it's going to be for you to make."

"Ugh. That's the last thing you should even think about. The how is for me to worry about, and besides," I threw her what I hoped was a contagious grin, "the bigger the challenge the better the adventure, right?"

I shrugged off my backpack and dropped it to the ground, then flipped my ball cap around so I was wearing it backward, before I started to jog. We'd just reached the edge of the lake, and this looked like the point where I had to guess she began her morning run.

"Hey," she called after me, cupping her hands around her mouth. "You're going counterclockwise. I always run clockwise around the lake."

I laughed and turned to run backwards so I could face her while I kept going. "Adjust to change, Isobel. Adjust to change."

She grumbled something I couldn't hear, then she hurried to catch up with me. Grinning, I turned to watch where I was going, though it was still too dark to see all that much. The sky was beginning to change colors. Orange, yellow and pinks peeked over the horizon and reflected off the surface of the calm water. A bird called in the distance. I breathed deeply, taking in the scent of damp earth and pine from the evergreen trees.

"God, this is breathtaking. No wonder you run every morning."

"It feels strange going this way," she muttered.

I laughed. "Like running it for the first time?"

She shot me an odd glance before gazing around her as if, yeah, she were seeing the scenery for the first time. Lips parting, she turned her attention back to me. "Kind of. Yeah."

With a wink, I offered, "Tomorrow we can run it clockwise and then toggle back and forth each day. Sound okay to you?"

"But…" I had a feeling she was worried about me hiking out here on foot every morning from three thirty to five, until she realized I didn't care. So she murmured, "Yeah. Okay."

It was the most satisfying feeling in the world whenever she stopped fighting and bickering with me to acquiesce or soften her tone. More rewarding than anything I could ever remember experiencing.

We didn't talk much after that. The peace of the awakening morning, plus the whole out-of-breath thing from running, kept conversation limited. I asked her how long she typically ran, she answered eight laps, which made it approximately two miles, and that was about all we said.

Since I wasn't used to running, she naturally kept pace with me. It made me wonder how fast she usually went and how much she had to slow herself to match my strides. I pushed myself as hard as I could, and yet I was still panting for breath and wanting to pass out right there on the path once we finished. But Isobel encouraged me to keep going, walk it off, until my heart rate settled.

Still, I had to clutch my chest and bend with my other hand on one knee for a good minute before I could straighten.

"Oh, damn," I gasped. "That was…that was amazing." Even as worn-out as I was, I don't think I'd ever felt so alive and energized.

When I stood upright, she held out an opened bottle of water. No idea where she'd been storing it, but I didn't care. I snagged it from her and gulped greedily.

"Thank you. You're a saint." I handed the bottle back, only for my mouth to go bone dry when she drank from the same spot I'd just put my lips against.

Tipping her head back, she closed her eyes and swallowed, her throat working through each gulp while a bead of sweat caressed her unmarred cheek before slipping down the side of her throat.

I went hard as stone, imaging myself licking the droplet away. Then she went and swiped her tongue over her bottom lip, catching some escaped water before lapping it back into her mouth. My skin prickled with such acute awareness I could already picture how it'd feel to push inside her and have the walls of her sex envelop me and contract from pleasure.

When a groan rumbled from my throat, Isobel turned my way.

Abruptly realizing I probably had the freaking Eiffel Tower poking out the front of my sweats, I bent and jerked my backpack from the ground where it had been waiting for my return and held it smartly over my lap area.

But the move only drew Isobel's attention down, which made me feel more exposed. I jostled the pack, explaining, "Change of clothes."

I'd only been trying to get her attention away from my crotch so she wouldn't notice how aroused I was, but when her expression fell, I wondered if she thought I was trying to make an excuse to leave because I didn't want to be around her any longer.

I opened my mouth to say…hell, I had no idea. I just knew I didn't want her thinking I didn't like her.

She beat me to the words, though. Turning her face slightly, so I couldn't see her scars, she motioned a hand toward the house. "There's a shower in the pool house if you want to use that to wash off before changing into your clothes."

"Okay," I started to agree, my mind still unable to stop picturing her flat on her back and opening herself to me. "Wait." I shook my head. "You have a pool house? You have a *pool*?"

Then I nearly smacked myself in the forehead. Of course they had a pool and a pool house. Every house as grand and huge and expensive as this one must have a freaking pool and pool house. I was mostly shocked because I'd never seen either before.

My shock was a good thing, though. It seemed to amuse Isobel. She softened her edges until she forgot to hide her burn wounds from me. "One of these days, you're going to need a full tour of the place."

I grinned. "If you agree to be my guide, I accept."

No idea why I said that. I realized how flirty it sounded as soon as the words left my mouth, but I couldn't regret it. Isobel drew in a breath as her face flushed and her mouth tightened in an effort to keep her emotions at bay. Then she glanced at me, and those blue-blue eyes of hers reflected all the hope and yearning I'd been feeling in my own chest since the moment I'd met her.

"We'll see," she murmured evasively. And I was forced to keep my backpack positioned directly over my lap area for the rest of the walk to the pool house.

chapter TEN

"It's not even six yet," Isobel said, jarring me from my thoughts of how best to hide my erection.

I glanced her way and lifted my eyebrows. "What?"

She flushed and waved a hand. "It's still over three hours until you're supposed to start work, but it'd be counterproductive for you to walk all the way home. You'd just have to turn around and start right back once you reached your door."

"Oh…. Yeah. I hadn't thought of that." Actually, I had. I'd been hoping to sneak inside her house and find some place to nap until nine. But now that she'd realized the time discrepancy, I wasn't so sure I could sneak a nap anywhere.

I couldn't be too upset about my ruined plans, though. I was a little too pleased she'd considered my situation enough to realize my dilemma. How very thoughtful of her.

I liked being on her mind.

"I bet my dad would be fine with you leaving at two today if you want to start work at six."

"You think?" I liked how she wanted to help me.

She nodded. "And tomorrow…I mean, if you still want to keep running, I can wait until seven. Then you could work from eight to four."

And I liked how she was willing to readjust her own schedule to fit me into her plans.

I liked all of this new side to Isobel, actually. Once she dropped the bitterness, she could be extremely nice. She was quite the dichotomy.

Flashing her a roguish grin, I couldn't help but tease. "So you've decided I make an acceptable enough exercise companion, huh?"

Her eyes went wide and she turned her face away before murmuring, "You'll do."

For Isobel, I considered those two words to be an endorsement for sainthood. It was a far cry from *who's the idiot in my rose garden.* Actually, it was hard for me to register this as the same woman who'd chastised me for trying to steal a flower from her.

I sent her a sideways glance. Since the sun was up, I saw her better. And damn, she looked fit and adorably sexy in the black yoga pants, long-sleeved running top and perky ponytail. She walked on my right so I couldn't see her scars from this angle, and it made me wonder if she'd done that on purpose. She did that a lot, I realized, sneakily maneuvering herself to keep them hidden.

I wanted to be insulted. I mean, did she really think I would treat her any differently because of them? But honestly, I got it.

Everyone had issues about themselves, parts they thought were ugly or humiliating, and aspects they wanted to hide away because those things made them feel vulnerable. People didn't generally let others see their vulnerable parts until they felt safe. You never knew if someone else would be disgusted, or think less of you, or if they'd use your weakness as leverage to hurt you. It was purely human nature and self-preservation to vet a person first before letting them prove to you that you could trust them enough to see if they'd continue to like you in spite of, or even better, *because* of your flaws.

So it must suck that the most vulnerable part of Isobel was right out in the open, on display for everyone to see. She didn't get to decide who saw her—well, I guess that wasn't true. She'd become a hermit to keep most everyone away. But the point was, having something she clearly didn't like about herself on full display took away a lot of that control and self-preservation. And it seemed to make her want to close other parts of herself away even tighter.

Which only made me more determined to gain her favor. One day, she'd look me straight in the eye without ever worrying about hiding anything. That was my goal.

"Here," she murmured, motioning in front of us.

I looked up, paying attention to where we were going, only to slow to a stunned halt. I didn't know why anything about Porter Hall should surprise me anymore, but this…this shocked the shit out of me.

"You gotta be fucking kidding me?" I blurted.

We'd just cleared the gravel path through the trees that led from the pond, only to step into an entirely new world. The pool…okay, the pool was actually not that impressive. It was smaller than I'd pictured it being and curved into a cute kidney bean shape. It was the pool *house* that left my jaw dropping. Not that house was an accurate word for the cave in front of me. And I'm talking a real, freaking cave here. They'd amassed an enormous pile of clay boulders, large enough for a small evergreen tree and some plants and bushes to grow up the side, to make the house. A waterfall gushed from over what looked like one entrance into the place with another round tube opening that had to be a slide.

I didn't know how I never caught sight of this before when I'd been helping Lewis work outside, but shit…I was thinking it was about time to take the full tour of this place.

"There should be towels and toiletries in the bathroom," Isobel told me as she pushed a button posted on the side of the rock wall.

My eyes grew wide as the wall separated to display the abundance within. It was nothing but rock floors, rock ceilings, rock walls and a rock bar that ran the length of the room. Even the twelve-foot hot tub was made of rock. With a fish tank, television, and fireplace embedded into the far wall, there was still enough room to host a doorway that led into what appeared to be the bedroom.

A gasp of pure awe left me.

"I could live here," I said, turning to gape at Isobel, wondering why *she* didn't live in here. "I mean…can I live here?"

She blinked at me, to which I felt the need to lift my hands and say, "Kidding," though really, I wasn't. I could seriously live here. No problem. This place—the entire property of Porter Hall—was pure awesomeness. I was beginning to wonder why Henry Nash was so worried about why his daughter wanted to hang out here all the time. Hell, I wanted to hang out here all the time.

"The bathroom's in there, through the bedroom," Isobel said. She suddenly seemed awkward.

I wondered if my amazed gawking at all the splendor made her self-conscious, or if she was coming to realize just how close we'd been standing. She turned her face to the side, hiding her scars. I wanted to tell her to stop, to touch her chin and force her to face me directly.

But she rotated away and left the pool house before I could summon the nerve.

Clearing my throat, I nodded to myself and stepped into the bedroom.

Yep, I could definitely live here. Quite comfortably. The bed was probably a queen size and about twice as wide as the sleeper sofa I'd been using since Mom had moved in with me and taken over my bedroom. A little depressed over the fact I couldn't sneak in here and take that nap on *this* bed, I found the bathroom and shook my head.

Again, it was all rock with half the space taken up by a shower full of glass doors and about a dozen different showerheads. I was already drooling for the experience when I shut the door behind me and began to peel off my damp running clothes as fast as I could. I tore off my hat then kicked off my shoes even as I shucked my sweats.

Figuring out how to turn on the various showerheads and control the temperature was a bit of a challenge. I froze my backside, then burned it, before getting things just right. And then…then I just stood there, getting pummeled by what felt like a million miniature wet massages.

"Heaven," I moaned, lifting my face to one spray. "Oh, God. This is heaven."

Deciding the stainless steel dispensers hanging from the wall contained the soap and shampoo I needed, I pushed a button and flooded my hand with foamy soap. It smelled woodsy, spicy and masculine. I lathered my body and rinsed. Then, I couldn't help myself, I soaped up again. It just felt so good. I could shower in here all day.

But it didn't take me long to remember who I was, and where I was, and what time it was. It'd be six soon, and if I wanted to start my workday at six, I'd better stop using all my employer's things and get to work.

A little ashamed of myself for dawdling, I rinsed and shut off the water before shaking myself dry. After opening the shower door, I hunted up a towel in the cupboard above the toilet.

On went fresh underwear, socks, and a clean pair of jeans. I'd had a little too much fun with all the hot water, so the room felt like a sauna. I took my work boots and a folded shirt from my backpack before gathering all my running shit and stuffing them inside. Then I opened the door to finish dressing in the less humid bedroom.

No sooner had I snapped the T-shirt open and lifted it above my head to slide it on than Isobel came through the doorway.

"I brought more towels in case there weren't any—*oh*!"

Instead of rushing to pull the shirt the rest of the way on, I lowered my arms but kept the shirt stretched across my chest since I'd already shoved my arms into the armholes. Only one shoulder, the tops of my biceps, and the side of my ribs were exposed to her.

That seemed to be enough to make her blush though. She hugged the towels she'd been holding to her chest and blinked at me.

Heat pooled under my freshly washed skin, building deeper, and lower.

"I'm already done," I said. "And yeah, there were plenty of towels. But thanks."

She moved her head up and down but didn't speak. Her eyes seemed stuck on my exposed flesh. My biceps particularly liked the attention. Without my permission, they twitched, not a full-out flex, but not a tiny flinch either. The damn things were definitely showing off, and it was enough to make Isobel jump and realize she'd been gaping. She turned to the side, so she was no longer facing me.

The strange thing was, she turned to the side where I could see her scars on full display, and I had to say, it did my ego good to realize my undressed state had flustered her enough to forget to hide them from me.

"That…" She paused to swallow. "That was fast."

To me, it had felt like the longest shower I'd ever taken, but I wasn't going to argue with her. I slipped the shirt on, taking my time and biting back a grin when I caught sight of her turning back to stare again.

"I wasn't sure how close to six it was," I said, putting

my back to her as I bent over to slip my shoes on. "I didn't want to be late to work."

She caught an audible breath before stuttering, "I…you…you're not late." She sounded somewhat breathless as I kept my jean-covered ass facing her way the entire time I laced up my boots.

When I was done, I snapped the hems of my jeans over the tops of my boots before straightening and turning toward her.

Her shoulders rose and fell before she added, "You're right on time."

"Great." I grinned and finger combed my hair a few times before calling it good and slapping my hat on. "You want to get back to the library and plan those bookshelves then? I did a little research this weekend and got a few more cool ideas, mostly dealing with molding and designs."

It struck me how painfully inept I was to make shelves in a place like this that hosted what had to be a multimillion-dollar pool house rock cave. But if Henry, and more importantly Isobel, didn't seem to mind, then I wasn't going to mind either.

Isobel started to nod. "I, okay. I…" Her eyes flared wide, gaze fixed on me. But when I moved toward her, she tripped a step back. "Actually, no. I…I think I'm going to take a quick shower too." Then I swear I heard her mumble under her breath, "*A cold shower.*" But I wasn't sure because she followed it so quickly with, "Why don't you head to the kitchen and beg some breakfast from Mrs. Pan? I'll meet you there, okay?"

"Okay," I said, nodding, my stomach growling happily over the prospect of food. "Works for me."

She started to spin away, only for me to realize she was going to abandon me there to find my own way back to the house. "Isobel, wait," I called, springing after her.

Stopping so fast I nearly ran into her, she spun back, only to stumble backward again when she realized how close I was. Eyes flaring wide, she gasped, "Yes?"

I cringed and offered her an apologetic smile. "How, uh, how exactly do I get to the kitchen from here?"

Chagrined, she blushed. "O-oh. Right. Here. I'll just take you there."

I fell into step behind her as we left the pool house, where I had to glance back one last time to get another look at all the coolness inside. At the end of the patio surrounding the pool, the familiar hedge maze sprang up. Isobel chose an opening and I followed her down it. It wasn't wide enough for two people so I had to stay a step behind her.

I think that made her self-conscious, which hell yes, it should, as I was totally checking out her ass in those yoga pants. She cleared her throat and asked, "You, uh, did you get any reading done this weekend?"

Surprised she'd brought up books and reading since we'd only corresponded about them through notes, I lifted my attention from her ass to her face just as she glanced back at me over her shoulder.

"I...yes, actually, I did. Thanks for reminding me." Transferring my book bag from my back to my chest, I unzipped the front pocket and pulled out *Brisingr*. "Finished it. Thank you again for the loan." I handed it to her, and she had to stop walking and turn slightly to receive it, which brought us closer together.

Her fingers accidently skimmed past mine when she took the book. "I..." Her gaze lifted to mine, and damn, those eyes looked so freaking blue while her lashes looked so impossibly long. I wanted to kiss her. I wanted to kiss her so fucking bad.

And then she went and wetted her lips, flicking her pink tongue out over them. I nearly lost it. But I refused to make the first move. This was her call. It killed me to remain as still as possible, but I did, trying to silently convey to her with everything inside me that I was totally okay with anything she might want to do to me.

Instead of stepping closer, she cleared her throat and jerked back. "I guess you'll need book four, then?"

I deflated a little with disappointment but managed to nod and even send her a smile. "Sure. That'd be great. Thank you."

With a nod, she turned away and hurried off. I nearly had to jog to keep up. She didn't speak again for the rest of the trip to the kitchen, and I didn't trust myself to say anything either.

When we came to an opening in the hedge path, we ended up on the patio where I'd first met Kit. Isobel approached the back door and went inside, leaving it open for me to follow.

When I did, I was surprised to see Mr. Nash in the kitchen, sitting at the table and eating his breakfast. I hadn't seen him eat in the kitchen since I'd come to work here. Granted, most days, except Saturdays, he was gone by the time I arrived. But the last two Saturdays, he'd just had a tray brought to his office for meals.

He looked up and smiled. "Morning, sweetheart. Did you have a good…?"

His voice died off as I entered and quietly closed the door behind me.

Mrs. Pan turned from the stove where she was flipping pancakes, and Kit, who'd been sitting across from Mr. Nash, dove under the table at the sight of Isobel.

"Shaw!" Mrs. Pan exclaimed. "What're you doing here so early?"

She stood frozen, spatula in hand, waiting for an answer, while Mr. Nash seemed similarly struck.

I swallowed, not realizing until that moment how it might look to spend time with Isobel outside work hours. But there was no way to hide it now. Besides, there was nothing seedy *to* hide.

Still, I couldn't help but send her a seeking glance to make sure she was okay with me outing our jogging sessions before I said, "I decided to go running with…"

It was on the tip of my tongue to be formal and call her Miss Nash, but then I thought, *why bother?* I wasn't hiding anything, so I finished with, "…Isobel."

Both the cook and Isobel's father seemed startled. I wasn't sure if it was from the informal address or the fact that I'd run with her.

Isobel cleared her throat. "Since he came in so early, I told him he could work from six to two today, instead of his usual nine to five. That's okay with you, isn't it, Dad?"

"Uh…" It took her dad a few more seconds to close his mouth before he slowly gave his head a dazed bob up and down. "Sure," he managed to answer. "Sure. Whatever you think is best, sweetheart."

Isobel nodded too. "Good. I'm going to go take a shower." She paused by her father to kiss him on the top of his balding head. "Have a good day," she said before sailing from the kitchen.

Mrs. Pan and her dad both blinked before they swung their attention back to me. "I…was that okay?" I asked, now that Isobel was gone. "Running with her, I mean."

Jarred from his shock, Mr. Nash jumped and immediately began to nod. "Yes, yes. Perfectly fine. I just…I didn't realize you two had…"

I drew in a breath. "We, uh, well, we talked quite a bit on Saturday while we were discussing bookshelves."

"Well…" Mr. Nash murmured. "That's…that's lovely."

His eyes glittered with an eagerness that made me uneasy. I suddenly wished he'd never found out about our run. I didn't want him thinking I'd done it because of our agreement. I hadn't even been thinking about that when I'd asked Isobel if I could run with her.

But the look on this face told me that was exactly what was on *his* mind.

I opened my mouth to—I don't know—correct him,

maybe. But Mrs. Pan interrupted.

"Can I interest you in some pancakes, Shaw?"

As I turned to her to politely accept, Kit chose that moment to crawl back up from under the table. Without saying a word, Mr. Nash patted him on the top of the head as if to soothe the kid, and I totally lost my train of thought, wondering why everyone allowed the boy to treat Isobel that way.

If it was the last thing I did, I was going to show Kit Pan there was no reason to fear Isobel.

chapter ELEVEN

By the time Isobel returned to the kitchen, freshly washed with her hair down, half-covering her face, everyone had finished breakfast, and even Constance and Lewis had arrived, eaten, and left again. Kit was off in Mrs. Pan's office—as she called it, though it looked more like a kid's playroom to me—while Mrs. Pan herself stood at the sink with a handful of tools, ready to hand them to me when I asked for them. And me…well, I was stretched under the sink, trying to figure out what was wrong with the garbage disposal.

I had just forked up my last bite of pancake when Mrs. Pan had tried to dispose of…well, garbage, I guess, and it had made the most god-awful grinding sound before the smell of burning electrical wires and smoke filled the kitchen.

Good thing the new handyman was on hand. Swallowing the last of my breakfast, I'd gotten to work. I had a little experience with garbage disposal repair. The one at the bakery had gotten jammed plenty of times. But this seemed worse than a stuck flywheel. The reset button hadn't done shit. Nothing seemed to be leaking and Mrs.

Pan had said nothing had been draining slow. So I guessed it must be an electrical problem.

"Wha...?" I heard Isobel's voice when she finally entered the kitchen.

I slid out from under the sink cabinet, explaining, "Garbage disposal."

Her immediate response was, "Don't put your hand down the drain."

I blinked, waiting for her to tell me she was joking. When she genuinely seemed worried I might actually try such a stunt, I sighed.

Really? She thought I was that slow, huh?

"Gee, and that was the next troubleshooting step I was going to try, too."

She had the grace to flush. "Sorry, I just—"

"No worries," I told her. "But it might be a bit before we can get back to bookshelf planning."

With a nod, she began to back away. "Yes, of course. I understand. Completely."

It didn't look as if she understood, though. I squinted at her as she retreated until she reached the opening of the kitchen.

"But what about your…" I tried to ask, except she was already gone. "Breakfast?"

"She doesn't typically eat breakfast," Mrs. Pan answered me.

I looked up at her, wondering if Isobel *would* have this morning if I hadn't just chased her off with my garbage disposal project. She'd yet to eat lunch with the staff since I'd been here. Sure, she'd been avoiding me for the past two weeks, but still…from Kit's reactions to her, I had a feeling she stayed away until everyone was gone before she scavenged for food.

Maybe her dad had been on to something. Aside from him and her brother, Isobel really did try to avoid people, even the rest of the staff. I don't think I realized how much progress I'd made with her until that very moment. I suddenly wanted to climb to my feet and race after her, force her back to the kitchen to eat with other people. But Mrs. Pan needed her sink back.

"Can you trade me for a flat-head?" I asked, holding out the Phillips screwdriver I'd been using to unscrew the main component.

We made the switch and I gritted my teeth as I wedged the screwdriver crowbar-like in between the gasket ring and main part of the machine to pry it loose. All the while, I kept thinking about Isobel, and the lost, abandoned look she'd had as she'd drifted from the kitchen. I hadn't abandoned her, though, and I couldn't wait to get back to the library to show her that.

Problem was, fixing the stupid garbage disposal ended up taking me the rest of the day. It took me a good two hours to decide the motor was shot beyond repair and there was no fixing it. Then I had to wait to get a ride from Lewis into town and buy a new one at the supply store. Installing it took the rest of the afternoon.

By the time I blew into the library, wiping grease stains off my hands and onto my jeans, Isobel was relaxing on her sofa, reading.

"Sorry it took so long," I gushed, feeling like an ass for leaving her hanging. "Are you ready to get back to work on those plans?"

But Isobel merely lowered her book to her stomach and said, "It's one forty-five."

I frowned. "Okay?" What did that mean?

She sent me a sad smile. "You leave in fifteen minutes. There's not really enough time to do anything today."

Oh, shit. I'd completely forgotten I was leaving at two since I'd gotten here so early.

"We might as well wait until tomorrow to return to the plans."

This time, I was the dejected one as I nodded and

left the library.

But I was back at seven the next morning, eager to go. We ran the path around the lake in the opposite direction than we had the morning before. And then I took another shower in the amazing rock cave pool house. After that, we ate breakfast in the kitchen, and yeah, Isobel ate with me, if you call granola and yogurt a meal. By that time, Mr. Nash had already left for work and Kit and Mrs. Pan were off elsewhere. So were Lewis and Constance. It was just the two of us.

We discussed the Inheritance series over a cup of coffee before putting our dirty dishes in the dishwasher and retreating to the library. This time, we put in about half a day's worth of planning before Constance showed up, needing help with a potted plant she'd accidentally knocked over. Turned out, it was more like a potted tree and the pot probably weighed three hundred pounds. I tipped it upright for her and she vacuumed away the spilled soil.

The rest of the week progressed in the same vein. We were interrupted constantly by either Lewis, Mrs. Pan or Constance, needing help. It was Saturday before we had a solid set of plans outlined with a calculation of how much wood and supplies we'd need. That was actually a nifty coincidence, though, since Saturday meant Mr. Nash was home.

Clutching my list of supplies in my hand, I made my way to his office and knocked, waiting until he called before I entered.

I didn't even get to the third item of the list, however, before he nodded and waved a hand, cutting me off. "Good, good. It sounds fine. Go ahead and get whatever you need."

"Wait, you want *me* to buy the supplies?" There was no freaking way. Even if he did plan to reimburse me, I couldn't even afford a tenth of everything we needed.

Henry glanced up from whatever he was writing.

"I'll set up an account at the lumberyard and give them permission to give you unlimited access to whatever supplies you want."

"Oh!" I said, surprised he would be so generous, but still… "Thank you, but, uh…" I winced, feeling like a failure.

Mr. Nash sighed. "What's the problem, Mr. Hollander?"

"It's just…" I flushed hard. "I'm sorry, but I don't have a truck…you know, to transport the supplies from the store to here."

"You don't?"

Jesus, this was humiliating. "No, sir."

"Oh. Well, right, of course. I guess I just assumed you for a truck man." Then he chuckled. "I suppose it would be hard to haul a pallet of wood in the trunk of your car."

"No, I don't have a car, either," I offered quietly.

Mr. Nash blinked at me. "You don't…" This time, I stumped him. "What do you mean?"

"I don't…I have no automobile at all."

"At all?" he repeated, clearly not understanding.

"Well, I did. But I sold it to help my mom with…" It didn't seem necessary to finish that statement. Understanding filled Mr. Nash's gaze.

"Then how have you been getting to work each day?"

"I walk."

"Oh," he murmured, his mouth falling open before he snapped it shut. Then he cleared his throat and glanced away. "Well, then…" He flung out his hand. "I'll have the supplies delivered. No problem. That's the list of everything you need, I presume?"

"I…" I looked down at the list in my hand, only to rattle myself back to the topic at hand. "Yes. This is everything." I handed it over. "Thank you, sir."

He grunted out his response, briefly scanning over

the items on the page before setting it on the desktop beside him. "I'll take care of it."

I nodded, thanking him again, and left his office.

On Monday, I arrived to work to find a shiny new black truck sitting in the driveway. I lifted my eyebrows, impressed, before walking past it to meet Isobel on the running trail. I wondered who was visiting that owned such a grand piece of machinery. But when I asked her, she only shrugged.

"No idea."

I thought it was odd that she didn't even seem to care whose truck sat in her driveway, but I shrugged it off, too, and stopped pestering her about it.

My question was finally answered when Constance found me an hour after our run, while I was rearranging things in the library, waiting for the lumberyard to deliver our supplies.

She handed me a lumpy envelope. "Before he left this morning, Mr. Nash asked me to give this to you."

"Okay," I said, frowning suspiciously as I took it. "Thank you."

I opened the top flap as the housekeeper left the room, only to find a note and set of keys inside. I frowned at the keys and pulled out the note.

Mr. Hollander,

It turns out lumber ordering is not my forte, but truck buying is. I'd feel much more settled if you used the truck outside to go purchase the bookshelf supplies yourself. It's a black Ford sitting in the circle drive in front of the house. I believe you won't miss it. There is a gas card in the glove box so you won't be responsible for paying for fuel, and I would appreciate it if you'd drive it to and from work from here on out, as well. It wouldn't be seemly if anyone saw you walking every day and got the impression I didn't pay my employees enough to even afford transportation. Thank you for your understanding.

Henry

My mouth fell open before I took the keys and gaped at them in disbelief.

"What're the keys for?" Isobel asked as she entered the library, munching on an apple.

I spun to her, the keys still weighing down my palm with disbelief. "Did you know about this?"

She glanced around, confused, before turning back to me. "Know about what?"

"I…I think your dad just bought me a truck?"

Slowing to a stop, she paused mid-chew to cock her head my way and give me a funny glance. I held up the note.

After reading it, she lifted her face, took in my pole-axed expression and grinned. "Well, why are you still standing there? Let's go check it out."

My eyes grew wide, yet I couldn't move. "But…"

She laughed. It sounded amazing and multiplied my shock by ten, unable to believe I'd made her laugh.

"But *nothing*," she encouraged, taking my arm. Yes, God, her fingers wrapped around the inside of my elbow caused sparks to shoot through my entire body. "Let's go."

I followed her helplessly. She seemed so happy for me, which made my own anticipation grow. Once we marched past the cupid statue and fish tank floor and in-door fountain in the foyer, she threw open the door and hurried out into the warm, sunny morning.

"Shit," I breathed, taking in the truck I was meant to use from here on out. Pulling to a stop only a few feet from it, I began to shake my head. "No. I can't."

Isobel turned back to me, her eyebrows crinkling with worry. "You can't what?"

"I…" Furiously waving my hand toward the truck, I stuttered, "This…I…it…I just can't. I can't drive this."

She blinked. "Why not? Don't you know how to drive?"

"Of course," I muttered, sending her a short scowl. "I just… It's so nice. It's *too* nice. I don't belong in a truck this nice."

When I went to take a step back, Isobel caught my arm. "Shaw," she warned, arching her eyebrows threateningly. "Don't you dare wig out. It's just a truck."

"Ju…just a truck?" I exploded. Just a truck. Right. And Porter Hall Estate was just a house. "It's a brand spanking new Super Duty F-450 *Platinum. That's* what it is! It's like the boss of badass trucks. Do you know how much this thing had to cost? Holy fuck, Isobel. What if I wreck it, or dent it, or get a freaking *scratch* on it?" I was afraid to even touch it, much less drive it.

In fact, I took a safe step back, worried my breath might stain the paint job.

Isobel blinked at me as if I were completely overreacting. "I'm sure it's insured."

I let out an incredulous laugh. "This is insane. You realize how insane this is, right?"

A shrug this time. "It's a work truck, Hollander. Not yours to keep forever."

I nodded. Yes, I knew this, but still…I was going to be *driving* this beast, this beautiful, spectacular road beast. My hands began to shake with nerves, the keys in my palm jangling. Holy shit, I couldn't believe I was holding the keys for it.

With a roll of her eyes, Isobel reached past me and opened the driver's side door. I flinched, afraid some kind of alarm would sound, warning me away. When it didn't, she lifted an eyebrow and shooed me forward. "Well, climb in. See how it fits."

"Oh, God," I whimpered, but slowly stepped forward before I gripped the door, planted my foot on the sidebar and hoisted myself inside. "Holy shit. It smells so new."

"Not too bad," Isobel agreed, hopping up onto the sidebar step so she could lean in and check things out. Her nearness distracted me. I breathed in roses over the new-truck smell and narrowed my attention on the ends of her hair that brushed my thigh when she leaned past me to examine the dash.

Forgetting all about my driving inhibitions, I found myself asking, "Want to go for a ride?"

Her face zipped up, surprised blue eyes meeting mine. "What?"

My grin widened. "Let's take it for a spin. I need to go to the lumberyard and buy all the supplies for the bookshelves, anyway. Why don't you come with me?"

She blinked and pulled back as if I'd just asked her to show me her tits. "Oh, no. No, I don't think—"

"Come on," I encouraged, taking her hand as the idea gained energy. Not only did I want her to come with me, but Mr. Nash would probably piss his pants if he found out I'd coaxed Isobel into leaving Porter Hall.

But she tugged her had free and took another step away. "No. I don't…I don't think so. I don't go out much."

Or at all, I wanted to add.

I sent her an expression full of begging eyes. "I'd feel better if you were there, making sure I picked out the correct wood, and stain, and—"

"I fully trust your capabilities in this matter."

I stared at her a moment before saying, "I'd still like you to come with me."

She shook her head.

I sent her a sad smile and capitulated, feeling as if I'd lost. "Some other time, then."

I might've lost this battle, but I was still determined to win the war.

chapter TWELVE

When I drove home that night, I expected red and blue lights to start flashing behind me any second with some cop threatening to arrest me for theft. I drove with my eyes more on the rearview mirror than on the road ahead of me.

By the time I made it into town, handcuff-free, my worry only gained volume. People didn't own rides as nice or new as this in my neighborhood. If I parked this thing on my street, I might as well paint a huge target on it. It wouldn't survive the night.

Swearing under my breath, I found a better neighborhood about a fifteen-minute walk from my own, where the cars and trucks started to look nicer and were safer to park on the street. I still felt wrong about leaving it there, so far from my apartment, but hell, it had a better chance here.

"You'll be okay," I said, stroking the paint job and reassuring myself more than I was the truck. Then I stepped back, took a deep breath, and hurried home. Once I reached the apartment, I remembered to check the mail slot on the first floor before heading up the stairs. There were about half a dozen letters, all from people we owed money.

Realizing it'd been days since we'd received a single late notice, I started to sweat and tore open the first letter. I was halfway up the first flight when I realized what I was staring at. Slowing to a stop, I gaped in disbelief.

I knew I'd made the deal with Mr. Nash, but a part of me had never fully believed he'd see to his half. Yet there I stood, slack jawed as I stared at the *loan paid in full* notice. It was exhilarating and kind of scary. I feared it couldn't be real.

Palms sweating, I tore open the second letter. Another loan paid notice.

Holy shit. He'd done it. He'd really done it. He'd paid off all my mother's debts.

With the third letter ripped open, I blinked, my eyes prickling with emotion. Every single thing had been paid off.

I covered my mouth with my hand and stared around the quiet stairwell, overcome.

She was free. My mother was finally free and safe.

If Henry Nash were standing there in that moment, I would've hugged him. He'd just saved Mom. To me, he was a hero.

By the time I made it up to my apartment, my relief and joy had left me somewhat drained and dazed. So I was even more flabbergasted when I opened my door, only to smell baking bread along with apples and cinnamon.

Oh God, it couldn't be. Not my mom's famous apple cinnamon rolls. They'd grown so popular around the neighborhood, they were actually the reason my sister Victoria had urged Mom into opening the bakery. Inhaling them now was bittersweet. It reminded me of how our life had been led into ruin, but it also told me Mom was up and about, actually baking.

I hurried toward the kitchen, worried I'd find her

hovering over the oven and hacking out the last of her flu. But when I came to the opening, I jerked to a surprised halt. Mom looked completely recovered from her sickness. She hummed to herself as she spread butter over the top of a still steaming bun. A limp remained as she moved toward a plate at the other end of the counter, but even her uneven gait seemed better than any movements she'd made since breaking her hip three months before. Her walker sat unused on the other side of the kitchen.

"Shaw!" she said, pleasure blooming across her face. "Are you hungry? I made enough to feed us for a week, I think." Then she laughed her tinkling laugh that always reminded me of fairy bells ringing or angel wings flapping. I loved my mother's laugh. It'd been too long since I'd last heard it.

Affection warmed my entire chest. Mom was back, better than ever. She was free from loans and she looked healthy and happy.

"I could eat," I said, approaching. "But first…" I wrapped my arms around her and gave her the biggest hug, even picked her up and caused her to laugh.

Patting my shoulder and then touching my cheek, she grinned. "What's all this about?"

I shook my head, not sure if I could voice how pleased I was by all our good fortune if I tried. "It's just been a good day."

She, of course, totally misunderstood me, not at all thinking I was happy because of her. "Something must've happened at work," she mused, her brown eyes, the same shade as my own, twinkling with joy.

I started to shake my head before I remembered, oh shit, yes. "Yeah, I guess." I gave a rueful shrug, almost too embarrassed to tell her my news. "Mr. Nash loaned me a truck to drive to and from work."

"Wow, that's nice." Mom turned to pick up the cinnamon roll she'd just buttered to hand it to me. "You won't have to spend so much time walking to that place anymore."

She said *that place* as if it were a nasty omen. I'd told her over and over again there was nothing shady about the Nashes, but she continued to doubt.

I took the roll and bit into it, moaning over the apple and cinnamon flavors that exploded on my tongue. Then I closed my eyes, enjoying the taste, before I swallowed. When I looked at Mom again, she was buttering another roll. I leaned against the counter and watched, taking another bite.

"Mom, nice doesn't even cover *half* of what this truck is. You don't understand." I went on to explain the model and year along with all the bells and whistles it contained. "I was so afraid to drive it home and park it in our neighborhood, I had to leave it outside the Denny's on Fifth and Grand."

"Oh, Shaw." She rolled her eyes. "You can be so dramatic, my sweet, precious boy. You make it sound like the Holy Grail when it's just a work truck."

I snorted and shook my head. "You sound like Isobel."

"Who's Isobel?"

I jumped at the question, because it hadn't come from my mother. Not realizing anyone else had been in the apartment, I jerked away from my casual lean against the counter and spun toward the new voice.

Gloria stood there, pointedly staring at me with her arms crossed over her chest.

"Jesus, where did *you* come from?"

She began to tap her foot. "I was in the bathroom, freshening up, when you came in. Who's Isobel?"

Righteous indignation stretched across her face, and she continued to glare at me as if I'd cheated on her. I narrowed my eyes and pinched my mouth together, refusing to answer, because it was none of her business who any of my acquaintances were.

But then Mom had to go and say, "I don't think I've ever heard you mention an Isobel before. Does she work for Mr. Nash as well?" Then she passed the newly buttered roll to Gloria, murmuring, "Here you go, dear."

When Gloria took it, answering, "Thank you, Mama," I almost lost my cool.

I did not like her calling my mother Mama. I didn't like her hanging out in my apartment all day. I didn't like her staring at me as if she had any right to me, and I really didn't like that I was going to have to answer her demanding question because now Mom wanted to know who Isobel was too.

Dammit.

"Uh, no," I said, frowning between the two women. The bite I'd just taken seemed to grow larger in my throat the more I tried to swallow it. "She's not another employee. She's Mr. Nash's daughter."

Mom smiled politely. Gloria scowled harder.

"I didn't realize he had any children," Mom said.

I nodded. "Yeah, he's a widower with a son and a daughter. The son lives elsewhere, though."

"How old's the daughter?" Gloria asked, her jealousy thick and livid.

I stared at her, my jaw ticking. I didn't want to answer her.

But Mom had to go and press, "Well?"

With a sigh, I muttered, "She's twenty-five."

Gloria snorted. "Twenty-five and still lives at home with her daddy? Wow, that's impressive."

I tipped my head to the side, drilling her with an insulted glare. "I'm twenty-eight and live with my mother."

Face flushing, she immediately began to stutter, "That's not…but your situation is unique. I'm sure Mr. Nash could *buy* his daughter another home to live in. Besides, why doesn't she have her own job and take care of herself?"

"She can't," I snarled, needing to defend Isobel more than I needed my next breath.

But I was so vehement about it, both women reared back in surprise before Mom said, "What do you mean, she can't? What's wrong with her?"

My instinctive answer was *nothing*. There was nothing wrong with Isobel. She was flawless in my eyes. But after my passionate *she can't*, I had to give them something.

"She, uh, well…she was in a house fire that killed her mother, and it left her…"

Mom pressed her hand to her chest. "Oh, that poor sweet child. Is she crippled?"

"No." I smiled a bit to myself, thinking about how in shape she was. After running with her for a week, I still couldn't keep up with her pace. She definitely wasn't crippled. "I mean, she doesn't use the fingers in her left hand much because of the burn wounds." I'd noticed that about her, anyway. "But mostly it's just…aesthetic."

"So she looks hideous?" Gloria guessed, a smirk of evil relish brightening her features.

"No," I said before I could check myself. Honestly, it was probably best if I let Gloria think Isobel *was* too revolting for me to have any interest in her. She'd probably hate her less, and I knew the two would never meet, but I didn't want someone to hate Isobel, even in spirit only. "I don't think the scars look that bad, but she's become quite self-conscious about them. She doesn't leave the property, like ever."

The two women stared at me a moment longer before Gloria self-righteously proclaimed, "What a lazy, entitled coward."

For the briefest moment, I was too shocked by her words to respond. Then I blinked and slowly said, "Excuse me?"

"She's so scared people might laugh at her looks that she's decided to live off her rich, fat daddy for the rest of her life and, what, eat *bonbons* while you shine her shoes? That's appalling."

"She's not appalling." I was so flabbergasted by the critique I couldn't check my words. "The way she pushes herself every morning during her run, and how tenaciously she tends to her roses, is the very *opposite* of lazy. Plus, she's been quite the trooper, helping me build her bookshelves. I think she carried just as many lumber supplies into the house from the truck as I did today. And who the hell cares if she lives the rest of her life on her daddy's money? Trust me, he can certainly afford it."

Lifting her chin, Gloria narrowed her eyes and sniffed. "I suppose you'll try to convince me it's *bravery* that makes her hide away from the rest of the world, too, won't you?"

"Can you honestly blame her?" I spat back. "Her life was irrevocably changed. She's just trying to deal with it the best way she can. Until you lose your mother in a fire and get half of *your* face melted off, you have no right to judge her so harshly."

"Well," Gloria said, her entire being rigid with sanctimonious outrage. "I think it's time I be on my way."

Finally, I agreed with her on something. "I think you're right."

"*Shaw*," Mom gasped, sending me a disappointed glare. "I invited Gloria to stay for supper."

Of *course* she had. Pulling my anger back together, I drew in a deep breath. "Sorry, Mother. I wouldn't dream of kicking out your guest." Sending Gloria a tight smile, I splayed out a hand. "Please, stay and eat."

With a satisfied little smirk, Gloria preened and tucked her hair behind her ear. "Why, thank you. I think I will."

With a single nod at her compliance, I took a step in reverse. "I hope you ladies enjoy your meal."

They both blinked. "What? But where are you going?" Mom asked.

I sent her a sad smile, completely ignoring the woman at her side. "I think I'll eat out tonight." I gave her a kiss on the cheek before adding, "Have a great evening, Mom."

With that, I turned away and started for the door.

Both Mom and Gloria called after me, but I kept going. Once I was outside and back in the stairwell of the building, by myself, I finally cursed under my breath. I wished I hadn't been so quick to defend Isobel. It felt as if I'd just painted a great big target on her back for Gloria to hate. It wasn't a big deal, of course—the two women would never meet. Gloria couldn't mistreat her to her face, and Isobel would probably never even be aware that someone disliked her now, because of me. But I still wished I'd been able to hide my feelings better.

What if Henry caught on to the fact I was starting to like her…a lot?

Damn, I was definitely going to have to learn to control myself better than this. Everything seemed to depend upon it.

chapter THIRTEEN

Planning bookshelf projects and reading about bookshelf projects were entirely different beasts than actually building fucking bookshelves.

"Dammit," I muttered, tossing down another board I'd cut a fourth of an inch too short. "I suck at this. I so totally suck at this."

You'd think routing fancy edges or aligning and screwing boards together would be the real challenge for me. But nope, I just couldn't measure and cut worth crap.

"Too short again?" Isobel asked from across the room, where she sat at the opened window and brushed wood stain across a freshly sanded shelf. Between us, the floor was covered in plastic drop cloths while sawdust fluttered in the air and the crisp scent of lacquer floated to me from the breeze the window let in.

"Yes," I mumbled, tearing off my hat to run a hand through my hair and trying not to lose my shit. But seriously, you'd think I'd learn not to fuck up the length so badly after the first five boards I'd cut wrong. Moodily, I jammed my hat back on.

"Well, this is only the sixth miss," Isobel said, dipping her brush into the metal can she held with one hand. "You've easily cut three times that number right."

I blinked at her, wondering when the hell she'd turned so optimistic and encouraging. And why was she being so helpful? From the moment I'd showed her my idea for the library, she'd been involved in this project one hundred percent, just as much as I was. In fact, *I* wasn't building these bookcases at all. *We* were.

The saw scared the shit out of her, so she didn't do any cutting, but she sanded and beveled and measured, and now she was staining. This was supposed to be *my* handyman job, but she'd worked and sweated as much as I had. And I had to say, it was nice. We'd bickered, and disagreed, and then agreed and complimented, and now we were encouraging each other, apparently.

"Why don't you take a break from cutting," she suggested. "I only have one more board to stain before I'm out of the ones that have been sanded."

Grateful to move on to something else for a bit, I started toward her. "You need some more sanded?"

She pointed her brush toward a stack of cut boards. "Those right there."

"On it," I said, happy for a change of scenery.

"I know it's not plausible, but I was hoping we could at least put up one range of shelves today. I'm excited to see how the new ones will look next to the old ones."

I grinned. Her enthusiasm was contagious. And adorable. I wanted to make sure she got whatever she wanted. With a grin, I said, "I bet we could get one up before the end of the day."

She snorted. "It'd probably take us another eight hours, working straight through, to get to that point, and you get off work in," she consulted her wrist, "two."

I shrugged. "I don't mind staying a couple hours longer."

Blinking, she stared at me as if I'd just suggested I

give her my undying love and devotion.

"But…you don't have to do that. You already work here nearly fifty hours a week as it is."

Sending her a grin, I merely said, "But I want to see one of the bookshelves up today, too."

Before she could argue the point further, I slid my safety glasses on, turned up the sander and drowned out her protests with noise.

We'd been working on the bookshelf project for about a week now. And throughout all the planning, brainstorming and calculating, we talked. We talked a lot. We talked about books, movies, and our favorite television shows. We talked about my family, my mom's situation, her lost bakery business, and my absent siblings. She wasn't as open about her family. She mentioned things about her dad and brother, but usually avoided conversation about her mom entirely, as well as the fire that had changed her life.

Occasionally, I asked her about her future, what she wanted to do with her life and if she ever planned to move out of Porter Hall on her own. But her eyes would glaze over with this faraway expression, and she would never go into any of that. So I'd change the subject.

But mainly, smiles and conversation flowed smoothly between us, just as it did for the rest of the afternoon.

At one point, Mr. Nash strolled into the room, saying, "Izzy, did you receive the note I left, letting you know I'd be late on Friday because I had a business dinner?" He was shuffling through a pile of mail in his hand, not paying attention to any of the progress we'd made.

"I saw it," she answered, her voice strained, because she was busy holding two boards in place for me so I could screw them together.

Henry finally lifted his face and blinked. He gazed about the construction zone we had going on before returning his attention to us. "Shaw," he said with some surprise. "I must not have been paying attention when I pulled into the drive. I didn't realize you were still here. It's two hours after your regular time to leave."

"We wanted to get at least one shelf installed tonight." I glanced at Isobel. "Ready?"

She nodded, her knuckles going white as she held everything in place while I drilled a screw through wood.

Henry moved curiously closer. "It's really coming along," he murmured with a note of surprise. "Looks professionally done, too."

"That's because Shaw is a perfectionist," Isobel announced, sending me a glance with a bit of censure but also pride in her teasing gaze. "He usually redoes a single piece five times before he's satisfied with it."

"I'm not that bad," I immediately argued, only to flush when she sent me an arch stare. "Okay, I might be that bad."

"You're totally that bad." She laughed before turning to her dad. "We've made it to this point three times already, only for him to insist we start all over again."

Shifting uncomfortably because I was sure Mr. Nash would get upset over how much lumber and supplies I'd wasted by doing that, I glanced up at my boss, only to see him gazing strangely between the two of us.

"Well," he murmured quietly, "it seems like whatever he's doing is paying off, so I say he should keep up the good work."

The meaning in his gaze was clear. Henry wasn't talking about bookshelves.

I glanced at Isobel and cleared my throat, worried she'd catch on to the silent message her father was trying to convey. After the past few days, I'd actually forgotten what my main purpose here was. I'd been too eager to see Isobel, spend the day with her, and work on our project together. Being reminded why I'd originally been brought to Porter Hall soured the beauty of the moment.

"It looks as if you've turned into quite the assistant,

sweetheart."

Isobel sent her dad a pleased but tired smile. "He probably needs about five assistants, but we're getting it done. Slowly."

Taking that as a cue that he was excused now, Henry shifted a step back. "I guess I'd better let you two get back to it, then."

I snorted as I pulled a screw I'd been holding between my teeth and plugged it into the end of the drill. "What a friendly snub to your own father that was."

Isobel flushed guiltily before sending me a scowl. "I couldn't help it. I wanted to get this done tonight, and he was slowing us down."

With a laugh, I shook my head and drilled the next screw into place before she could accuse *me* of slowing us down.

An hour later, we had the first shelf pieced together and standing upright. The next step was anchoring it to the wall.

"The stud wall should be right here," Isobel murmured, marking an X on the wall with a pencil as her stud sensor beeped.

"You sure?" I asked, approaching with a tape measure.

She swept out her hand, inviting me to find out for myself. "Well, why don't you drill a hole and see if it hits a stud?"

The idea had me startling to a stop, but Isobel continued. "Can't hurt anything since all this space is going to be covered by bookshelves, anyway."

I shrugged. Good point. "Okay." I put the tape measure away and retrieved the drill. But as I pressed the bit to the wall directly over the small pencil mark, I froze.

Staring at my hand I had braced against Sheetrock, I couldn't seem to make a hole.

"Okay, you can start," Isobel said behind me.

Could I? Really? I wasn't so sure. This suddenly felt

big.

"Anytime now," she added, only to huff a second later. "Seriously, Hollander, you don't have to wait."

"I know," I muttered, still not getting to work.

"Then why aren't you?"

"I *will*." I held up the hand I'd been pressing against the wall, hoping to quell her impatience. "Just give me a second."

"A second for what? You know how to use a drill, right?"

"Yes!" I spun to nail her with the full impact of my indignant glare. She knew I knew how to use a drill; she'd been watching me use one all damn week. Then I realized she'd been heckling me on purpose, trying to get a rise out of me, and I scowled.

Lifting her eyebrows to meet my scowl, she set her hands on her hips. "Just what is the problem?"

"I told you..." It was hard to say from between clenched teeth, but I managed. "Give. Me. A. Second."

"And I asked... For. What?"

"Oh my God!" I lowered the drill and backed away from the wall, losing my cool. "For...for... You know, you are the most annoying woman on the planet. Can you not even wait ten goddamn seconds for me to deal with this and let the gravity of it actually sink in?"

She blinked a moment, before more quietly asking, "The gravity of what?"

"The...*that*!" I motioned toward the bare wall. "This. Everything. It's all finally hitting me. These shelves are going to be permanent."

She sniffed out a degrading sound before nudging my arm and grinning through a teasing eye roll. "Don't be so sure about that. I give them a couple weeks. In fact, I predict we'll be calling a real carpenter in here within the month to fix your mess."

"Wow," I muttered. "Thanks for your vote of confidence."

She shrugged, even though her eyes sparkled with her tease.

"It's just..." I sighed and ran my fingers through my hair. "This is the first thing I've ever made that's going to last. And it's going in *this* house, this huge, amazing grand house where freaking *millionaires* live. Long after we're both gone, these shelves will still be here, a piece of history."

She made a sound in the back of her throat and wrinkled her nose. "Again, debatable."

I ignored that, needing to get this feeling off my chest before I could start drilling anything. "It's like I'm making my mark on the world." My chest filled with a sense of purpose. "I mean, I've always loved archeology stuff and the history of things, learning about cultures. Studying *that* had always been my big passion, but this...today...it's like I'm the one actually providing a piece of my own life for future archeologists and it's...well, it's pretty freaking cool. I wonder if someone hundreds of years from now will look at my shelves and comment on them, maybe speculate on why I made them the way I did or wonder about the life I lived. It's almost...humbling."

Isobel blinked at me.

I blinked back, realizing how much I'd just exposed. A sense of alarm filled my gut. After Gloria and even kind of my mom had belittled my passion for artifacts, I'd always pushed it down and tried to hide it, thinking it was stupid and trivial. I fully expected Isobel to make fun of me for getting so sentimental and weird, too.

But she just studied me with the oddest expression before turning to look at the bare wall as well, as if never having seen it before.

A second later, she spun away and moved off. I gazed after her, wondering what that meant, what she thought of me now, and where the heck she was going. She paused at the study table and pulled open the drawer under it before riffling around and coming up with a thick black permanent marker.

"What…?" I wrinkled my nose, confused, as she returned to me.

She didn't say a word, just stopped in front of the wall, lifted the marker and started to draw in huge block letters:

Isobel was here.

A slow grin spread across my face.

When she turned back to me and arched a lofty eyebrow, I nodded my approval and thanks. She hadn't made me feel like a freak; she'd joined me, making her mark as well.

Biting my lip, I took the marker from her and wrote above her phrase, adding:

Shaw and…

She snorted and pressed a hand to her mouth, holding in a laugh. "Now you have to change my *was* to *were.*"

I looked up, reread everything, and flushed. "Oh yeah." Lifting the marker again, I marked out the *a-s* after the *w* and added *e-r-e* above it.

When I stepped back to check out the result, I winced. "Oh, great. Now it looks like total shit."

"Yeah," Isobel agreed, nodding. "Maybe you should put those shelves up to cover it."

I shook my head at her dry sarcasm, even though I was still amused by her witticism. "Smart-ass," I muttered, biting my lip to hold in the grin.

Then I lifted the drill, and bored a hole through the wall of Porter Hall's library.

chapter FOURTEEN

Weeks passed, the library transformed, and a routine sprouted between Isobel and me. We'd run, I'd take my dream shower—I was becoming increasingly spoiled by those showers—then we'd eat breakfast together after everyone else had eaten and cleared out of the kitchen, and after that, it was off to the library for renovation time. In between the woodworking part, we painted the walls a glossy eggshell color and installed more lights.

I asked Isobel if she wanted me to find some professional painters and electricians to take care of that part, but she'd admitted she liked this do-it-ourselves thing we had going on. It made it more meaningful to her. That had me grinning until she added, "Besides, you're such an anal-retentive perfectionist, I'm sure you'll do fine."

So I read more books and learned about wiring, and it ended up I only electrocuted myself twice before all the new lights were installed.

We were finishing the last bookshelf one Tuesday when Kit skipped into the library, calling my name, except it sounded a lot more like he said *Saw* because of his missing front teeth. "Mom said to tell you—"

But then he caught sight of Isobel on the other side of the room, adjusting the space between shelves, and he ran out again.

I huffed out a breath and set my hands on my hips. "That kid pisses me off. I hate the way he acts around you."

"Oh, give him a break," Isobel chided, not even looking my way as she lowered the shelf another inch. "I'd be afraid of me too if I were him."

Shaking my head, I stared at her as she worked, amazed she could defend someone who never treated her right. "Has anyone actually ever forced him to get to know you so he can realize you're perfectly normal?"

She finally glanced my way and lifted a mockingly insulted eyebrow. "Only perfectly normal, huh? How depressing."

I sighed and then grumbled, "You know what I mean. He shouldn't be allowed to treat you like that."

"It's fine, Shaw. Leave it be."

"No. Not unless you can look me in the eye and one hundred percent tell me his behavior doesn't bother you."

She turned to look me straight in the eye, only to frown. After a sniff, she muttered, "I said it was fine."

"He's creepy, if you ask me."

With a laugh, she shook her head. "Creepy? Because he's scared of a scary-looking woman?"

"You're not scary-looking, and yes, creepy. The first day I met him he was drawing a dead animal with blood pouring out of it with sidewalk chalk on the patio outside the kitchen."

She shrugged. "Sounds like a typical little boy to me."

I sent her a get-real scowl. "I never drew pictures of bloody things."

"I have a feeling you weren't a typical little boy, either." That was true, but it disgruntled me to think of how accurate it was. "I think I remember a couple gruesome drawings by Ezra a time or two."

I opened my mouth to keep arguing, because typical or creepy, the fact of the matter was he kept hurting her with his behavior, and I wanted it to stop. But Kit's mother strolled into the room, all grins, followed by a scowling Lewis. Each carried a tray laden with food.

"Woohoo," Mrs. Pan called cheerfully. "I sent Kit to tell you lunch was ready, but he said you were both hard at work, so I decided to bring you trays so you both will remember to eat *sometime* today."

"And she forced me to be her servant boy," Lewis muttered, following her to the table where they each set down their trays.

"Thanks, Mrs. Pan." I abandoned the bookshelf I'd been anchoring to the wall, because the mention of food made my stomach growl. A quick check at the time revealed it was after two in the afternoon.

Damn, Isobel and I really had gotten lost in the project, hadn't we?

"It was our pleasure." The cook beamed at me, clasping her hands to her middle before she elbowed Lewis in the side, making him mumble something not so pleasant under his breath. Then she turned to take in the room. "I wanted to get a peek at your progress, anyway, and I must say, wow. You two are doing an amazing job."

"Thank you." Isobel neared the food as well, looking about as hungry as I felt. "I think it's coming along nicely."

"It doesn't look like the same room at all. You can't tell which ones are the old shelves and which are the new."

Isobel and I shared a glance, pride glazing our eyes. We really had kicked ass on the room. I could point out a dozen mistakes I'd made, but overall, yeah, it looked fairly awesome.

"Didn't there used to be a door over there?" Lewis

asked, pointing toward a wall full of nothing but shelves.

Before we could answer, Mrs. Pan whirled toward him, scowling. "Shh!" she hissed. "It's rude to ask a question like that."

The old man only blinked at her before scratching his head. "It is?"

I chuckled. "It's all right. And yeah, the door's still there. Check this out." I hurried toward the bookshelf so I could pull open the hidden doorway and reveal the other room to the cook and groundskeeper.

They were suitably impressed. Lewis even gave a whistle of awe. Then Mrs. Pan praised the rolling shelf ladder we'd installed the day before, right before she smacked Lewis's hand when he reached for a grape sitting on one of the lunch trays.

"Don't you dare steal their food, you old fart. You already had your lunch."

"But you didn't give me grapes," Lewis whined.

Huffing, she grabbed hold of his ear and twisted, making him howl as she marched him from the library. "You want grapes, I'll give you grapes. But you won't be stealing them from either Miss Nash or Shaw. Do you hear me…"

Their voices became indistinguishable as they moved further down the hall. I stared after them, shaking my head and grinning. "They're kind of like oil and water, aren't they?"

Isobel shrugged as she popped her own grape into her mouth and took a seat at the table. "Love is a strange and curious thing."

She lifted the lid off the tray that sat next to her bowl of grapes. The steaming mashed potatoes and sliced pot roast slathered in brown gravy made my mouth water, so I instantly sat across from her, even though her comment had me blinking out my confusion.

"Love?" I said.

She picked up her fork, only to pause and glance at

me as if I was being the confusing one. "What? Isn't it obvious? They're totally crazy about each other."

I pointed toward the opening of the library where Mrs. Pan had just dragged Lewis from the room by the ear. "We're talking about the same two people, right? The cook and the groundskeeper."

She rolled her eyes. "Yes, I know exactly who we're talking about." Then she plunked a forkful of mashed potatoes into her mouth.

I was too busy gaping at her to dig into my own food. "But they hate each other. They're always at each other's throats."

Isobel finished chewing, swallowed, then took a long drink of iced tea. As she sat the cup down, she answered, "I don't know what to tell you; I guess that's just how their relationship works. But Lewis has had a crush on Mrs. Pan since he came to work here. And she's been trying for the last five years or so to hide her own feelings in return for him."

I glanced down at my food and blinked some more. "Really?" All the while, I wondered why I'd never gleaned such things from them myself.

"I wonder if she feels guilty about falling for the next man who filled her late husband's position here," Isobel mused, her voice full of sorrow and sympathy. "Mr. Pan was such a warm, wonderful man. It can't be easy for her to move on and love again. And it must be equally hard for Lewis to stand back and wait until she's ready. I feel bad for both of them."

Lifting my face to watch her as she ate heartily, I stared at yet another version of Isobel I'd never seen before. This intuitive, empathetic side was a wonder. But the more she explained Lewis and Mrs. Pan's plight, the more it really did make sense why they treated each other the way they did.

It made my chest ache for them. If the two were in love, it only seemed right that they should be *together.*

Needing this to happen, and needing it with a fervency that was strong and totally foreign to me, I sat up straighter and announced, "We should set them up."

Isobel finally stopped eating to blink at me. "What?"

"Let's…I don't know." I sat forward, growing more eager the longer the idea brewed. "Let's force some contact between them that creates an opportunity for them to, you know…develop into that stage where they can finally be together. Make one of them take the first step."

I'd meant it to sound like we were only providing an opening for Lewis and Mrs. Pan to do what they already wanted to do, but my explanation kind of reminded me of some of the things Mr. Nash had said about Isobel and me when he'd hired me. I glanced at her, wondering—

But, no. He'd specifically said he didn't want to buy her friends. So there was no way he'd been trying to buy her a boyfriend.

Was there?

A split second of fury hit me, wondering if that thought had ever even crossed his brain. His daughter was a beautiful, amazing woman. The idea that he might even consider forcing some man to pretend to have feelings for her was not cool.

But, no, that wasn't what he'd been trying to do, so I calmed my heels and shook my head. When I focused on Isobel, she was gazing at me as if I'd gone insane.

"How do we *create* an opportunity?"

I shrugged. Romance was not my forte. "I don't know. How do couples usually hook up?" It'd been too long for me to remember the dating world.

Her eyebrows arched in a silent, *You're asking ME this question? Really?*

Which got me wondering how many romantic encounters *she'd* had. If she'd sequestered herself into this house since the accident, she would've only been seventeen when she'd basically abandoned the dating pool. It didn't seem right. She should've gotten the privilege to have men fight for her, woo her, romance her, make her toes curl. She deserved that. She deserved the flattering attention from an interested pursuer, the heady rush of desire, the anticipation and thrill. It wasn't right that she hadn't gotten to experience any of that for the last eight years.

"What about leaving a poem for her and saying it's from him?" she suggested.

I tipped my head, thinking that idea was similar to the books and seeds I'd left on her sofa. She'd never said anything about them, but warmth spread through me. What if that was why she thought "Lewis" leaving something for "Mrs. Pan" was romantic as well? I liked that thought. I liked it a lot. A big grin spread across my face.

"Great. Or he could leave her a flower or something," I added, brainstorming from her idea.

Isobel nodded. "Yes! Lewis is an outdoorsy guy. That would make more sense."

My eyes grew wide, and I snapped my fingers before pointing at her. "One of your roses. That would be perfect."

She pressed a hand to her heart. "*My* roses?" From the look on her face, one would've thought I'd just suggested she rip a kidney from her back and donate that to the cause instead.

"Don't you think it'd be worth it?" I pressed, curious just how attached to her flowers she really was. "Mrs. Pan would love it. And your roses…your roses are amazing, Isobel. That kind of beauty is meant to be *shared*."

Her brow crinkled, telling me my argument had gone a little overdramatic, but then her shoulders fell. "Okay, fine. We can use a couple of my roses."

chapter FIFTEEN

I'd only suggested one, so the fact that Isobel was willing to give up a *couple* of her roses made my eyebrows lift, impressed.

But she must've mistaken my expression as me thinking I considered her offer meager. So she sighed. "Fine. I can put together a full dozen."

Holy shit. I hadn't thought she'd go that far. But I smiled. "Mrs. Pan is going to love this."

Still appearing put out, she huffed, "Which color?"

"I don't know." Again, this was out of my territory. "What do the different colors symbolize?"

I thought she'd give me another look that told me she had no idea about that either, but nope. When it came to roses, Isobel knew her shit. "Well, red is obviously for love, passion, beauty, courage, or respect. White roses are for purity, innocence, silence, or secrecy."

I shook my head. "Nah, we don't want it to be a secret admirer thing. She needs to know they're from him."

Nodding in agreement, Isobel ticked off another finger. "Dark pink is for appreciation and gratitude. Light pink is admiration, sympathy, grace, joy, and sweetness. Orange is fascination, desire, or enthusiasm. Peach is appreciation, closing the deal, or getting together."

"Seriously," I murmured, staring at her in awe. "How do you know all this?"

Isobel just kept going. "Coral is for desire. Lavender is love at first sight. Yellow with red tips are friendship and falling in love. A mix of red and white roses means—"

"Okay, okay, okay," I cut her off, waving my hands. No way could I remember any of that. "Let's just go with the simple red roses."

She shrugged. "Works for me."

Then she stood up, abandoning her meal, and started toward the door as if to go fetch the roses that very moment. I scampered to my feet and followed her until we reached the entrance of the garden. She left the door open behind her, which I probably could've considered an invitation, but I wasn't taking any chances.

The *"I don't want anyone else messing around in my garden. Especially him"* demand she'd given that first day had been explicit. I wasn't going to break the rule unless I was just as explicitly told it was okay.

Rocking back onto my heels, I clasped my hands behind my back and patiently waited for her to notice I was no longer behind her. She picked up a pair of gloves and scissors, then said something I couldn't hear, before she whirled around and scowled at me.

"What the heck are you doing out there?" she called, frowning irritably.

Feigning surprise, I pressed a hand to my chest. "Oh! Am I allowed to enter?"

Her glare was dry. "Get in here."

I grinned, happy to get on her prickly side. Then I stepped a foot inside, only to breathe in a lungful. "Damn, it smells good in here."

Isobel ignored my wonderment, already turning to the roses and eyeing them with a sad longing. "It's going to have to be long-stem," she decided.

I fluttered out an unconcerned hand. "Whichever ones you feel as if you can part with." I refused to participate in the actual choosing. They were her babies; she was going to have to be the one to decide which left the nest.

I turned to the pink vines to my left; I swear they smelled the best.

Behind me, I heard a snip, then another. She was actually doing it. Pride filled my chest. Refusing to look, mostly because I was scared I'd lose my own nerve and make her stop if I saw any kind of tortured expression on her face, I once again clasped my hands behind my back and began to walk the row, studying all the different types.

When I noticed a couple obvious non-rose greens growing amongst the bushes, I lifted my eyebrows. "What's this? Is this…holy shit, is there a *weed* in your rose garden?"

Isobel appeared at my side, only to grumble under her breath and immediately pull the weed from the ground. When I blinked at her, trying not to grin, she scowled back. "What?"

I shook my head. "Nothing. Just surprised you let one grow that big. The first time I was in here, everything was so immaculate and flawless. I thought it wouldn't even be possible for a weed to—"

"I've been a little busy lately," she snapped, sending me a death glare before returning to the flowers and clipping savagely. "The library never would've gotten renovated if I'd let you do it all by yourself."

Since she wasn't looking my way, I let my grin grow. To me, it was a good sign that she no longer spent every waking hour in here, perfecting her flowers. It meant she was learning to live a little. Her father would be pleased with this progress. But more importantly, *I* was pleased by it.

My step a little lighter and smile a little brighter, I wandered to the end of the row until I came to a shelf holding about two dozen tiny pots full of moist soil and miniature green leaves splitting out of about half of them.

"Ooh, what're these?"

Isobel briefly glanced up from her work before turning back to her clipping. "Those are the seeds you gave me."

My lips parted in awe. But shit, it was thrilling to realize she hadn't thrown them out, and even more exciting to learn she'd actually gotten them to grow.

"Really?" I stepped closer. "Holy shit. They're actually growing. I can't believe it. Look at those cute little baby leaves." I wiggled my pointer finger at them as if to tickle their stems, even though I didn't dare to actually touch them in fear I might kill one.

"Those cute little baby leaves are called cotyledons."

Of course she would know that. I grinned, amused by her formality. "Well, whatever they're called, I just want to bounce them on my knee and smoosh their chubby little leaf cheeks. They're freaking adorable."

Isobel laughed. Honest-to-God laughed. "You're so strange."

As long as she was laughing in true amusement, she could call me anything she wanted. I shrugged, grinning even wider and feeling like I was on top of the world. "I can't wait to see the roses. Black with blue tips sound pretty cool."

Isobel went back to studying the red roses before she clipped another for Mrs. Pan. I could tell she was trying to pick the best, and that made my chest expand. She had such a good heart.

Then she said conversationally, "You know there's no such thing as black with blue-tipped roses, right?"

My mouth sagged open, before I blinked and shook my head, unable to believe what I'd just heard. "Say what again?"

"Roses only come in shades of white, red, yellow and purples or variations and mixes between those. Anything else is artificially created."

Still slowly shaking my head back and forth in adamant denial, I said, "No…no, that can't be right."

My absolute unwillingness to believe such a thing amused her. "It is." She clipped another rose for Mrs. Pan.

I gaped at her. "But…" Spinning wildly, I found a rose that was an exception to her rule. "There!" I pointed. "You have a black rose, right there."

Her lips tightened as she held in a smile. "Look again, Hollander."

I stormed to the rosebush in question and knelt to its level before the redness of it began to show through. "I'll be damned," I murmured in awe. "It's not black; it's just a dark, dark red."

When she laughed for the second time in the last minute, getting a kick out of my shock, I looked over at her. "Wait, then…those seeds?" I whirled to take in the buds sprouting from the tiny starter pods.

"Whatever they are, they aren't midnight supreme roses, that's for sure," Isobel admitted, "because there's no such thing as a black and blue rose."

I gulped, shocked and mortified that my gift had been…it'd been… "But the lady who worked in the flower shop said…she said…"

Sending me a wince of genuine sympathy, Isobel murmured, "Whatever she said was a scam. She had to have known black and blue roses weren't possible."

"But…" I shook my head, feeling like a big gullible idiot. "I read all these rose books on roses, and *I* didn't know. Maybe she didn't either. Maybe—"

"Wow," Isobel murmured, watching me kind of

sadly. "You just can't believe anything bad about anyone, can you?" It looked as if she felt sorry for me—*me*—so I scowled defensively.

"She might not have known," I cried. "She was so nice and helpful, and—" I threw up my hand, remembering. "She gave me a discount. What kind of scammer gives a discount?"

Isobel wrinkled her nose before saying, "Probably all of them, to convince suckers like you that they're kind and benevolent souls."

I scowled at her moodily, wanting to argue my case. But there wasn't much to say except, yeah, I was a total idiot sucker who'd gotten taken in by a freaking scammer. I hissed out a huff. "I can't believe this." My gaze strayed to the baby rose plants. "I wonder what color they'll turn out, then? Or if they're even rose plants."

"Oh, they're definitely roses," she assured me. "But your guess is as good as mine on the color."

Reaching out, I just barely grazed one of the new leaves with my fingertip. "I guess our babies are going to grow up and surprise us all." Grinning tenderly, I added, "I kind of like the sound of that. You grow big and strong, baby roses. Show the world you're better than any fake midnight supreme rose bush."

I glanced toward Isobel to share the joke with her, but she was gazing at me with the strangest expression. "What?" I asked, immediately reviewing what I'd just said in my head. Yeah, it'd been strange, but all just teasing fun, until I remembered the words, *our babies*, as if we were their parents.

An immediate heat stirred through me. The idea of raising anything with Isobel, even just a rose, was intimate and bonding. I gazed back at her, wondering if she felt the same connection stirring between us.

Face flushing, she cleared her throat and suddenly looked away, focusing on the roses in her hands. "Get your ass over here, Hollander," she said, "and help me pick off the leaves and thorns. This was *your* idea."

"Right." I cleared my throat and made my way to her. "Do we really have to take off the thorns?"

She sent me a look as if that were a stupid question. "We want it to appear as if he really likes her, right? Taking off the thorns is a sign he's serious. If he's willing to go through all the work of stripping the stems to protect her valuable fingers from getting pricked—"

"Okay, I'm sold," I told her, lifting a hand. "The thorns gotta go."

"Here." She held out the roses she'd already picked out and plucked. "There's another set of gloves in the—"

But I was already reaching out with my bare hand, and yep, pricked myself right in the thumb with a damn thorn. "Ouch! *Shit.*"

I plunged the injured appendage into my mouth and sucked the blood away. Isobel sighed as if dealing with a misbehaving child. "Gloves," she repeated. "Right there."

I fetched the gloves, but soon found out they weren't my friends either. I had no idea how Isobel worked with these clunky things on. I couldn't get a good grip on the flower because it felt as if I was crushing it if I held it too hard, and it was damn near impossible to slip gloved fingers into the handles of the scissors and then get them to work properly. I glanced repeatedly toward Isobel to see how in the world she was handling them with such aplomb, but it was something I just couldn't master. I was more of a hands-on kind of guy, I guess.

"I'll just deal with the thorns," I finally muttered, ripping the gloves off and picking up the shears with much more ease.

Isobel snickered to herself but said nothing. I scowled her way, except she looked so content and at home snipping flowers that all my grouch dissolved. It didn't even bother me—much—when I pricked my finger again thirty seconds later.

We worked in comfortable silence until the flowers were ready. Then Isobel bundled them together and found a yellow ribbon on her shelves to tie them with.

"Should we leave a note with them?" I asked. "So she knows they're from him?"

Isobel gazed at the roses a moment before nodding. "Yes. Definitely."

So we trekked back to the library to find some paper and a pen, where Isobel immediately handed me both. "You write it."

"No way." I shoved the paper back at her. "I have awful penmanship."

"Doesn't matter. It's probably more male than mine. Mrs. Pan would never believe Lewis wrote the note if we left it in my looping, feminine scrawl."

"Good point." I made a face. "Dammit." Taking the pen and paper from her, I grumbled, "What do I say?"

She shrugged.

I sighed and wiped the back of my hand across my forehead, already feeling too stressed to deal with this task. "Okay, fine. What's Mrs. Pan's first name?"

A blush lit her cheeks before she confessed, "I have no idea."

"Oh, Jesus." We were doomed. Until an idea hit me. "Ooh, I got it." I bent to set the note on the table and began to write, "To the best cook and mother I know. Thank you for being you. You make coming to work each day less about income and more about getting to see you. Lewis."

When I glanced up, eyebrows lifted, to gauge what she thought of that, I caught my breath when I saw the look on her face. She stared at me as if I'd written some of those parts about me and her instead of about Lewis and Mrs. Pan.

The scariest thing was, I had.

I swallowed and straightened before folding the note and extending it her way. We never took our eyes off each other as she slowly received it and brought it to the bundle of roses she was still holding to her chest.

"Thank you," she murmured as if thanking me for writing those words to her and not for handing her the note.

I nodded, unable to speak.

Another moment of intense staring continued before we both glanced away.

She cleared her throat. I rubbed the back of my neck.

"Maybe, we should, uh…" I fumbled awkwardly before motioning toward the door. "I mean, do you think it's a good time to plant the surprise now? She shouldn't be in the kitchen at this time of day."

"What?" Isobel's lips parted as her blue eyes met my brown. Then she blinked rapidly and glanced down at the roses. "Oh…right." She shook her head from the trance she'd been in. "Yeah…I mean, yes, now's a good time."

So we stealthily stole our way to the kitchen. I led the expedition, checking around each corner first before waving her to follow with the roses. The kitchen was indeed empty, though the most lovely baked bread smell floated from the oven where it appeared Mrs. Pan was cooking homemade loaves.

I motioned Isobel into the room. She hurried to me, her eyes wide. I swear I could hear her heartbeat thumping as fast as mine was. We were such nerds, getting this big of a kick out of planting romantic gifts for other people. But hell…it was fun.

"Where?" She whispered the word, glancing around the kitchen for the perfect spot.

I started to shrug, but stopped short when I heard a sound at the back door.

"Shit! Here she comes," I hissed, probably whispering too loud as I grabbed Isobel's arm and hauled her out of the kitchen with me. She squeaked out her worry and surprise, tossed the roses on the table, and stumbled after me.

We tripped to a halt just outside the entrance at the same time and stared at each other with wide eyes, silently communicating how glad we were that we hadn't gotten caught when I realized I was holding her wrist of the scarred hand. The skin was rough against my thumb and I wanted to explore more, shift my finger further along her flesh to investigate all the unique ridges, but she didn't seem to realize what I was touching, and I didn't want to bring it to her attention in case it freaked her out. So I held my breath and stayed as still as possible as I watched her face, while she listened to Mrs. Pan's footsteps move through the kitchen.

We could tell the moment she saw her present. A gasp filled the kitchen and spilled out into the hallway where we were hiding.

"Well…" she breathed, clearly pleased. "I'll be." The quiet shuffling told us she'd probably scooped the flowers into her arms. "Oh, God. They smell so good."

Isobel and I shared an excited, gritted-teeth grin. I tried to sneak a peek into the room to see the cook's expression, but Isobel caught the sleeve of my shirt and jerked me back out of sight.

I grinned at her just as the back door opened and Mrs. Pan suddenly raged, "Lewis, you stupid old fool, what have you *done*?"

Okay, that didn't sound pleased or appreciative at all. I shared a confused glance with my cohort, only to find she looked as stunned and worried as I felt.

"What?" Lewis asked, his voice full of the same confusion. "What'd I do?"

"You *stole* roses from Miss Nash's garden? Are you insane? If she found out about this, she'd have her father fire you for sure. I can't believe you were such an idiot."

My mouth fell open and so did Isobel's. We hadn't foreseen this kind of problem. But the shit was about to hit the fan, and it was all our fault. Our experiment was supposed to nudge Lewis and Mrs. Pan together, not push them apart.

"What do we do?" I mouthed, frantic worry flooding my veins.

"I didn't steal any flowers," Lewis claimed, the tone in his voice saying he was scowling and ready to put the cook in her place.

Setting her hand against her heart, Isobel rushed past me and flew into the kitchen. I started after her, ready to confess all to Lewis and Mrs. Pan, but what she said stalled me in my shoes. "Mr. Lewis, I've decided I don't want cash for the flowers you purchased from me. I'll just have my father deduct the amount from your paycheck. All right?"

"I…uh…" A blank-faced Lewis stuttered and gaped a moment before he glanced at the roses in Mrs. Pan's arms and then back to Isobel.

The cook flushed a deep, embarrassed red before gushing, "Oh Lord, Lewis. I'm so sorry. I didn't realize you'd actually *bought* them for me. That's so considerate. I love them." She hugged them to her face so she could take a deep whiff of them. Then she smiled at the groundskeeper appreciatively. "And you even took all the thorns off. Thank you."

Lewis's Adam's apple bobbed before he gave a slow nod and just as sluggishly answered, "You're…well, you're mighty welcome, Mrs. Pan. It was my pleasure." Then he sent a grateful, flush-faced nod to Isobel. "Thank you, Miss Nash."

Isobel gave a short, businesslike nod and whirled on her heel before briskly stalking from the kitchen.

She strode right past me, but it didn't take me long to pick my jaw up off the floor and hurry to catch up with her. We were nearly to the library before I managed to say, "That…that was brilliant."

I wanted to kiss her. I wanted to drag her into my arms and hug her before kissing the breath straight from her lungs. She'd made the entire situation completely real by remaining her haughty, high-brow self, and Mrs. Pan hadn't had a clue at all that it'd been a setup. Then Lewis had fallen into place perfectly, knowing when to save his hide and impress his gal. I wanted to pull Isobel into my arms and laugh and dance with her.

Instead, I offered her a huge grin and a high five. "You rock. You so totally rock."

Her lips finally tipped into a smile and her blue eyes glowed with triumph before she slapped her palm against mine.

And that was the moment I'm pretty sure I fell flat in love with her.

chapter SIXTEEN

A day after our matchmaking endeavors, Isobel and I officially claimed the library shelving project complete. I had wanted to call everyone into the room immediately and show it off, even though most of the staff had stopped by periodically to follow our progress, anyway. But Isobel wanted everything cleaned and all the books shelved before our "grand opening."

So while I removed the drop cloths and ladders and tools, Isobel dusted and began to vacuum. When it came time to shelve the books, our great debate about how to organize them started.

"This is where I had the mysteries before," Isobel started, narrowing her eyes as if daring me to disagree.

I just grinned, ready to play. "But this is a darker corner. Don't you think mysteries should be in the darkest, most mysterious part of the room? And romances belong by the light, since they're, you know, light and full of love with happy endings and stuff."

She blinked at me as if I'd lost my mind. "You have the strangest logic I've ever heard."

With a wink, I chuckled. "But you like my idea, don't

you?"

Scowling a moment longer, she chased it with a huff before she bit her lip and gazed around the room. "Okay, fine. The romances should go by the windows. But the mysteries need to be on the bookshelf covering the hidden door, and the horror novels can go in the darker corner."

My mouth fell open before I pointed and said, "Even better. Perfect."

So we got to work, carrying piles of books from the center of the room where some had been stored for the building project to their respective areas. After five minutes, I noticed a pair of eyes peeking around the opening of the library watching us.

I had no idea how long Kit had been there, but our mundane book carrying had clearly fascinated him.

"Hi, Kit," I said good-naturedly. "Why don't you come help us?"

Isobel paused what she was doing and turned to see the boy. When he realized her attention was on him, he gasped and disappeared.

"That does it," I muttered, setting down the stack I was holding and charging after him.

"Oh, leave him be," Isobel called. "Seriously. *Shaw*! What the heck are you doing?"

I held up a finger. "I'll be right back."

Then I raced from the room and reached the boy before he could make it to the kitchen. "Hey!" I caught him by the back of the shirt, pulling him to a stop.

I winced when he stumbled off balance from the abruptness and almost fell. Shit, I hoped no one had seen that. But when he looked up at me with big, scared eyes, my reason for chasing him down resurfaced.

"Why'd you run off?" I asked, shaking my head cluelessly.

He peered down the hall as if looking for signs of Isobel before turning back to me and whispering, "She looked at me."

"Yeah." I nodded before giving him a wink. "And you didn't turn to stone. That's a good sign, isn't it?"

Considering that a moment, he finally gave a slow nod. "Yeah. I guess."

"Here." I grasped his hand and urged him to follow me back toward the library. "Just meet her. She's actually very nice."

"But—"

"Trust me, kid," I told him, looking him straight in the eye. "I wouldn't let anything bad happen to you."

He gulped audibly before whispering, "You swear?"

"On my life."

After giving me a nod, he followed me willingly but hesitantly back to the library, but as soon as we hit the doorway, he pressed himself to my hip and hugged my leg.

"I found us some more help," I announced to Isobel, grinning as if a trembling, scared child wasn't clinging to me for dear life.

Isobel sent me a reprimanding glance, silently commanding me to stop torturing the poor child.

I ignored it. "Isobel, this is Kit. Kit, Miss Isobel Nash."

Kit peeled his face from my thigh and slowly turned his attention to her.

She smiled at him, even though her lips trembled. She had her hair pulled back and face on full display. I knew it took everything she had to keep from hiding her scars from him, but I think we both realized he had to see them openly before he could combat his fear of them.

"Hey, Kit," she said. "Are you really here to help? Because I have some important rare books I need put on this shelf over there, and I need someone special to do it."

The muscles in Kit's body relaxed fractionally; I felt every one of them because he seemed to have them all plastered against me. "I…I guess," he mumbled.

Isobel's face brightened. She looked more beautiful than I'd ever seen her before. "Great," she said, "these books are super important to me. They're first edition fairy tales with hand-drawn pictures. They're really good pictures, too." She began to gather an armful of crumbling old books. "Did you know, in some of the original versions of Cinderella, the wicked stepsisters cut off parts of their feet to fit them into the glass slipper?"

Kit perked to attention and stopped holding my leg entirely. "Really?"

"Yep. And they have pictures of it. It's really gory and bloody."

"Sweet." The kid bounded away from me, hurrying toward Isobel as she opened the book on the top of her pile and started to flip through pages.

"Here it is." She knelt down next to him.

Kit's eyes grew wide as he stared. "Gross," he cooed in absolute awe.

Isobel glanced up at me and grinned. "And, ooh, you should see the picture of the woodcutter cutting open the stomach of the big bad wolf in Little Red Riding Hood." She flipped a few more pages until they came to the one she was looking for.

"Awesome." Kit seemed to vibrate with excitement as he asked, "Are there any more?"

"Well." Isobel bit her lip before her eyes sparkled. "Yes. They have one of the witch burning in Hansel and Gretel just after Gretel pushed her into the stove."

As she began to flip pages, Kit glanced up to study her face. "Did it hurt a lot?" he asked, sympathy clogging his voice. "When *you* burned in the fire?"

Isobel slowly stopped flipping pages. She turned to look at him before admitting, "It was the worst pain of my life."

Kit nodded slowly, his eyes large but full of understanding. "Do you think my dad and your mom hurt a lot when they died?"

Shit. I hadn't meant for things to take this turn. I'd only wanted the boy to stop treating her like a monster. But he was suddenly taking it somewhere I wasn't sure Isobel could handle going. I started toward them, to stop the kid, even drag him away from her if I had to. But Isobel lifted her hand in my direction, asking me to stop as she kept her attention on Kit.

"I think it hurt, yes," she admitted, her throat working through what had to be a difficult swallow. Then her chin lifted a fraction of an inch. "But then I think it stopped and was over quickly. For me, the pain lasted for months and months, because I survived. For them, it was only for a few moments. That's the only consolation I can give myself when I think of them. At least their pain stopped."

The kid watched her a moment longer before his head slowly moved up and down. "I think you're right," he agreed.

I drew out a long, relieved breath, glad the moment hadn't ended as awfully as I had feared it might. Just as I set my hand against my heart and finished blowing out a breath, Mrs. Pan appeared in the library.

"Kit! There you are. I've been looking all over for you, child. It's time to…" Her words trailed off when she realized who was sitting next to her son. She blinked once, then twice. Suddenly, she flushed and began to stutter, "I…I'm so sorry, Miss Nash. Is he bothering you? I can—"

"No, no," Isobel rushed to assure her, setting the book aside and pushing to her feet before brushing off her knees. "We were just looking at pictures in some old fairy tales."

"They're so cool, Mom. You should see what the wicked stepsisters did to their feet to fit into Cinderella's slipper."

"I…well…" Mrs. Pan shook her head and flushed before she seemed to remember why she'd originally come into the room, looking for him. "I will later, darling. For now, we need to get you down to the school and enrolled into third grade."

"Oh man, really, Mom? Already? But summer break just started."

"I'm afraid so. Then we'll need to go shopping for school supplies and new shoes after that."

"Can we get ice cream too?" the kid begged, a natural negotiator.

His mother squinted as if she had to think it through before saying, "Maybe."

To Kit, I guessed that meant absolutely.

"Yes!" He fisted the air and started toward his mom, only to jerk to a halt and turn back to Isobel. "Thank you for showing me your book, Miss Isobel. Do you think I could come back later to look at more pictures and help you put the books back on the shelves?"

I swear Isobel's bottom lip trembled before she gave a slow nod and smiled, her eyes glassy and emotional. "I'd like that very much," she said, her voice so hoarse she nearly whispered the words.

"Cool." Kit leapt forward and gave her a hug.

Mrs. Pan turned slightly to the side so she could discreetly wipe the corner of her eye, while the kid pulled away from Isobel, calling, "See you later." Then he remembered to wave my way. "Bye, Shaw."

"See you later, kid."

And then he was gone, racing from the room at full bore.

"Kit!" his mother cried after him, chasing him into the hall. "Don't run in the house."

As their pounding footsteps faded from the room, I risked a glance toward the woman standing there, still staring at the doorway as if overcome.

"You okay?" I asked, edging closer to her.

She blinked, coming out of her daze, and looked up at me. "What?" Then she shook her head. "I mean, yes, of course." A smile bloomed across her face. "Did you see him hug me?"

"I did."

She touched the side of her waist as if she could still feel the pressure of him squeezing her. "He smelled like bologna," she murmured distractedly.

I chuckled, moving even closer to her. "Typical kid smell, I bet."

She nodded, her hand moving to the side of her arm. "Yeah. Probably." She looked up at me again. "He didn't seem afraid of me at all by the end there, did he?"

I shook my head. "Not at all."

Another smile lit her face. "That was pretty amazing."

You're amazing, I wanted to say.

I stayed next to her, waiting, not sure what to do but remaining nearby in case she needed…well, anything.

"I guess we should get back to shelving these books," she murmured, sounding as if she were still a little lost.

She knelt and gathered the heaping pile she'd set down in order to go through the fairy tale books with Kit, and tried to stand with them in her arms.

"Here, let me help." I reached out, but she shook her head.

"No, I've got it." And she tried to stand again, but I was still attempting to relieve her of them.

We were both determined, and it kind of caused a collision in which we bumped into each other and lost our footing. The books in her arms went flying, we tripped over another pile sitting nearby, and to the floor we went.

"Shit!" I cursed, landing on top of her, face-first, while plastering her back to the floor with a full impression of the woman under me, breasts, hips, thighs, legs. "I'm sorry. Oh God, I'm so sorry. Shit. Are you okay?

Isobel?"

I sat up, the feel of her breasts smashed into my chest following me.

When I looked down at her, she blinked but didn't move or speak. She just stared up at the ceiling and curled her hands up against her collarbone.

I sat next to her and hovered over her. "Are you okay?" I repeated, fearing the worst.

She started to nod, making a stray piece of hair that had come out of her ponytail fall into her face, a few strands tangling with her overlong eyelashes.

Unconsciously, I brushed them from her eyes, asking, "Are you sure? You're not talking."

"I'm—" She gasped when the tips of my fingers traced lightly over her scar while I was sweeping her hair aside.

"What?" I asked immediately, starting to freak out. "You *are* hurt, aren't you? Where?"

"No," she said, shaking her head. "No, I'm not—I'm not hurt. It's just… you…"

"What?" I demanded, ready to rush her to a hospital if I had to.

"You touched my scars," she breathed. Then she blinked up into my eyes. "No one ever does that."

My mouth fell open before I said, "Oh, God. I'm sorry. I didn't realize they were that tender. I didn't mean to hurt you."

She let out a small laugh and began to sit up. "You misunderstand. It didn't *hurt*. I don't feel much of anything there anymore since the nerve endings were damaged. It was just…*weird* that someone voluntarily touched them."

I watched her wipe another piece of hair from her face. "A good weird or bad weird?" I finally dared to ask.

She paused then nodded. "A good weird."

The way she said it made me wonder if it might hurt her feelings when people purposely avoided the scars. Of course, making fun of them and degrading her for them would be upsetting to her, but maybe pretending they weren't there was another form of condemnation in her book? Maybe she just wanted people to accept them.

I began to reach out without thinking, only to stop myself a few inches from her face. "I mean," I said, shaking my head in apology. "Is it okay if I…?" The words fell gently from my lips.

Isobel blinked wide surprised eyes before she slowly nodded her head up and down. "O-okay. I guess. If you're curious."

I swear, we both held our breaths as I slowly reached out. As soon as my fingers made contact, we released the air in tandem.

"It's not as bad as it used to be," she told me. "I had a lot of laser surgery, a compression mask, massage therapy. But it's the best they could get. My dad spared no expense."

"Did it hurt?" I asked. "I mean, all the surgeries and work they did."

She shrugged, which I'm sure meant yes.

I smiled. For the haughty, pampered snob I'd taken her for the first day we'd met, Isobel was actually quite modest.

"I have this itching urge to say it really doesn't look that bad, because honestly, you still have all your hair, your ears aren't like hanging half down your neck and the skin isn't really that discolored. There's some bumps but no major craters or anything." I looked into her wide, watchful eyes. "But I have a feeling that would be the wrong thing to say, wouldn't it?"

She nodded her head. "It really would."

I nodded as well. "Then I won't say it. But honestly, it doesn't dominate what I see when I look at you. Sometimes, I'll even forget you have them. And I'll turn and look at you, and they'll surprise me all over again." My grin turned playful. "You hear that, scars?" I told them.

"I know you like to hog all the attention away from my girl here, but I gotta tell you, she's still prettier than you are ugly." And then I leaned in and kissed her cheek, pressing my lips directly against scar tissue.

Damn, she always smelled so good. I think roses were my new aphrodisiac.

But I didn't get long to enjoy this up-close-and-personal experience of her. She gasped again, and jerked against me, reminding me I'd just freaking put my mouth on her.

Oh, shit. I'd just kissed Isobel. On the cheek, but still…

Eyes wide, I pulled back and gaped into her face, realizing she looked as stunned as I felt. "I…I'm sorry," I gushed. "I don't know what I was thinking." Oh, God. What the hell had I just done? "Are you going to tell your dad?"

She stared at me and pressed her hand to the scar as if I'd just slapped her instead of kissed her. And then I had to wonder if I had. What if some of the shit I'd just blurted came out all wrong and upset her instead of made her feel better?

Shit, oh, shit, oh, shit. I'd fucked up epically, hadn't I?

She pushed to her feet to stand above me, still holding her hand to her cheek and staring at me as if I'd just plunged a knife into her back. Then she murmured, "Of course I won't tell him," and she rushed from the room.

chapter SEVENTEEN

Isobel didn't return to the library for the rest of the day. At first, I was okay with her absence. I mean, hell, I needed a moment to regroup, too.

I'd kissed her. Things had changed. We'd probably never get back to the place we used to be. And this new direction could either lead somewhere very good, or very bad. So, yeah, it was scary. I got that. I understood her need for a moment to herself.

Maybe even an hour or two to her herself.

But when four o'clock rolled around, it was time for me to leave, and she'd never reappeared. I had tried to place as many of her books on the shelves as possible, hoping I didn't put something somewhere she didn't want it to go, but it just felt all wrong doing it by myself. We'd started working on this together; we should've finished together.

The worst of it came the next morning at seven, when she didn't show up at the lake to run. I stood on the running trail, *our* running trail, hands on my hips as I turned a slow circle and glowered at the amazing sunrise.

Dammit, she'd even ruined dawn for me. I couldn't

appreciate the pinks, and purples, and oranges in the sky without her.

Not about to let her retreat from me again, not the way she had the first two weeks I'd been here, I stormed toward the house.

I didn't need to go inside to find her, though. As I approached the back, I saw a light on in the rose garden. So I veered that way. Even as I approached the entrance, I could see her inside, crouched among bushes as she gave her flowers a hundred and ten percent of the attention they needed.

Opening the door, I stalked inside.

"Morning," I said, trying to conceal my anger so she wouldn't know how truly furious I was. I hoped I sounded pleasant enough.

Her head jerked up, blue eyes blinking. Then she went back to work. "Morning."

I watched her pluck a weed and then patiently fill the hole its absence had created with some fresh soil. Folding my arms over my chest, I chewed on the inside of my lip, silently willing her to look at me again. She didn't.

After drawing in a deep, calming breath, I said, "Missed you on the trail this morning."

She shrugged. The damn woman merely shrugged. "I didn't feel like running."

Okay. Fair enough. There were plenty of mornings I could've slept in and would've stayed in bed another hour. But I *hadn't*, because I knew she'd be there waiting on me, *counting* on me to run with her, just as I'd counted on her to be there *this* morning.

And just like that, my anger snapped, fresh and new.

"Can we just talk about it?" I demanded, my tone no longer polite.

At last, Isobel glanced up. "Talk about what?"

I sent her a dry stare, not impressed by the act of ignorance.

"The kiss," I bit out, watching her flinch at the word.

But she went back to work, using the back of a small spade to press the new earth into the old. "What about it?"

Well, at least she was allowing me to say what I wanted to say, which was exactly what I planned to do, anyway. "Everything feels awkward and stiff now. Maybe it's just me, but I don't think it is. You've avoided me ever since it happened. And now, you won't even look me in the eye."

She jerked her head up, looking me straight in the eye, even though her eyebrows pulled together with annoyance.

I knelt beside her, softening. "Just tell me if you're okay or not."

"I'm fine." She trilled out a fake laugh and then wrinkled her brow as if she couldn't believe I was even worried.

I lifted my eyebrows. "Are you sure?"

Another fake laugh. "Yes, I'm fine, Shaw. Whatever you're imagining, it must really all be in your head, because *nothing* is wrong."

My shoulders fell, disappointed she wasn't going to talk about it. I refused to give up, though. So I said, "Bullshit."

Her eyes widened. "Excuse me?"

"You heard me. I said bullshit. If nothing is wrong, then why do I feel so shitty? Why do I feel as if I've made some horrible, awful, terrible mistake? You would tell me if I had, right?"

"Of course, but you didn't—"

"*Yes*, I did. Something is wrong, and it's my fault. I don't know how I know it, but I know it, and I can't figure out what it is. So you just need to buck up and tell me, so I'll—"

"Oh my God, you stopped, okay? You *stopped*."

At first, I thought she was telling me *to* stop, as in

to shut up because my rant was driving her bonkers. But then I realized she was speaking in the past tense.

I blinked, thrown all off track.

"What?"

She flushed a deep purplish red with embarrassment. "Nothing," she was quick to say, turning away.

But I caught her shoulder and urged her back around. "No. You said I stopped. I stopped *what*?"

Closing her eyes, she bowed her head. "Nothing," she insisted. "It's stupid and silly, and I don't want to talk about it."

"Isobel," I murmured in quiet reprimand, leaning toward her until our brows were nearly touching. "I don't care if it's the wackiest thing in the world, I want to know. I *need* to know."

Finally, she looked up, lifting her face to show me the fear and uncertainty in her blue eyes. "You stopped kissing me," she said in a low voice that shook with nerves. "You stopped and pulled away and then apologized like…like you *regretted* it."

My lips parted as shock punched all the air from my lungs. "No," I gasped. "Oh, God, no. Isobel…Jesus, no, that's not why I apologized. I didn't regret kissing you. I *don't* regret it even now."

Her eyes looked so blue, and large, and confused. "Then why did you say sorry?"

"Be-because I was worried I had offended *you*."

She shook her head, frowning. "Huh?"

I laughed. But when her brow puckered as if she thought I was laughing *at* her, I sobered. Tenderness and even relief filled me.

"Oh, you crazy girl," I murmured, cupping her face in my hands, one palm settling against smooth warm skin, the other cradling ragged, torn scar tissue. "If only you could look into my head right now and see how much I think about you, see *what* I think about you, you would never doubt my willingness to kiss you ever again. You absolutely own everything about me. I would not regret kissing you at any time, anywhere, in any sense. I would kiss you in the morning or at night, or in the dark or full daylight."

With a laugh, she buried her face in the front of my shirt. "You're starting to sound like Dr. Seuss."

Since it'd made her smile, I ran with it, murmuring in her ear. "I would kiss you in a box with a fox or on a house with a mouse. I would kiss you in a—"

She cut me off by lifting her face and smashing her mouth to mine. Then she grabbed two fistfuls of my hair, anchoring me to her. My surprised grunt was muffled against her lips, vibrating between us. Then her tongue touched mine, and I was gone. Done. Lost in passion.

She smelled so good, felt so soft, tasted like fruit—something citrusy—and made the most fetching whimper to ever touch my ears. I swear it reached right down into my pants and bitch slapped my dick awake. I was suddenly hard and throbbing, focused on nothing but her. She gasped my name and this primal urge to feast on her filled my senses.

I broke my mouth from hers, working my way down her neck. I couldn't even tell you if I was on the scarred side of her throat or not, I just knew she felt amazing against me, still clutching my hair and tipping her head back to allow me better access. I wanted all of her right then. My attention went lower, and she made a hiccupping sound of surprise when my lips touched the swell of her breasts through her shirt.

Blinking myself somewhat back to reality, I looked up into her face. "This okay?" I asked.

She nodded, breathing heavily. "Yes. Of course, I just...we're so out in the open. I feel exposed."

I looked around, realizing where we were. Immediately, I whipped my hands off her. "Oh, shit. We're in the...I'm at work. I'm making out with someone on the job." Not just *someone*, my boss's daughter.

Henry was going to kill me and then fire me for this if he ever found out about it. Probably in that order.

Isobel merely grinned. God, why did she have to look so beautiful when she smiled like that?

"You don't technically start work until eight, and it's barely seven thirty now."

I stared at her, listening to her words, but for some reason, they didn't make me feel better.

"I need to tell you something," I blurted, not even planning to say that, but my mouth…the stupid fucking thing had a mind of its own. "And I don't think you're going to like it."

God…damn. Why couldn't I just keep my trap shut?

Isobel sank away from me, her eyes going wary and untrusting. I reached for her without thinking but she evaded my touch.

It gutted me. I hadn't even confessed yet, and she was already withdrawing.

Pretty sure I was about to fuck myself over majorly, but unable to lie to her in any way, not even a lie of omission, because my guilt would drive me insane, I pulled my knees up toward my chest and wrapped my arms around them. I probably looked like a lost little child about to confess my deepest fear, but I sort of felt like one too.

"What?" she demanded. "Just say it."

Closing my eyes, I admitted, "I was brought here because of you."

chapter EIGHTEEN

The silence that followed my confession was resounding. It echoed around in my head until sweat misted on my brow.

I opened my eyes to find Isobel watching me, her expression bleak.

She shook her head. "What do you mean?"

Glancing down at my hands, I began to pick at a piece of skin coming loose around a callus on my palm.

"I told you before, I originally went to your dad because of my mom, right?"

She nodded. "What? Is that not true?"

"No, it's true," I said. Then I drew in a deep breath and began my story.

"I went to him because she owed him money. He'd given her a loan for her bakery. I swear, she owed *everyone* money. I have no idea how a single person could rack up that much debt, but she kept it from me for as long as she could. By the time I learned about it, it was out of my control. I sold my truck, sold her house, sold most of our furniture. And it still wasn't enough. Not nearly enough. After I moved her in with me, she tripped on the stairwell outside my apartment. I live on the second floor, and they've always been steep steps. I wish I could've moved us somewhere safer, but I'd been working at Pestle."

Isobel nodded in understanding. "But they went out of business," she said for me.

"But they went out of business," I repeated, nodding too. "Then Mom lost the bakery, and suddenly we were making no money, so I couldn't afford to move us. And after she broke her hip, I had to be there for her almost every hour of the day. It took her a few months before she was able to get around on her own, enough for me to safely leave the apartment and look for work. But by then, pretty much everyone who'd been let go at the shoe factory had filled all the available jobs around. Bills kept coming in, the one from Nash Corporation included. Mom had talked about how she'd gotten to speak to Henry Nash personally when she was given the loan for her bakery—and he was the richest man I knew that I thought I might get to speak to in person—so I thought maybe he'd let me in to see him too."

I paused to glance at Isobel, gauging her interest, her mood. For the most part, she seemed patient and not too upset.

But I knew that wouldn't last. Fearing her ultimate reaction, I drew in a deep breath and dived back into my story.

"I was so desperate. You have no idea how desperate I was. When I was able to get a meeting with your dad, I thought…" I shook my head. "I'm not even sure what I thought. I'd worked so hard all my life only to fall into debt and poverty. It was humiliating and humbling. It stripped most of the pride right out of me."

Wincing, I admitted, "I was ready to do anything to get out of this slump. And…well, I was sure someone as rich and powerful as Henry Nash had to be crooked at the core, that he had to have about a dozen undercover, black market, blackmailing deals going on with people.

So I went to him to offer myself up as…as one of his thugs, I guess."

Isobel blinked before a smile cracked her face. "Wait. You seriously thought my *dad* was crooked? Really?" She snorted before beginning to laugh outright. "Oh my God, that's so funny. My *mobster* dad." She laughed again.

I scowled. "It's not funny. I mean, I didn't *know*!"

"What the heck did you think he was going to say—'Sure, I just met you but come be my evil minion henchman.' Oh, Lord."

She threw her head back, giggling so hard tears streamed down her cheeks. I sat there, brooding, and waited it out.

"I so wish I could've seen how that conversation went. How did you even *ask* such a question?"

I shrugged, feeling ridiculous for ever thinking Henry could be some kind of mob lord. "I just told him I'd do anything," I muttered moodily.

No way was I going to tell her what I'd first feared he wanted from me when he'd hired me. She'd probably bust her gut right open from the power of her laughter.

Her brows wrinkled as she shook her head. "So…he just gave you a job?"

I sniffed. "In my defense, I was pretty damn convincing."

"Oh, I'm sure." Pressing the back of her hand to her brow, she tried to mimic how dramatic she must've thought I had sounded. "Please, sir," she wailed. "I'll do *anything*."

My face grew uncomfortably hot. "I got the job, didn't I?"

She straightened, sobering. "You did," she murmured thoughtfully. Then her face began to drain of color, and on a whisper, she said, "Yeah. You did. Why did you get the job?"

Realizing she'd caught on as to the why already, I

sighed. "He didn't tell me what he wanted me to do. He just gave me the address to Porter Hall and said to be here by nine the next morning. I had no idea what I was supposed to do; I showed up ready for anything. Absolutely anything. So when he told me he just wanted me to be the new handyman, I was relieved. You have no idea, Isobel. It felt as if I'd been pardoned from a death sentence and allowed to live after all. I still had no clue about anything other than being a handyman when the first place he sent me was the rose garden."

I looked around me, breathing in the scent of her roses, and feeling sad for the first time since I'd come in here.

"Oh, God," Isobel murmured, knowing exactly where this was headed. Pressing her hands to her face, she looked up toward the ceiling and gave a harsh laugh. "Of course he sent you to my roses. Where else would he send you?"

She was beginning to fall apart, so I talked faster. "He didn't tell me anything about you, he just mentioned it was his daughter's garden and he wanted me to keep your flowers in tip-top shape. But then you…you showed up, and you seemed so adamant that he should know you wouldn't want anyone in there. I confronted him after you left his office."

"And let me guess," she said, her eyes filling with tears as she spilled out another bitter laugh. "He finally clued you in to your *true* duties here. Oh my God." Pressing her hands to her face again, she choked out, "All this time. I thought we were actually becoming friends."

"We were! We *are*." I reached for her hands, but she pulled them away.

"Friends?" she said in a small, distraught voice. "But you were *forced* to spend time with me against your will."

"No, not against my will. You're making this out to be more lurid than it really was. Nothing was forced or unwanted. I was desperate, Isobel; I would have done any number of unpleasant, maybe even illegal things to pay back my mother's debt. So when he said he just wanted me to spend time with you, I thought I'd hit the jackpot."

But she shook her head. "You just don't get it. He's tried to buy me friends before, and it—"

I grabbed her hand before she could keep it away from me and I pressed it against the center of my chest. "I know. But that's not what he did this time. He told me from the beginning I didn't have to try to befriend you. It wasn't like those other times before."

She looked at me, her eyebrows pinched as if doubting but maybe, finally ready to listen to what I had to say. "Then what exactly was it like?"

I smiled. "I believe his exact words were for me to break up the monotony of your day. I could make you mad or make you laugh, as long as I made some kind of contact to force you into a little human interaction."

Her expression grew thoughtful. She was trying to decide if she wanted to buy my story or not, if she *liked* my story or not.

I sighed. "He knew it was wrong to try to buy you friends before; he admitted that to me. He realized he wanted people to like you because of who you were, not because of how much he could pay them, so his instructions to me were actually *not* to become your friend."

Shaking her head, she admitted, "That doesn't make sense."

With a smile, I admitted, "Yeah, it didn't make much sense to me either. But he thought…" I winced.

"What?" she urged. "Just say it."

I groaned away before admitting, "He thought you'd be attracted to me, and it'd help distract you from how lonely you felt."

Her lips parted. She stared at me for an uncomfortably long time. Then she licked her lips and said, "So…my dad bought me eye candy?"

I shrugged, my face flaming hot. "Pretty much,

yeah. I think."

"Oh my God." She groaned and covered her eyes with both hands. "This is so humiliating."

It had to be as embarrassing for her as it was for me, but I couldn't handle her feeling discomfited. Shifting closer, I touched her shoulder, trying to comfort her, make it better. "What I don't think he counted on, and hopefully he still doesn't know, is that I was attracted to you right back."

"Don't," she whimpered, shaking her head. "Please don't say that. That's just the Stockholm syndrome talking."

With a laugh, I shook my head and pressed my forehead to hers before gently easing her hands away from her eyes so she'd look at me. When I got a peek at blue heaven from between the longest eyelashes ever made, I confessed, "No, that's my heart talking."

She sucked in a hard breath, but I knew she couldn't believe me. Not yet.

"Think about it, Isobel," I urged her. "I just had to make sure I was in your presence during a scheduled time. I didn't have to come in early to run with you, or stay later to build bookshelves with you. I didn't have to open up to you and tell you about my life, my biggest dreams. I didn't have to fall in love with you. I did because…because I couldn't help it."

"Wait. You did *what*?" Her eyes grew big as if horrified. "What did you just say?"

I couldn't repeat the words. My hands were already shaking and my voice was beginning to wobble. "I went further than he asked me to go. Got closer than I think he wanted me to get. And the fact of the matter is I'm worried as fuck what he's going to do when he finds out just *how* close I've gotten to you. He told me he didn't want me to befriend you; what the hell is he going to do when he learns I've fallen in—"

I shook my head and gulped for air. "What if it

pisses him off and he fires me, breaks our deal and takes back all the loans he paid off for my mom? Hell, what if he tells me I can never see you again? Because that's what freaks me out most. My mom and my own livelihood are at risk here, and all I can think about is how much I don't want to lose you. Christ, I'm so messed up right now, I don't—"

"Shh." She pressed her fingers to my lips, stopping the flow of words.

I lifted my gaze to her. She gave me a gentle smile. "Don't worry. I'll never let that happen to you."

I kissed her fingers. "You believe me, then?" Worry still choked me, but hope was beginning to spring eternal. "You believe that this thing between us is real and has nothing to do with your dad?"

She swiped a piece of hair tenderly across my forehead and stared into my eyes. Then she nodded. "Yeah. I believe you."

"Oh, thank God." I sank into her, closing my eyes and resting my brow on her shoulder. "I was so sure you were going to drop me flat when I told you the truth. You have no idea how worried I was."

"I'm glad you told me. Thank you for trusting me with the truth."

I looked up and smiled. "I trust you with my heart. Giving you the truth was easy."

chapter NINETEEN

I might've followed Isobel around the rest of the day like an eager little child. I just had this pitch in my stomach, telling me not to let her out of my sight. What if she suddenly changed her mind and decided not to believe me after all? I mean, all she had to go on was my word alone and no physical proof whatsoever. Or what if she decided she felt deceived after all? Or she decided she didn't like me? Or—

Okay, I might've been a tad paranoid. But could you blame me? I'd just bared my heart to this woman, fully expecting her to stomp on the organ and throw it back into my face. That's what I deserved. But, no. She'd taken it all surprisingly well and believed me when I had nothing to back up my story. I wasn't sure if I could trust such an easy resolution. And so instead, I probably annoyed the hell out of her by refusing to leave her all day.

Thank goodness she didn't seem irritated by my neediness.

But I think she understood what I was doing, and she took full advantage of the situation. Knowing how eager I was to please her, she started asking personal questions, the really embarrassing, uncomfortable ones guys never liked girls to ask them, like how many girlfriends I'd ever had and when my last relationship had been.

I'd fumbled and stuttered, not sure how to answer, because honestly, it'd been so long I couldn't even remember how many months it'd been. Definitely over a year since I'd been out with a woman, maybe going on two. So that's what I told her.

Except, the return look she shot me was full of suspicion, making me throw my hands into the air and insist, "I'm serious. I've had a pretty long dry spell. For the last few years, Gloria's chased off any female who's even looked as if she might be interested in me."

To which she tipped her head and squinted. "Who's Gloria?"

I groaned. "Oh, God. Don't get me started on Gloria."

So of course, she got me started on Gloria. Ten minutes later, I was still complaining about the bane of my existence as I followed Isobel into the conservatory for the second time that day.

"...And then she said, 'I understand, Shaw.' But how the hell *could* she if she came back a week later, acting as if I didn't just totally blow her off? I'm telling you, this whole Gloria thing is driving me nuts. Why won't she just leave me alone already? She *knows* I'm not interested in her."

Isobel looked amused as she pulled on her gloves. "Probably because she also knows you're too nice to come right out and hurt her feelings with a hard brush-off."

I sniffed. "But *why*? I don't get why she likes me in the first place. The few times I ever did try to open up to her and let her in to see the real me, she didn't like what she saw. She thought my dream to become an archeologist was silly. Her words. Freaking *silly*. I was serious as all get out and she laughed in my face over something that was important to me. So honestly, if she doesn't care about what I want or need in my life, how the hell can she expect me to care about anything *she* wants? And why are you looking at me like that?"

Isobel shook her head, her eyes glittering as if entertained but also crinkled at the corners as if she were learning me, learning the most basic components about me.

"I'm not even sure where to start," she murmured thoughtfully.

With a sigh, I leaned against a wooden beam wall of the greenhouse. "I'm that messed up, huh?"

"No." She shook her head slowly. "You're not messed up at all. You're just..."

When she didn't immediately answer, I swallowed, feeling as if she really did have something negative to say about me, something that told me how awful I was for not wanting anything to do with a girl who obviously adored me. God, I *was* a terrible, awful man, wasn't I? The way she kept studying me made me squirm inside.

"What?" I demanded. "I'm just *what*?"

She shook her head. "You're so delusional. You say you don't know why she likes you in the first place, so it's hard for me to get past that part, let alone consider the rest of what you said."

"I don't...what do you mean by that?"

"You're a handsome guy. You're a handsome, kind, considerate, *likeable* guy. And maybe a little too humble for your own good. Anyone would be drawn to that alone without ever getting to know the real you."

"I'm not—" I wanted to argue, because hell, I really wasn't that stand-up of a person. I was just...me. There were about fifty things wrong with me I could immediately start listing off the top of my head.

"And you have a good heart," Isobel continued. "With as honest and sincere and kind as you are, people know they can trust you with just about anything, even their deepest darkest secrets. I'm just curious why more women in your neighborhood than just this Gloria lady aren't after you as persistently as she is."

I blew out a breath before clearing my throat, suddenly uncomfortable from all the praise. "You know I wasn't angling for quite that many compliments, right?"

She shook her head. "I know you weren't angling for *any*. I'm just telling it like I see it."

My breath caught in my throat. She really did see me the way she described. It registered through my system like a shock. "Well, whatever the reason, it's making me want to kiss you right now." I pushed away from the wall to stroll near her.

She snorted and rolled her eyes. "Trust me. I didn't say it to—"

But it was too late. I grasped her hand and tugged her against me. "I'm going to kiss you anyway." Then I dipped my head and brushed my mouth across hers.

Our lips shifted, clung and then pressed together before I cupped her face and deepened things. Tongues danced, bodies closed in, breaths quickened. My fingers slipped down the sides of her neck, then her back until I was clutching her ass. Damn, it felt even better against my fingers than it looked in yoga pants.

When a moan sang from her throat, I lifted her slightly, rubbing us together, letting her feel my arousal, taste my passion.

"I can't get enough of you," I admitted, trailing the tip of my nose along the front of her throat. Her scent clouded my nostrils and we both shuddered.

Hand clasping my shoulder, her fingers bit through the cloth of my shirt as she tipped her head back and gave a husky laugh, taunting me. "Too bad you're on the clock."

Earlier, I'd made a strict rule there would be no hanky-panky between us while I was working. I was adamant about it, wanting to remain honorable and trustworthy to her dad. But to Isobel, I swear it became a challenge to tempt me at every turn.

"Dammit," I muttered, stepping back. "You put on that ruby-red lipstick on purpose, didn't you?"

She smiled, her eyes glinting with mischievousness.

Chuckling, because I really couldn't mind her seduction attempts at all, I shook my head, murmuring, "Evil. You're just plain evil." Then I leaned closer and more quietly added, "I like it."

Her eyebrow arched primly as she glanced down at the obvious tent in my pants. "Yes, I believe you do."

I sent her a wolfish grin. "I won't be on the clock forever, you know."

Her smile and giddy laugh did my heart good. Touching her, kissing her, dreaming about going further was all good and well, but being able to make her laugh…that was the true triumph. She'd changed so much since the first day I'd been here, and I couldn't help but swell with pride and accomplishment, knowing I'd been the one to nudge her from her shell. And I was the one to reap the benefits of it too, because once she was free from her insecurities, she was amazing.

Cheeks still flushed with pleasure, she cleared her throat and turned away from me. "What were we doing in here again?" she asked as she faced a silver rack sitting against the wall. "Oh right. Planting the baby rosebushes."

"Our babies," I immediately cooed when she picked up a seedpod where the tiny sprout was getting bigger. Instead of one inch tall as they had been when I'd first seen them, they were now three inches. "Aww." I couldn't help it, my heart melted. "They're so cute. Can we name one Groot?"

Isobel sputtered a laugh and shook her head. "We can't just name one." Then she sent me an impish grin. "The others would get jealous."

"So it's settled." I snapped my fingers. "We must name them all. This one can be Shaw, Jr., and ooh, that one looks like a girl. She'll be Isobel, Jr."

She snickered. "How the heck do they look like girl or boy plants?"

I shrugged, simply enjoying the playfulness of the moment. "No idea." I pointed to another. "We'll have to name one Margaret after my mom, and…" I glanced up. "What was your mom's name?"

Gaze softening and eyes glittering with emotion, she swallowed before softly saying, "Annalise."

"Annalise," I murmured. "That's pretty. I like that name."

Her smile was watery and grateful. "It's my middle name."

I shifted a piece of hair out of her eyes, and she didn't even flinch when I accidentally brushed past her scar. "Then we should name them all Annalise."

She made an amused sound, but sadness lingered in her eyes, which I was sure was what prompted her to turn away. "So, where do you want to plant them?"

I shrugged. "I don't know. Wherever you think best." She kept gnawing on her lip as she studied the garden, unable to make a decision, so I pointed to the first bare patch of ground I saw. "What about there?"

Isobel stiffened, her entire bearing charged with tense distress. "Not there."

When she immediately turned away, I crinkled my brow and turned to study the ground. "Why not there?"

She said nothing. I touched her back. "Isobel?"

She drew in a breath before answering. "That was where I died."

My lungs seized. Then I shook my head. "Come again?"

It took her a while before she faced me. When she did, she looked even sadder than she had when she'd said her mother's name. "It was my fault," she admitted. "The fire."

My lips parted. Lifting my hand to cup her scarred cheek, I murmured, "My God. I had no idea. What happened?"

She shifted her attention to the bare section of earth. "I had a boyfriend. Eric. He was..." I removed my hand from her. She sent me a dry glance. "Well, at seventeen, I thought he was everything. My first serious boyfriend. I thought he'd be my last. My happily ever after." With a roll of her eyes, she muttered, "I thought I loved him."

I nodded as if I understood, except I couldn't stop my stomach from churning. She was talking in the past tense, and it had happened eight years earlier, but none of that mattered. I hated this Eric douche, and I wanted to smash his face in, for no other reason than Isobel had once fancied him above all others.

"What happened?" I asked, my voice low and my feelings restrained under tight control.

"Mom found my birth control pills," she confessed. "We fought. She told me I was too young to be sexually active. I told her it was none of her business, and then she...she grounded me."

Shaking her head, she glanced at me with a slight smile. "She'd never grounded me before. I'm not even sure if she knew what a real grounding entailed. Neither did I, really. But I didn't care what it meant. I was the spoiled princess of the manor, Henry Nash's only daughter. I'd always gotten whatever I wanted. So no way did I accept her punishment."

I shook my head sadly, imagining a young, pampered, entitled Isobel. And as I did, I still felt bad for her. Not even a spoiled brat had deserved the fate she'd landed.

"It was so stupid," Isobel went on, her eyes glazed and focused on the past. "I wanted to sneak out to see him, so I climbed from my window and jumped down to the ground. I forgot all about the candle in a jar I'd left burning on the desk right in front of that window. The curtain must've gotten swept into the jar when I'd opened the window. I'm not sure. I just remember looking back up there once I climbed down to make sure my mom hadn't spotted me, and that's when I saw the orange blaze behind the glass.

"I ran back inside, but oh God, do you know how fast a fire spreads? By the time I reached my room, it was entirely engulfed. I couldn't just beat out the burning curtain, like I thought I could. I thought I could run and find a fire extinguisher, but my brain felt like it was working through molasses. All my thoughts went into slow motion. I panicked and ended up running to my mom for help, or to warn her, or I don't know. I just knew there was a problem, so I got my mom.

"When we left her room, the fire had already reached the hallway and was eating up more rooms. We could barely see the bright orange through all the smoke, but my mom grabbed my arm and then…then this flaming beam came crashing down toward us."

When she paused to gasp for breath as if the smoke was still stealing her oxygen, I took her hand. She didn't seem to notice, even though her fingers squeezed around mine.

"I'm not sure if the rest is real memory or things I've heard that happened mixed with dreams I have about that night. But the dreams feel so real like an honest-to-God-memory; they haunt me more than fuzzy things I recall when I'm awake. In them, I'm trapped and burning alive. It hurts like nothing I can describe, so I scream, thinking I'm going to die. I try to find my mom, but I can't see anything. Then I hear her calling my name above the crackling flames. She sounds so desperate and scared, but I don't know where she is."

Isobel finally realized I was holding her hand and she gently pulled her fingers away to cradle them to her chest. She shook her head.

"Mr. Pan saved me. He must've kicked the beam off me, because these arms suddenly scooped me up and carried me down the stairs. He brought me out here, right to this very spot. The first time I came back here after the fire, there was still a human-sized burn patch in the grass where I had lain."

She placed her hand against the bare patch, her eyes filling with tears.

"In the dreams, Mr. Pan was breathing hard, his face full of soot, and his skin bubbling and bleeding where he'd burned himself to free me from the fire. I reached for him, begging him not to leave me, but he said he had to go get my mom."

"I waited there for them, unable to move, listening to the fire consume my house, smelling my own burned skin and experiencing the worst agony of my life. I really thought he'd be able to get her and bring her back out. Finally, I passed out. I remember waking a few times when the ambulance and paramedics arrived. I remember being lifted onto the gurney. I vaguely remember bits and pieces of the inside of the ambulance. I tried to ask about Mom and Mr. Pan, but I couldn't talk very well. They said my heart stopped three times, and I coded before I was brought back again. The first time was when I was lying here in the grass, waiting for my mom to escape from the fire I'd started."

"Jesus, Isobel." I shook my head and reached for her, pulling her into my arms.

She rested her head on my shoulder.

"She died because I was spoiled and selfish. Mrs. Pan's husband, Kit's dad, *died* because I wanted to pout and break the rules. My childhood home burned to the ground because I just had to see my boyfriend."

I wanted to argue and tell her those weren't the reasons why. But I knew she wouldn't believe me. No one could convince her of this; she would have to convince herself someday. I could only be there to hold her through it until the guilt and misery passed.

"What happened to him?" I asked. "Eric."

"Oh, he left me," she said, her voice bland and unconcerned. "I was too hideous for him to deal with after that."

I stiffened and pulled back to see her face. "Are you fucking kidding me?"

She shrugged and lifted her face. "No one blamed him, least of all me. That was before all my surgeries and graphs. I look tons better now." Then she touched her own scars. "Remember that comment you made about how my ear hadn't melted halfway down my neck? Well, it actually did, but they were able to move it back to the proper place. I looked awful. Horrific. I can't fault Eric for leaving."

Well, I could. I didn't give him any kind of pass at all for taking off. The jerk bastard piece of shit. "A misplaced ear is no reason to leave a girl."

"He was only seventeen," she tried to explain.

"I don't fucking care," I muttered. "He's an ass."

Her smile was affectionate. Pressing her palms to my chest, she looked into my eyes, eyes that told me they loved me, and she said, "You're such a good person; I can see why it's hard for you to understand imperfection in others. Eric wasn't—"

"I'm not that good," I argued, shaking my head. "And I'm damn well not perfect. There's nothing special about me at all. I make just as many mistakes as the next guy. But I'm not going to forgive some douche who left you after you were scarred no matter how much you defend him. He's an ass."

She chuckled. "You already said that."

"Well it bared repeating."

"You make me happy," she murmured, smoothing her hand up my chest until she wrapped her fingers around the back of my neck. Then she leaned in until her mouth was only inches from me. "You make me feel light.

And free."

"Strange," I murmured, pressing my forehead to hers and swallowing to combat the urge to kiss her. "You always make me feel heavy. Heavy and hot. So damn hot."

I burned for her.

"Shaw?" she whispered.

"Yeah?" I whispered right back, my body thrumming and pulse quickening.

She licked her lips. "It's five minutes after four."

"Oh, thank God." Officially off work, I crushed my mouth to hers.

Drawing her into my arms, I hauled her against me. When her breasts gouged my chest, I groaned. When my arousal prodded her hip, she gasped. Our hands gripped and tugged at each other while our teeth clashed and tongues tangled. I gripped her ass, securing her to me, while she rubbed her hip against my front, making me growl a throaty curse of pleasure.

Neither of us heard the door from the house open.

"What the hell is going on?" a voice snarled.

Isobel and I leapt apart before spinning to face the new arrival. Shame and fear filled my veins as Henry set his hands on his hips and narrowed his eyes.

"Dad," Isobel gasped. She wiped the back of her hand across her mouth before glancing my way. I caught her eye, and we shared an *oops* mingled with an *oh fuck* look. Together, we turned back to him.

I looked down when she took my hand. Our fingers interlaced, and for some reason that eased me. No matter what happened, we were a united front.

"I kissed Shaw," she announced.

That was obvious, and yet I still very nearly pissed myself when she said it.

"And I like him. A lot." She used my hand she was holding to jerk me closer to her, all the while not taking her eyes off her dad. "He likes me too. Do you have a problem with that?"

Henry narrowed his gaze on his daughter, then glanced down at our connected hands before he looked up, right into my eyes.

I gulped, unable to decipher what he was thinking.

"I'd like to talk to Shaw in private," he said to Isobel as he kept his gaze steady on me.

But Isobel shook her head. "I don't think that's necessary."

"But—"

"He already told me about the reason he was brought to work here as a *handyman*."

Henry pierced me with a deadly glare. "Oh, did he?"

He kind of looked as if he wanted to castrate me.

"And I'm not mad at you," Isobel continued. "You were worried about me; I can respect and appreciate that. I'm not happy that you brought another person here specifically for me, to keep me *company*, or for whatever reason you did it, but since your misplaced intentions actually turned out for the best, I can forgive you and move on."

"Well…" Henry seemed momentarily boggled before he nodded, saying a humble, "Thank you. I'm glad you realize I was coming from a place of love and only wanted you to be—"

"I know, Dad."

Her quiet words seemed to affect him dramatically. His face flushed, eyes watered, and he began to cough. Then he nodded, cleared his throat, and shifted his gaze back to me.

"Nevertheless," he drew out slowly. "Shaw is my employee, and I would like to speak to him. Alone."

I nodded and started to step forward, but Isobel tightened her grip on my hand, keeping me next to her.

"Only if you promise his job isn't at risk and you won't do anything to harm his mother," she said, trying to negotiate with her father for my sake.

After a sharp scowl my way, Henry turned back to

her. "He really did tell you everything, didn't he?"

"Yes." With a nod, she added, "And I believe him."

"Thank you," I told her sincerely. I opened my mouth to let her know how much that meant to me, but her dad interrupted.

"In my office, Hollander. Now."

Leaning over, I smacked a quick kiss to Isobel's scarred cheek, then I hurried after her father.

Henry waited to speak until we reached his office. And even after he shut the door and turned to me, his gaze flashing with outrage, he kept his voice low, as if he were afraid Isobel was listening at the door.

"This wasn't part of the agreement," he hissed.

"I know, sir." Keeping myself military stiff, I nodded. "I didn't mean for it to happen."

He narrowed his eyes, studying me shrewdly. "You didn't mean for *what* to happen, exactly?"

"Isobel and me."

"And what is happening *between* you and Izzy?"

I crinkled my eyebrows. "That's really not your business," I said slowly.

He didn't seem to care for that answer. His face a mask of anger, he marched closer, waving his finger in my face. "This is an outrage. I brought you into this house to make her feel alive again. Not to…not to…"

"And I did," I said evenly. "You can't deny how much more active and social she is now."

He growled and narrowed his eyes.

So I added, "And in return, she made *me* feel alive again. I know I wasn't supposed to get as close as I did to her, and I know with my station in life, I'll never be good enough to—"

"Dammit, Hollander," he growled. "Don't make me out to look like a snob. I brought you here because of her, just to get her to open up. It wasn't supposed to become some grand romance. You weren't supposed to pretend a friendship."

"I didn't. I didn't pretend anything." But he kept going as if he didn't even hear me.

"You weren't supposed to seduce her, and you damn well weren't supposed to—"

"Fall in love with her?" I cut in, anger vibrating under my skin. "I'm sorry, but you never made that clear. It wasn't in the contract, and it certainly wasn't something I could control."

I swore, if he could, Henry would've exhaled fire from his nose. His glare was scorching. With a slow snarl, he bit out, "So you're going to play the love card, are you?"

I blinked, confused. "It's not a card. It's the truth."

"Is it?" Isobel's father asked quietly, his gaze boring into mine. "Or is this the desperate man who came into my office thinking he finally found his ticket to securing his future in the arms of my wealthy, vulnerable daughter?"

Something in me snapped. There was no other way to explain it. I couldn't stand there and let him—or anyone else—question my feelings. Stepping threateningly close, I glared into his blue eyes that were the same shade as Isobel's.

"I will let you question my affections one time, and this one time only. But don't ever make that mistake again. She is your daughter; you *know* how amazing she is. Do you honestly think I was able to spend the last two months in her company without noticing it too? Without falling for her? You're smarter than that, Mr. Nash. You could put her out on the street right now, without a penny to her name, and I would take her in, happy to have her with nothing but the clothes on her back. Isn't that why you hired me in the first place? Because you knew that was the kind of man I am? I *love* your daughter. And if you want to fire me and break our agreement because of it, *fine*. I'll find another way to take care of my mother. But it won't stop me from feeling the way I do about Isobel."

Henry stared at me long after I'd finished talking. Then he blew out a long breath, ran his hands through his thinning hair, and fell into the seat in front of his desk. "I hope this doesn't make me a fool, but I actually believe you."

He still hadn't answered my most pressing question. So I asked, "So did I just lose my job here or not?"

With an amused sniff, he glanced up. He looked tired, but resigned. "No. But my original warning stands. If you hurt her, you're gone."

I nodded, perfectly fine with that. "I'd sooner cut out my own heart," I promised.

chapter TWENTY

Isobel pounced as soon as I exited her dad's office. "Well?" she demanded, grabbing my hand.

Her worry made me grin. "Well, what?" I teased, leaning in to shift my nose across her cheekbone.

Huffing out her impatience, she nudged me back far enough to see my face. "Well, what'd he say? Did he try to fire you? Pay you off? Chase you away? Keep us apart?"

With a laugh, I tugged her into my arms. "No, no, and no. He already promised you he wouldn't fire me and…what? Pay me *off*? Are you kidding? He's pretty much already paid me off by taking care of my mother."

"But—"

"And how exactly did you think he'd keep us apart? We're both adults. That's not even…" I shook my head, cracking up over her concerns.

Isobel sniffed and shoved against my chest. "Stop laughing. This isn't funny. He could've—"

"He couldn't have done anything to keep me away from you." Then I winked. "He has no mob ties, remember?"

She shook her head slowly, not amused. "Don't tell me you weren't as worried as I was when you went into that room. Your face was pale and hands were shaking. He could've threatened your mother's security."

"But he didn't," I murmured, burying my nose in her hair. "So it's all good."

"What *did* he say?" Calming against me, she softened her voice.

"He just wanted me to convince him I genuinely liked you."

She looked up into my eyes. "And did you?"

My grin was immediate. "I convinced you, didn't I? Of course, I convinced him."

Letting out a sigh, she nodded. "It's true, you *are* rather convincing. It almost makes me believe you may genuinely like me after all."

"Oh, you..." Realizing she was teasing me, I lifted my eyebrows in mock warning. "You're just begging for me to tickle an apology out of you, aren't you?"

"What? *No.*" Her eyes went wide, and she immediately backed away, holding her elbows tight to her sides, pretty much letting me know exactly where she was the most ticklish. "You wouldn't."

"Take it back, and I won't." I advanced, holding up curled fingers that were prepared to tickle. "Tell me I'm not just being convincing, that I'm merely being honest."

She backed away slowly, shaking her head. "But what if you *are* just an excellent actor?"

"Isobel," I growled. "I'm warning you." I reached out and she squealed her surprise. "Okay, okay. I know you like me. You're not just saying it."

I pulled her into my arms and pressed my brow to hers. "Prove it."

She stopped tightening against possible tickles and straightened to look into my eyes. Then she stared at me a moment, her face uncovered and scars on full display. Lips relaxing into a smile, she cupped my face in her hands and kissed me.

Behind us, a throat cleared. We reluctantly pulled apart to glance over and find Henry in the doorway of his office, watching us. This time, getting caught didn't make us leap apart. Instead, Isobel and I shifted closer to each other, facing him side by side.

Henry's gruff, censuring stare eased when he looked at his daughter. "You do seem happier," he finally relented.

Her entire presence brightened. "I am."

Henry gave a single nod. "Then so am I." After a single approving nod my way, he disappeared back into his office, where he closed the door.

I blew out a relieved breath. Isobel turned to me, her smile letting me know she was onto me. I'd been even more worried about my conversation with her dad than *she'd* probably been.

But what she said to me was, "Are you going to go straight home, or do you have plans this evening?"

The question was odd enough to make me pause and focus on her face. She looked expectant and hopeful, her eyes already begging, which let me know she wanted something from me. My blood pulsed with anticipation. I moved toward her, ready to give her anything.

"I don't have plans," I said, focusing on her mouth. "Why? Did you want me to stay?"

She bit her lip. "Actually, no. I'd like to go somewhere. Do you think you could take me?"

I shook my head, certain I'd misheard her. "What?"

"I said, I'd like go—"

"Are you kidding me?" I shouted. "*Yes!* I'd love to take you somewhere. You mean, out of the house, away from Porter Hall, right? This is so…holy shit. Where do you want to go?"

She bit her lip. "It's a surprise."

I blinked. "A surprise?"

With a nod, she cleared her throat and glanced

away. "So…are you in or not?"

Nodding freakishly hard, I said, "Of course I'm in. Wherever you want to go, I'll take you. Gladly."

"When's the last time you left Porter Hall?" I asked, glancing toward the passenger side of the truck as we waited for the gates to swing open and let us out of the driveway.

Isobel bit her lip as she thought about the answer. "About six months ago, I think." She shrugged. "I had a checkup with the doctor."

"And before that?"

She kept her gaze fixed out the front windshield, but her hands sat tightly clasped in her lap, revealing her nerves. Leaving the property was a big deal for her. I reached out to cover her cold, trembling hands with my warm, steady ones, letting her know I understood. When she glanced over, I sent her a bolstering smile.

"Which way?"

She told me the address of where she wanted to go. I nodded, because I knew the area. Strangely, it wasn't too far from my apartment. Then I tightened my grip on her knuckles and pulled onto the roadway.

The trip into town was quiet. I kept thinking I needed to start some brilliant, witty conversational topic, but the more I tried to think up something interesting to say, the less my brain spun ideas. Suddenly, I realized I was nervous. Not because I was going out into public with Isobel, but because she trusted me enough to take her there.

What if someone said something or did something to offend her and she never attempted another outing again? It was my responsibility to make it worth her while, to make her want to try again. This duty felt massive and almost too heavy for me to bear.

I wanted her to enjoy her time away from Porter Hall.

"Hey, what's that?"

Isobel's voice shook me from my thoughts. Glancing in the direction she pointed, I grinned.

The entire sidewall facing the road of the abandoned brick warehouse we passed bore a striking painting of a wolf grinning out at all the cars that passed. Next to it, a quote read:

The best way to find out if you can trust someone is to trust them.

"That's the work of Black Crimson," I said. "You like it?"

"It's breathtaking," she murmured. "And the quote sounds like someone famous should've written it."

"Someone famous did write it. Ernest Hemingway," I said. When she glanced at me, I shrugged. "I had to look it up after the first time I saw the painting."

Nodding, she glanced back over her shoulder to take in the last of the masterpiece before we'd driven past it completely. Turning forward again, she asked, "Who's Black Crimson?"

I shook my head. "No one knows. He's the city's famous—or maybe I should say infamous—graffiti artist. He only works in black, white, and red spray paint, and all his masterpieces usually depict some kind of meaningful message. They're signed B.C., which is how he became dubbed Black Crimson."

Isobel wrinkled her nose. "I'm sure B and C are for the initials in his name, not for the colors in which he works."

"Probably. But no one knows, so they just call him Black Crimson. Rolls off the tongue better than B.C., I guess."

She turned to watch me seriously. "What do you think of them?"

"I like them," I said honestly. "I hate how the city paints over them. They're not evil and have actually seemed to lift the morale of the people, especially the ones who were so affected after the closing of the Pestle shoe factory. Plus, someday, I can picture a future archeologist uncovering them and trying to figure out the meaning and culture behind them."

Isobel stared at me silently before nodding her head. "That's a good answer. I think I like them too."

I don't know why her agreement pleased me. It wouldn't have mattered if she'd liked them or not, but it just felt good to know we were of the same accord. It made me feel as if we understood each other better.

"Want me to take you past my favorite one? It's not too far from where we're going. We can swing by it on the way."

"Yes." She nodded. "I'd like that very much."

Her answer was so formal, I burst out laughing before answering, "Indeed, my lady."

She reached across the center console to nudge my arm and roll her eyes, all the while grinning over my tease. "Just drive."

I did but still had to smirk as I went. Making a slight detour from our original destination, I turned down a side street until we passed the town's historical museum. The outer wall facing the street held no windows, deeming it a perfect place for Black Crimson to strike. In this picture, he—or she—had painted a tower with some long flowing hair streaming out the balcony at the top. It flowed all the way to the ground. Some hapless guy had tried to climb the hair, but he must've lost his grip because he was flailing in midair, ready to drop to his doom.

The quote for this picture said:

Don't take life too seriously. You're not getting out of it alive.

From the passenger seat, Isobel burst out laughing. "Oh my God, that's hilarious." Holding her side, she rolled to face me. "Who is it a quote from?"

Her eyes glittered with joy and I had to admit, it felt nice, knowing she realized I'd made sure to find out the answer to that question already.

"Elbert Hubbard," I said. "Or at least, it's similar to one of his quotes."

She nodded. "Does all of Black Crimson's art illustrate some fairy tale or another?"

I sent her a curious glance.

Motioning behind her, she explained. "Well, that one was obviously Rapunzel. And the one before was the Big Bad Wolf, right?"

"Holy shit," I cried, gaping at her before shaking my head and returning my attention to the road. "I think you're right. I remember another one having some guy leaning over a sleeping woman and one had a mermaid on it, which must be—"

"The Little Mermaid," she murmured for me.

I nodded before saying, "Huh. I wonder why I never caught on to that before."

"Well, the pictures look pretty contemporary. No one is wearing chainmail and suits of armor or big, flaring dresses with tiaras, which usually clues a person in to a fairy tale."

"True," I allowed before winking over at her. "Or I just needed someone like you around to notice the obvious for me."

My praise made her blush. I turned another corner at a light and halfway down the block, we came to the address she'd given me, but even before I pulled to the curb, my eyes flared with shock at the flower shop where I'd found her fake midnight supreme rose seeds.

"Hey," I said, my surprise evident. "I've been here before. It's where I bought the—"

"I know." She grew serious as she gazed out the truck window at the building. "The name and address of the place was stamped on the back of the package of rose seeds you gave me."

"Oh." I frowned, only more confused. "So…why are we here then?" I would've thought she'd want nothing to do with a business that offered such a hustle.

"I was a bit upset at the woman who owned the place for scamming you the way she did," Isobel explained with a shrug. "So I bought her out of business."

I stared at her, blinking before I shook my head and laughed, unable to take her words literally. "You did *what*?"

She shrugged. "The woman didn't deserve to own a flower shop if she treated her customers the way she treated you, so I bought her out. And now…" She tipped her head to the shop and met my gaze. "I own a flower shop."

"I…" I laughed again, not sure what to think of this before bursting out, "Are you actually serious?"

"As a heart attack," she said. "So…are you willing to help me with this project, or not?"

I shook my head, dazed. "Help you with what? Holy shit, I can't believe you just up and bought a business out from under someone. Do you even know how to run your own shop?"

"No." She started to grin. "Of course not. I've been a shut-in at my home since I was seventeen. But my dad and brother can give me pointers, plus…" I swear, her lashes fluttered as she looked entreatingly at me. "You helped your mom run her bakery, right?"

"Only for a few months," I argued. "And it ended up going out of business. I don't think that makes me such a good referral."

"Nonsense," she argued. "You'll do fine. You can be

the face of the company and deal with customers. I'll work in the back, arranging flowers and…you know, do whatnot."

Whatnot.

It was enough to make me laugh again. Not because it was funny. It was just…stunning, a scratch-my-head-in-wonder-and-laugh kind of shock.

"You're really serious about this," I repeated, not asking this time, but stating.

She nodded. "What? Don't you think it'll work?"

"I don't…" Shrugging, I gave her my honest answer. "I actually have no idea. I mean, of course, I'd be willing to help you, no matter how risky it was. But what about your dad? I'm kind of indebted to him and signed a contract saying I'd work for him for the rest of my life."

"But your agreement was for you to spend time with me, which you'd be doing."

"I…" I wrinkled my brow before slowly saying, "Yeah. I suppose that would be one way to put it. But—"

"Then we'll talk to Dad and see what he says."

I laughed again. "What about you, though? You never leave the house, yet now, suddenly, you want to open a flower shop where you'll be exposed to customers all day? Do you really think you could handle that?"

She lifted her chin primly. "I believe I already told you, dealing with the customers would be *your* job, not mine."

"But you must know sometimes you wouldn't be able to help it. If I got busy, or sick, or had a question only you could answer… There would be some exposure."

She seemed to deliberate that before giving a slow nod. "I suppose I could handle some exposure. It's time."

"It's a big step," I told her. "Like jumping straight off into the deep end, instead of slowly wading in until you're comfortable. Are you sure you're up for it?"

She nodded. "I'm sure." Then she blushed. "You make me feel ready for anything."

I blew out a breath, honored by such a statement, but also intimidated. What if something went wrong? Would she then blame me? Besides…

"I'm still baffled here," I admitted. "What even prompted you to do this?"

"I told you—"

"Yeah, yeah. You wanted to stop that lady from deceiving anyone else, but that didn't mean you had to keep the place once you bought it. You could spice it up, then turn around and sell it for a profit. Or put someone else in charge of running it, instead of making it some do-it-yourself project."

She drew in a slow breath, before meeting my gaze and admitting, "You made me want more."

"What?" I whispered.

"With the bookshelves," she prompted, "and running every morning together, and just everything. I've felt more alive these past few weeks than I have in years, maybe in forever. And it's made me feel cooped up in that big house. I suddenly felt this urge to get out and *do* something, to make a living, to just…live. I want to do this, Shaw, because…because I actually want to *do* something. Like you said once, I want to make a difference in the world and leave my mark. Even if it's just to make people smile when they buy my flowers. That would be enough for me."

My lips parted in awe. I wasn't sure why, but in that moment, I couldn't think of anyone else I admired more in the world. To watch her go from being the vulnerable, standoffish scarred woman in the rose garden only to bloom into the amazing creature before me was nothing short of a miracle.

I was mesmerized.

"Then I'll help you," I heard myself say. It didn't matter what it took or how we'd convince her father to allow my assistance, I would help her. *That* I knew for sure.

She grinned as if I'd just pulled down the stars for her, then she threw her arms around my neck and opened her mouth to mine.

Our tongues met first, then our lips, our hands. But she was still too far away. I started to tug her over the cup holder and into my lap before a passing car honked. I had no idea if they were honking at us or something else, but it still cooled me off enough to let her go and pull away. Breathing hard, I wiped my mouth that still tasted of her.

"That's probably as far as we should go in public," I said, blushing, before I sent her a rueful glance of apology for nearly mauling her in front of anyone and everyone who bothered to look into the cab of my truck.

Isobel met my gaze, her blue eyes serious. "Then take me somewhere private."

My stomach dipped with disappointment. "You want to go home?"

"No…" She shook her head and her kiss-stained lips curved into a smile. "Not yet."

chapter TWENTY-ONE

Oh, holy shit. Holy shit. Did that mean what I thought it meant?

I had no idea, but my libido certainly started assuming plenty. Instantly hard, I shifted in my seat to make more room in my pants before clearing my throat and tipping my head toward the flower shop. "Didn't you want to go inside?"

Isobel glanced over her shoulder toward the store she'd purchased. Gaze disinterested, she turned back to me. "No."

Air puffed from my lungs. "So, you…just…anywhere?" I asked.

When she nodded, I had to concentrate on exhaling again. "Okay," I said. "Okay."

I put the truck in drive and pulled back into traffic. We drove for about five more minutes as the day slid into dusk and my headlights came on. At first, it was aimless. I wasn't sure where to take her that would be private. Mom was at my house, and well…that's as far as my brain could travel. Until I remembered the closed and abandoned shoe factory I'd worked at for nearly ten years. The loading dock back in the shipping department had been pretty secluded, and with the place closed down, it'd be absolutely deserted now.

A chain-link fence surrounded the lot, but vandals and looters had long since broken the padlocked cable keeping the rickety entrance closed. The gate hung open limply by one hinge. As we drove through, Isobel sat forward with interest. It'd only been eight months since the factory had closed, but grass and weeds had already grown up between the cracks in the asphalt parking lot, making the place look as neglected as it was. I rolled the truck slowly over broken beer bottles and around the main building to the back. It seemed creepier now that no life or light shone from within. Cracked and shattered glass in the windows only helped along the desolate sensation.

"Damn," I murmured, shaking my head. "I didn't realize it'd feel so dead around here."

Empathetic to my mood, Isobel quietly asked, "Where did you work?"

"Back here," I answered, pulling into a tight squeeze between buildings to arrive at a courtyard where the loading dock still stood.

When I saw the work of Black Crimson on one wall, I sucked in a surprised breath. "Well, that's new."

The painting portrayed a woman pointing a flashlight into a dark corner only to illuminate a man who was holding up his hand to shield himself from her. The poor dude looked as if he had an abundance of hair, long mane, shaggy beard and all. Or maybe it was a bear, not a man. I wasn't sure. But he definitely didn't want her looking at him.

The quote next to the painting read:

Darkness cannot drive out darkness; only light can do that. Hate cannot drive out hate; only love can do that.

"Oh! I know who said that." Isobel brightened. "It was Martin Luther King, Jr." She smiled over at me. "I wrote a paper about him in high school."

I nodded, putting the truck into park and killing the engine. Silence and then darkness greeted us as I turned off the headlights. In the fading daylight, you could barely make out the graffiti on the wall.

"I wonder which fairy tale that couple's supposed to be," I mused aloud, still studying the artwork.

Isobel turned to me, blinking. "You can't tell?"

"What? You *can*?"

Her smile was a pure tease and absolutely stunning. Instead of answering me, she said, "I have a present for you."

I blinked. "You do?" Then I laughed and shook my head. "Why?"

She shrugged, looking embarrassed and abashed as she tugged a small box from her purse. "It's nothing fancy. Just a…a thank-you gift, if you will?"

"Thank you?" I murmured, growing intrigued. "What am I being thanked for?"

"For being you. For being kind to me when I didn't deserve it. For showing me not everyone cares so much about appearances. For showing me the world isn't such an awful place after all. For making me want to live again."

My lips parted. "Isobel," I whispered, speechless and dazed. "I…" I started to shake my head, unable to take credit for so much. It didn't seem possible I could make that big of an impact on anyone's life. But from the way she was looking at me, I couldn't deny the possibility either.

Overwhelmed to learn I'd influenced her that much, I blew out a hard, bracing breath, trying to keep myself together.

Isobel misconstrued my reaction completely, though. She probably thought I didn't feel the same about her or something, but she muttered, "You're right," and started to shove the box back into her purse. "I don't know what I was thinking. This was stupid and silly. I shouldn't—"

"No!" I covered her hand with mine to stop her from withdrawing. When she fell quiet and peeked up from frightened blue eyes, I slowly opened her hand and took the box from her palm.

"Thank you," I said meaningfully before I dropped my gaze and slipped off the lid. The case looked as if it would hold a piece of jewelry, but when I peered inside the only thing that peered back was myself, in the reflection of a small pocket mirror.

It looked old and well used. Knowing there had to be a story behind it, I drew it out carefully and shifted my thumb over the clouded glass before lifting my face. "Who did it belong to?"

As if transfixed by the looking glass, Isobel blinked, her gaze reflecting beauty and yet pain. Then her eyes lifted to mine. "My mother. It was one of the few things we saved from the fire that belonged to her. She'd had it tucked away in the family safe along with some pictures my father later framed and hung on the wall in his office. But this…this was the only real thing that was left of hers."

I sucked in a breath. "Oh, Isobel, no." I pressed the mirror back into her hand. "This is important to you. It's *priceless.* I don't deserve something so special."

She just stared at me, her lips beginning to tremble. "It is special," she agreed, "and important, and priceless." Her voice then went so low I had to strain to hear her confession as she added, "Which is exactly why I want you to have it."

With my heart expanding two sizes too big for my chest, I folded my hand over hers, trapping the miniature mirror between our fingers. "Are you sure?"

She nodded. "I wouldn't want anyone else to have it.

And I thought…" She drew in a deep breath before continuing. "I thought that whenever you were sad, or in pain, or it felt as if everything was wrong and ugly in the world, you could just look in here, see yourself, and know there's still beauty left, something worth living for. Because that's what you've done for me, just by being you. You've made me want to live again."

I floundered.

Nothing I could say in return would ever measure up to that. And I didn't even want to. I just wanted to live in that moment where someone thought I was something.

Eyes growing damp, I blinked repeatedly before spilling out a rusty laugh. "Whoa," I said before leaning toward her and pressing my brow to hers. Then I interlaced our fingers around the mirror.

"No one's ever made me feel the way you do," I admitted.

Her gaze lifted. "Same here."

With a groan, I disconnected our foreheads so I could slant my mouth across hers. She opened up to me, slipping her tongue around mine and clutching the front of my shirt in her fist as I circled the back of her neck with my free hand and sank my fingers into her hair.

Without looking at what I was doing, I placed the mirror into the cup holder in the center console as smoothly as I could. Then I hauled Isobel across her seat and into my lap.

She laughed against my mouth before moaning and pressing her ass down on my erection. I sucked in a breath and arched up my hips to help her out. Our bodies ground against each other, sparking out an electrical current that arced between us.

"Holy shit," I gasped, trying to catch my breath.

Heat collected under my skin and seemed to explode from me when she grappled with my shirt before wrenching it up over my head, pulling off my hat with it. Then her hands were on me, exploring and gripping muscles, digging into flesh, sliding lower toward my navel.

Feeling the need to reciprocate, I tugged at her shirt until I managed to pull it off. The black bra underneath cupped proud, plump breasts, and for a moment they were all I saw, until I leaned in to kiss the tops of them. That's when I finally noticed the scars. They trailed over her shoulder and halfway down her torso.

"Damn," I murmured, sucking in a breath. "That must've hurt."

Skimming my fingers over them, I looked up into Isobel's face to get a better sense of how much pain she must've endured, and yet I was still unable to imagine the severity.

Hooking my hand around the back of her neck, I drew her forward and pressed my mouth to hers. "I wish I could give you twice the amount of pleasure for every second of pain you've ever suffered."

Isobel sifted some hair across my forehead with her fingers. "You're making a pretty good dent so far," she assured me with a soft smile.

I kissed her again. And then again. And again. Our mouths clung until I grasped her shoulder, only for my fingers to come into contact with warm bare skin. Needing to investigate this further, I began to kiss my way down along her throat, then over her collarbone, and finally down to the uppermost swells of her breasts.

Glancing up at her to make sure she approved, I slipped the straps of her bra off her shoulders and pulled the cups down. Her nipples were hard and tight, a dusty rose color. I groaned before pulling one into my mouth and sucking.

Isobel whimpered and clutched my head. I glanced up at her, without letting go of her breast, to make sure it was a good whimper. Her eyes were as blue as a stormy sea and full of wanton need.

I moved to the second breast, only to glance up

again, needing to know she wanted this as much as I did.

She smiled and cupped my cheek. "Why do you keep looking at me as if you think I'm suddenly going to pull away and stop you?"

Because I kept worrying she was suddenly going to pull away and stop me.

"Just making sure you're real, that this is really happening," I said.

Blue eyes lightened with mischief. She pulled her bottom lip between her teeth and started to skim her hand down my chest. "You need confirmation of reality, huh? What about this? Does this feel real enough?"

She cupped me through my jeans, and my dick jumped to attention, straining and throbbing to reach her fingers through the material.

"Holy hell." All the blood in my head rushed south, racing toward my lap. When Isobel slid the zipper down, I went lightheaded and clutched her hair before pressing my face to her temple. "Careful. It's been a while since—*fuck*."

Her fingers wrapped around me, and I almost lost it. I had no clue what the hell she'd done to her hand, but I swear to God, no palm had ever felt that good clutching my cock before. She glided her fingers up and down like any other hand would, and yet rockets blasted behind my eyes.

Unable to properly process so much ecstasy, I could only stare into her eyes and feel. Experience. Enjoy.

Appearing confident and pleased with herself, she licked her lips. "I want to feel all this"—and she made me catch my breath as she gave another long stroke from tip to base— "inside me." Then she held up a condom between two fingers. "Think you can do that?"

Hell yes.

I plucked the package from her hand and had it opened, then wrapped around myself in about five seconds flat. When I looked up to grasp her hips and pull her down on me, I finally realized we were both still clothed from the waist down.

"Fuck, this isn't very romantic, is it?"

She didn't seem to care. Eyes alive with excitement and anticipation, she answered, "It's better than romantic. It's exhilarating."

Catching the waistband of her pants, she began to peel them down her hips. I watched, enthralled. "God, you are so beautiful."

She merely beamed, a goddess in her prime. "If you want any more clothes off, now's the time to take care of that."

The woman made a good point.

Rushing to join her in her nakedness, I bumped my elbow on the door handle. She cracked her knee against the steering wheel. We laughed and leaned into each other, absorbing the amusement of our awkwardness from one another.

"First time I climbed inside this truck, I thought it was the biggest damn vehicle I'd ever been in," I said. "Why does it suddenly seem way too small?"

Isobel grinned into my eyes and smoothed her fingers through my hair. "Let's get into the back."

"Yes. God, yes," I said, only to groan and press my face into her shoulder and mumble, "No. Fuck, no. Our first time shouldn't be in the back seat of a truck your *dad* owns."

"So…you think we should go back to my place…that my dad owns?" She lifted an eyebrow. "Or go to yours…that your mom owns?"

I started to correct her, telling her it was *my* apartment, not my mother's—a fact she already knew—when her words struck a funny bone. "Hell, we both still live with our parents. How lame is that?"

"Totally," she agreed, only half paying attention because she seemed more focused on the path of her hand as she drew her fingers across my chest. "We should climb into the back seat and console each other for being such losers."

After snorting out a laugh, I nipped at her chin with my teeth. "You know I'm not going to tell you no if this is what you really want." Because it was what I really wanted too, ideal location or not.

I started to add a *but*, except Isobel beat me to the punch.

"Oh, thank God." She hopped off me and started to wiggle herself over the seats and into the back, flashing me her million-dollar ass in the process. "I thought I was going to have to get violent and force you."

I shuddered as a vision of her brand of violence entered my head. It consisted of teeth biting into my shoulder, fingernails clawing my back, thighs of steel suffocating my hips, and her scream of release bursting my eardrums as I pumped into her. Holy damn, now I actually wanted her to get forceful.

Setting my hand on her backside—because, how could I resist?—I helped her along, making her tumble into the back with a surprised oomph. "Violate me any way you like, my little beast," I told her before joining her, tackling her onto her spine and pinning her beneath me. When I grinned at her, she gaped up at me with wide, surprised blue eyes.

"In fact," I leaned in to nip at her jaw with my teeth, "do your absolute worst. I dare you."

Her gaze warmed, it flooded with challenge, and the next thing I knew, she was clutching fistfuls of my hair and yanking my face down to hers. The kiss that followed was hard, brutal and one of the hottest kisses of my life. I swear she bit me. I even tasted blood.

Growling out my pleasure, I found her knee and opened her for me before fitting my hips between her spread thighs. My cock found its way to her opening, and it rested there a moment, anticipating that first thrust. My mouth began to water and my balls drew up taut.

As she sucked on my tongue, Isobel tightened her thighs around me, gripped my ass and arched up, impaling herself.

I threw back my head and roared, surging forward, deep into the tight wet heaven she provided.

God, it felt so good. I ground against her, relishing the sensation and making her whimper before I pulled out and spiked back in, repeating the move over and over and over again. She arched up to meet me, and our bodies slapped together, losing all semblance of sanity as we surged toward each other, our needs primal and urgent.

Staring into my eyes, she sucked her bottom lip in between her teeth and tightened against me. It was my breaking point. Sweat popped out of my brow. I lost control. I was going to come.

Gritting my teeth to hold it off as long as possible, I pressed my forehead to hers, looked back into her dazed blue eyes and rasped, "Come with me, Isobel. Come…"

When she shook her head and bit her lip, letting me know she was close but still not ready, I touched her clit and flicked my thumb across it, teasing her toward her release.

She gasped, dug her fingernails into my ass and began to spasm as the walls of her sex constricted around my cock. I grinned at her and pushed deep into her, emptying myself of everything but her.

chapter TWENTY-TWO

I couldn't stop glancing across the cab of the truck as I drove back to Porter Hall.

Isobel anticipated every stolen glance and met my gaze before she sniffed out a laugh and rolled her eyes. But then we both burst out with crazy, delirious grins. I bit my lip before I returned my attention to the road. When I reached across the interior of the truck without looking, she took my hand and interlaced our fingers.

Damn, I felt giddy. Light-headed. Downright decadent. It was the best feeling in the world.

"I don't want to take you home," I admitted, even though that's exactly where I was taking her.

Night had fallen and I could only see her face in the bluish glow from the screen of the truck's dashboard. Yet I still had no trouble making out the hope in her expression when she said, "You can stay the night…if you want."

I was tempted. Of course I was tempted, but then all the reasons why I couldn't stirred in my head, and I ended up wincing. "I don't think I could get comfortable snuggling with you under your dad's roof. And I need to get home to my mom, anyway, make sure she's okay."

She nodded, even though I could practically smell the disappointment ooze off her.

"I'd invite you back to my place, but…" I winced again. "My bedroom is currently the living room and I've been sleeping on the most uncomfortable pull-out sleeper sofa ever made."

Isobel blinked. "And how long has it been since you moved your mom in with you?"

I shrugged. "Not that long. I'd like to find us a new place. Preferably something with two bedrooms. But…we'll see."

"I've never met your mother," she suddenly murmured.

I glanced at her. She looked as if she'd been left out of something important. Drawing her hand to my mouth, I kissed her knuckles. "We'll have to fix that, though I already know she'll love you."

Her smile showed relief and delight.

When we pulled into the drive, I rolled down the window to hit the call button on the gate. It took nearly a minute for anything to happen, and then the iron bars began to open.

Henry opened the front door and stepped outside to stand on the front steps as I pulled around the circle drive to the front door, my headlights splashing over him. Then he started toward us even before I could brake and kill the engine.

"He doesn't look pleased," I mused, unbuckling my seat belt.

"I know," Isobel said, sounding similarly confused. She shared a glance with me. "I wonder what that's about."

"Think he knows what we did?" I whispered.

She sniffed but didn't say yes or no.

Henry pulled open the passenger side door, gasping, "Isobel," as he reached for her.

"Dad?" She took his hand and let him help her down from the truck. "Is everything okay? You look upset."

"Upset? *Upset?*" he roared. "I've been looking *everywhere* for you. You've been missing for hours."

"I..." She shook her head, seemingly perplexed, while I frowned.

"You didn't tell him where you were going?"

Her gaze shot to me as I joined her and her dad next to the still opened passenger door. "No," she said before blinking. "You told him yourself; we're adults. Why would I—"

"Because you don't typically *leave* the house," I explained. "Of course he'd worry. *I* would've worried if you had suddenly disappeared without a word after eight years of never going anywhere."

"Thank you," Henry said, nodding as he whirled to his daughter and pointed my way. "What he said."

"But I...I..."

At a loss for words, she merely stared at her father and then me before I cleared my throat and offered, "Maybe you should let him know whenever you go out, just until he gets used to the idea of you coming and going again."

"Yes, exactly," Henry added. "It never even occurred to me you had left the property. I thought you'd gotten hurt, or fallen into the lake, or...I don't know. I just knew I couldn't find you. And it was awful."

"Well I'm home now," she started slowly before wincing. "And I really didn't mean to worry you, Dad. I'm sorry I did."

Henry nodded. "It's already forgotten. I'm just glad you're here now, and okay." But he remained standing there between the two of us, his gaze shifting from me to Isobel as if maybe—oh, Lord, I hoped not—he could see exactly what we'd been doing.

"So...you two went out?" he finally said.

"Yes. It was a lovely time." She grinned and kissed

Henry's cheek. "And you'll never guess what. We're going to open a flower shop together and sell some of my roses. Shaw told me my flowers' beauty was meant to be shared. I haven't been able to stop thinking about that ever since. So I want to. Share them, that is. I'm going to start my own shop."

"Darling, that's…" Henry shook his head before clearing his throat. "That's great. I'm so proud of you. But are you certain it's not too soon to—"

"I'll be fine, Dad. Don't worry. But I do have a question."

"Oh?"

"I want Shaw to work for me, except he insists he belongs to you and can only do what *you* tell him to. So can you give him permission to work there with me, instead of here with you?"

"I…" Henry turned to me and stared for a moment before saying, "I believe I could willingly give you over into Isobel's hands for employment, though I can't say any of the other staff will be happy about this. They've become quite dependent on your handyman skills."

Unable to fully believe this twist in plans, I nodded. "I'm sure it'll be months before we get the shop opened. I can keep coming here as usual until then. Maybe I can even help you find a new handyman to replace me."

"I'm not sure we'd be able to find anyone to fill the shoes you leave behind, but that sounds like a fine idea to me. Thank you, Shaw."

Isobel grinned and clapped her hands together. "It's settled then."

I gulped, not sure how to take everything in. Things seemed to be changing at warp speed. And they were once again too good to be true.

Neither Nash seemed concerned or worried about fate intervening with something drastic, though.

"Izzy," Henry declared. "To celebrate how proud I am of these huge steps you're taking, I want to send you two out to dinner this weekend. On me. I'll take care of all the arrangements."

"Dad, you don't have to—"

"I insist!"

Isobel and I exchanged glances. She shrugged. So I shrugged, and that was enough for Henry. He set one hand on my shoulder and one hand on hers, grinning at the both of us. "I'll admit I was worried earlier this evening when I realized how close you two had become, but after seeing how happy you are and how willing you are to get out and experience the world again, I'm beginning to think this was the best damn thing that could've ever happened."

I gulped, worried he was really over tempting fate and certain he'd take a weapon after me if he knew I'd just had his daughter in the back seat of his truck. But I remained silent as I watched father and daughter grin at each other.

"Thank you, Dad," Isobel murmured, pressing another kiss to his cheek. Then she turned to me. "And you." Her hand gripped the front of my shirt before her voice dropped seductively low. "I'll see you tomorrow." Then she hauled me down for a kiss.

Our lips barely touched, the pressure only a promise of more to come. But it still made my body stir. I felt that light-headed giddiness again as she pulled away.

"See you," I said as she turned away and started inside.

Henry let me stare after her until she'd disappeared behind the door before he cleared his throat.

I jumped, having forgotten he was there. Certain he was going to tell me his true feelings about my relationship with her, I tensed.

But all he said was, "I think I'll set you up with reservations at Urbane for this Saturday."

I nodded, relieved. "Okay. Thank you, sir. But, uh, do you know how much a meal there usually costs? I'm not sure I can afford—"

"I said I'd take care of it," Henry announced.

But I growled, "The hell you will," making us both jerk in surprise and gape at each other.

I flushed, unable to believe I'd just said that to my boss. "I mean…" Face hot and heart pounding, I explained, "With all due respect, sir, *I'm* the one taking her there, right?" It was a pride thing. I should be the one to fund dinner. Not Henry.

"But I said it was my treat. I never meant for you to—"

"I want to," I said quietly.

He stared at me a moment before giving a respectful nod. "At least allow me to help you dress yourself for the occasion."

I glanced down at my usual ragged jeans and T-shirt, only to feel another rash of shame. Nothing I owned would suffice for a night out with Isobel at the posh Urbane restaurant. "Yeah," I relented. "That would be fine."

He nodded, looking relieved, before he pulled a phone from his pocket. When whoever was on the other end answered, he immediately barked, "Hollander's taking Izzy on a date this Saturday and has nothing suitable to wear. Can I count on you? Great. I'll send him over now."

He hung up and tossed out an address for me to remember. "Go. Get yourself set up."

My eyebrows lifted. "What? Right *now*?"

He blinked as if confused by my shock. "When else?"

As he waved me away, I just stared at him. He sighed. "Indulge an old man, will you? It's been too long since Izzy's been out on the town. On an actual date. I want it to be special for her."

Those were exactly the words I needed to win me over. With a nod, I relented. This really would be the first date she'd been on in eight years. I wanted her to have the best too.

I arrived at the address Henry had given me about ten minutes later. It was another lovely home, located on Porterfield Lane, but it wasn't as big as Porter Hall. It was still impressive, though. As soon as I parked, the front door came open, and Isobel's brother stepped outside.

I don't know why I was surprised to see him; it made perfect sense that Henry would send me to a man who owned half of a clothing company.

Stopping on the front steps, Ezra crossed his arms over his chest. "Was this date *your* idea or my dad's?"

I sighed as I strolled toward him. "Well..." I started.

A smile flickered across his face. "That's what I thought. Why am I not surprised he had to go and meddle in your relationship?"

With a shrug, I answered, "You know your father well."

"Yeah, I do." He sighed and stepped aside to motion me into his home. "Did he even bother to give you the fatherly, respect-my-daughter-or-die lecture, or was he so excited that she was actually doing something for a change that he completely forgot?"

"He did," I said. *Kind of.*

Ezra sniffed. "Doubtful. That's why I think I'm going to have to give it, instead." Flashing out his finger, he pointed and narrowed his eyes. "Don't disrespect my sister, or I'll kill you. And don't let anyone else disrespect her either. Got it?"

I lifted both hands and gulped. "Got it."

Narrowing his eyes a second longer as if to make sure I was sincere, he finally dropped his hand and relaxed. Then the easygoing Ezra I'd first met reappeared.

"Okay, then. Let's see what we have in my closet that might fit you?"

I started to follow him down a hall, only to stop. "Wait, what? I'm borrowing *your* clothes?"

He snorted and kept walking away. "What the hell did you think you were doing when he sent you this way?"

Huh, now that he mentioned it, I hadn't been thinking at all. With Henry Nash involved, calling the shots, I could've been headed to a tailor's house to be fitted for some custom-made digs.

Ezra was rapidly disappearing ahead of me, so I hurried to catch up. He entered a room, and when I followed him inside, I stepped into his bedroom. But he wasn't there.

"Where…?"

"In here," he called from a doorway deeper in the room.

I went forward to find a walk-in closet.

"Any certain color you want?" he asked conversationally, filing through suit jackets hanging from one wall. Yes, an entire *wall* full of suit jackets.

Shaking my head, I watched numbly as he shrugged over my response and took one down. "See if that fits."

He tossed it my way. I caught it against my chest, and held it there before reluctantly trying it on. It was a damn good fit, not too snug in the shoulders, not too big in the waist and barely half an inch short in the arms, which only made me feel more uncomfortable. Was I really going to wear some other man's clothes?

Ezra skimmed his gaze over my torso before shrugging as if that would do, and he turned to a carousel full of ties.

I quickly yanked the jacket back off, feeling as if I had cooties now. "Is it just me or is one guy borrowing clothes from another guy just plain weird?"

"Hell yes, it's weird." Ezra picked out a handful of

ties. "Which is why you're signing an NDA before you're allowed to leave my house."

I snorted. "As if I would ever tell anyone about this, anyway."

"Good." He turned to me, holding up half a dozen ties. "Which one?"

Dear God.

"Hell if I know," I answered, honestly.

He sighed. "Look, you've got to give me something here. Do you want to look nice for my sister or not?"

I shook my head. "Dude, you're the one who works in the fashion industry."

His scowl was immediate. "I'm *administrative*."

I lifted my eyebrows, letting him know that made no difference to me. His closet was bigger than my entire apartment and was full of custom-made, name-brand clothes. He *had* to have more fashion sense than I did.

Grumbling under his breath, Ezra picked out a tie and flung it at me. I looped it over my shoulder and watched him mutter some more as he chose a dress shirt and pants.

"Wait until I'm out of here before you try the pants on," he instructed before leaving me alone in his closet.

I did, hustling to do so as soon as he was gone.

Again, everything fit eerily well. The pants were a smidge too short, but not enough to look bad. I shifted around in everything, relieved it felt comfortable, and yet oddly aware I wasn't in my own clothes.

Just as quickly, I took everything off and pulled on my holey jeans and T-shirt.

Slipping the suit back onto its assorted hangers, I draped everything carefully over my arm and left the closet. Ezra wasn't waiting in the bedroom, so I entered the hall and found him in the front room, pacing the floor and scowling at something he was reading on his smartphone.

"That wasn't what I meant, and you know it, *Lana*,"

he growled as he jabbed his finger angrily against the screen, pounding out a response to the message he'd obviously just received.

I cleared my throat.

He glanced up, then lifted his eyebrows, waiting for a report on sizes.

I made the okay sign. "Everything fits perfect," I said and nodded my gratitude, because I really did want to look good for Isobel, even if I had to wear someone else's clothes to accomplish it. "Thank you."

He nodded and started to follow me toward the door when I headed that way. "You know this is her first date in eight years, right?"

I slowed to a stop and gulped before facing him again. "I know. Any good advice?"

"Yes." He pointed at me and narrowed his eyes. "No sex with my sister in my suit."

With a frown, I growled, "I'm serious here, man."

"So am I," he argued. "You seem like a decent guy. I'd *seriously* hate to have to kill you if you get out of line."

"And I'd hate to have to die," I spit back. "But in all *seriousness,* I want this to be amazing for her. It's your turn to give *me* something here."

"Man…" He shook his head and tossed me an amused grin. "I think you have Izzy pegged better than anyone. You'll do fine."

I blew out a breath, bolstered by his faith in me and yet still uncertain. "You think?"

Ezra laughed. "I only spent five minutes in a room with you two together, and it was obvious as hell. Now go get ready for your ball already, Cinderella."

Wrinkling my nose, I shook my head. "I'm not Cinderella." Then, because I was lame and couldn't think up a better retort, I said, "*Y-you're* Cinderella."

Ezra blinked. "That has to be the worst comeback in the history of comebacks. Seriously, Hollander, in what universe would *I* be Cinderella?"

He had a point. But I couldn't be bested, so I shrugged. "I just saw your closet. Clearly, you have a shoe fetish. One of those fancy loafers *has* to be missing its pair."

"Weak," he told me, chuckling. "Now go, before your lameness becomes contagious." But he was grinning affably as he said it.

I waved him goodbye before I realized we hadn't discussed one thing. "Oh! Hey, when do you want this back?" I held up the suit.

He made a face and shuddered. "Are you nuts? You're probably going to have sex with my sister in that suit. I never want it back."

I rolled my eyes. "If it makes you feel better, I'm sure I'll take the suit off before I have sex with her."

Then I walked out the front door, unable to stop snickering.

How was *that* for a lame comeback?

"Damn you, Hollander!" he yelled after me. "You laugh it up now, you little bastard. We'll just see who has the last laugh when I'm standing over your grave."

chapter TWENTY-THREE

The next morning, I woke early, eager to see Isobel. I made myself lie there for a good half hour until it was the usual time I got up. Then I pulled on my jogging clothes, stuffed another outfit into my backpack, tucked my new mirror into the front pocket, and checked on my mom who was still sleeping peacefully, before I hurried out the door. It took me about ten minutes to reach my truck, when it typically took about fifteen. And then I made it to Porter Hall in about half the time I usually spent driving.

The gate opened a minute later, letting me in, and I pulled around the back to my parking spot.

Isobel hadn't made it out to the lake by the time I jogged up to our starting spot. I paced and stretched, impatient for her to show. When I finally heard the crunch of gravel as she approached, my body clanged with awareness.

"Hey," she called, her voice full of pleasure when she caught sight of me already here. "You're early today—mmph!"

I cut her off with a kiss, tugging her into my arms

and plastering her body to mine.

"Are you sure you want to run today?" I asked breathlessly when we came up for air. "I can think of another way to exercise."

Her eyes flared with heat before she bit her lip. "What did you have in mind?"

"Sex in the pool house shower," I said, nipping my way down her throat as I confessed something I wanted to do every time I stepped into that shower: her. "Then in the bed. Then in the hot tub. Not necessarily in that order."

She shivered in my arms and ran her fingers through my hair. "I think you're successfully tempting me."

I grinned against the swell of her breast. "We have a full hour before I need to clock in." Then I bit her nipple right through her jogging shirt and sports bra. "Just think of all the ways I could make you come in a full hour."

She gasped before taking my hand and tugging me back up the trail toward the pool house. "Okay. I'm sold."

We were both laughing—okay, fine, giggling—by the time we reached the rock cave.

As soon as we were closed inside, Isobel ripped her running shirt up over her head, and I was quick to follow, peeling off mine. We watched each other giddily, racing to see who could get naked first.

Isobel won, whooping over her triumph as she called, "Hot tub first," and raced over to dive into the bubbling warm water. I hurried in after her, tugging her onto my lap as soon as we were both submerged. She turned to face me, straddling me so she could wrap her legs around my waist. We kissed, and my chest slipped against her slick breasts, warm water spilling between us with each shift of our bodies.

She worked her hips until she was pressing her entrance right against my cock. Hard and throbbing, I tried to push my way inside but the damn water worked against us. Plus, I realized I had no protection, even though I'd seen some in a drawer in the bathroom once. That was too far away, so I reached between us and messaged her clit, kissing her shoulder as the heat and vibration of the water brought her to an orgasm.

Her fingernails bit into my arm as she came apart. I gasped with her, my body on fire. The sounds she made, the expression on her face, the way she trembled against me, it was the biggest high. I felt powerful and pleased as she started to settle and relax against me.

"That was so hot," I said into her scarred ear, before kissing it. "You are so fucking beautiful."

She looked up at me. "Did you say something? I don't hear as well from that ear."

My lips parted. I'd never known that. I knew she couldn't use her hand quite as well on the left side, but I'd never known about the hearing. I leaned in and kissed her gently.

"I said I love you," I told her.

Her face softened. "I love you, too."

"Let's continue this in the bedroom. I want to be on a bed the next time I'm inside you."

I stroked Isobel's hair as she rested her head on my shoulder and breathed evenly. She was completely limp and relaxed and yet I somehow knew she was still awake.

"Have I told you I could live here?" I asked, abandoning her hair to run my fingers down the side of her arm. "I could so totally live in this pool house for the rest of my life."

Her chuckle vibrated through my chest. "Yeah, you've mentioned it once or twice before."

I turned onto my side to face her, our noses only inches apart. "I want to live here with *you*." That was a new part of my declaration: the addition of her.

It made her cheeks radiate with pleasure. "Really?"

I started to grin over the daydream until something in her expression made me pause. I'd just been spouting wishes aloud, but the way she brightened had me wondering if she thought I'd just suggested we actually move in together. Freezing, I stared in her eyes, not sure what to say.

Living with her in this pool house would be an absolute dream come true. There was no denying that. But I couldn't see how it could become a true possibility. First of all, it wasn't my place to be inviting her to live with me here, and even if her father did allow us the opportunity, it would be a step down for Isobel and too big of a step up for me. I wasn't sure I could handle being so far below her financially and socially. Which made me wonder how our relationship was going to continue at all. She might not have a problem with me being poor, but I couldn't say I cared for being the destitute one, the one who couldn't pull his weight. What if she began to resent me for dragging her down or started thinking I was some kind of gold digger? Not too long ago, I had thought my pride was dead, but it turned out, I did have some, and being so far beneath her didn't sit well with me.

Then, there was my mother to think of. I couldn't just leave her, even though I knew she'd financially be okay now.

As I looked into Isobel's hopeful blue eyes, I had a moment where everything between us seemed absolutely impossible. Our future felt doomed. It sent a flurry of panic through me. I didn't want to lose her. The world felt better when I was with her. We'd become a team, doing most of my handyman tasks around the house together. And I loved finally being able to touch her, and kiss her, and— But shit. I couldn't picture a life between us, not where we could get married, have babies, and live happily ever after.

It scared me. It was only a split second of fear; I'm sure I would've gotten over it in the next breath, and been fine again. But Isobel saw it in my eyes. She saw my hesitation, and she knew I hadn't been seriously suggesting we move in together.

The problem was I also knew she thought it was because I didn't *want* to live with her. When she sat up and reached for her shirt to cover her chest, I sat up with her, another form of panic flooding me. I wanted to say something, reassure her, convince her I loved her with everything I had and wanted to be with her more than I'd ever wanted to be with anyone. But if I voiced any of my reservations, I feared she'd see them as excuses instead of reasons, and she'd think I wasn't being honest about my feelings. What if she thought my issues and concerns were unsubstantial, and she tried to brush them off as no big deal? They *were* a big deal to me. I could suddenly picture this huge argument between us where she told me I was being an idiot—even though I already *knew* I was—and me denying it, and her wanting to throttle me, and me feeling more insecure, and all of it splitting us apart.

Except by remaining silent now, I think she assumed I didn't care enough about her.

"Isobel…" I tried, reaching out to touch her back.

She stiffened against my hand. It broke my heart, but I didn't give up. I scooted in behind her and wrapped my arms around her from the back before setting my chin on her shoulder.

"I don't know how to show you how much you mean to me," I admitted. I didn't know how to fix this.

She turned her cheek toward me. "What?"

Realizing I was on her scarred side, I transferred my chin to her other shoulder, then kissed her cheek. "What're we going to do today?" I asked as if nothing were wrong. "It's almost eight." Time to become the Porter Hall handyman.

She turned around to face me, and for a moment, I feared I'd see hurt in her eyes, but instead she grinned. "I think it's about time I gave you the grand tour."

Chuckling, I shook my head. "I think I've just about seen everything by now, haven't I?"

Blue eyes glittered as if amused by my ignorance. "Ah, but you've never heard about all the history behind everything you've seen."

I perked to attention. "History?"

Her smile said *just you wait.* "Yeah. Like the chandelier in the entry. Were you aware it came from Germany, where the Gestapo had taken it from a hotel in France during World War II?"

My mouth dropped open. "No freaking way," I breathed. "I've changed lightbulbs in that thing." I swear my fingers started to tingle, realizing I'd touched something Nazis had touched. My archeologist-loving heart began to beat a little faster.

Isobel watched me as if she knew exactly what I was experiencing. "Every piece in this house holds some kind of historical significance. Dad doesn't usually buy anything unless there's some kind of meaning or story behind it."

No wonder why I'd always liked Henry. "It's like a museum," I uttered, flabbergasted.

With a laugh, Isobel began to pull her clothes on. "Pretty much. Dad allows school bus loads of children to come in every fall and spring to take a tour. It's one of his charitable contributions to the community, along with giving out a high-risk loan to one worthy candidate each year."

I met her gaze, and the look in her eyes told me something. Something I hadn't considered before. "He knew he'd never see that money from my mother again, didn't he?" I guessed.

She shrugged. "He rarely gets reimbursed from any of them, so he writes them off as donations."

I shook my head. "But…he helped her out again, paid off the rest of her debt and…" I stopped talking when Isobel began to shake her head.

"Last year, he helped your mom out. This year, I think *you* were the candidate he chose to help."

My mouth fell open. I started to shake my head, except I really couldn't deny it. It made sense. Except…why? Why would he help *me*? I wasn't—

"He was going to help someone anyway," Isobel murmured, answering my unspoken question. "I guess he saw something in you he thought needed it most."

I gulped, not sure how to deal with this honor but also growing more determined than ever to prove myself worthy of it. "Wow," was all I could manage to murmur.

Fully dressed, Isobel approached me and took my hand before going up on her toes to kiss my cheek. "Come on. Let me show you everything."

Half an hour later, I was even more staggered by Porter Hall than when I'd initially laid eyes on the place. Turned out, the cherub statue that had nearly impaled me that first day had once sat in a garden in Rome. And the fountain in the foyer had belonged in a spa house in ancient Bath, England.

I soaked in every word Isobel said as she showed me around, telling me who'd painted which portrait and from which exotic location they'd purchased each rug. Even the crown molding in one room had been removed from the home of some Russian monarch.

"And this," she said, leading me into a new room where the only centerpiece seemed to be a rickety, ancient school desk-looking thing covered in peeling green paint, "…is Henry David Thoreau's writing table. He's Dad's favorite philosopher. So he was excited to purchase it from the Pratchett Museum to keep them from going out of business when they had some trouble with funding. He only paid eight thousand for it."

I shook my head as I gave a low whistle. "That is so crazy. I can't believe one dinky, ugly little table could be worth so much. Looks as if a stiff breeze could blow it to pieces."

"Meh. It's sturdier than it looks." She grabbed it by both sides and gave it a healthy shake. When my eyes bulged from my head and I swear my heart tried to pound its way out of my chest over her rough treatment, she laughed. "Oh my God. The look on your face when I did that was priceless."

"Yeah," I wheezed from winded lungs. "About as priceless as the table you just tried to shake apart." Turning away from her, I wandered around, studying the pictures on the wall, most of them photographs of Henry David Thoreau or facts about him.

"God, this place is amazing," I murmured, running my finger over a framed biography. "All the history, the stories, the different cultures. When I first came here, I thought all this gaudy shit was just a rich-people thing. But to learn the meaning behind each item…" I shook my head in awe as I gazed in wonder toward Isobel.

She wrinkled her nose. "A rich-people thing?"

I swallowed. Shit. I hadn't meant to insult her.

"Yeah, you know…" I shrugged, only to realize, nah, she really didn't know. Flushing, I sent her a wince. "It's hard to describe the jealousy and declining self-worth a guy like me feels when he enters a house this…" I spread my arms to encompass the room, not sure how to properly define it. "This grand."

Seemingly unoffended by my try at explaining myself, Isobel faced me seriously, before she leaned against Thoreau's desk. "If you could decide between being poor but beautiful and popular and loved by everyone, or rich beyond your wildest imagination but so hideously disfigured to the point no one wanted anything to do with you, which would you choose?"

I stepped toward her and set my hand on her waist before murmuring, "We make ourselves rich by making our wants few."

Her lips parted as if that was the most profound thing she'd ever heard. And it might've been, since it had originally come from the lips of Henry David Thoreau. Which was why I couldn't continue to take credit for it.

I pointed past her toward the wall with my free hand. "At least that's what Thoreau says." She glanced back to find the quote printed and framed above the desk.

"Oh." Scowling, she whirled back to poke me in the gut. "You cheated. That's a cheater's answer."

I laughed and leaned in to kiss her temple. "Then I'd choose whatever option brings me back to you each day. Rich or poor, I don't care. I just want you."

The breath rushed from her lungs. Lifting her fingers, she drew a piece of my hair between her fingers and gently brushed it out of my face, whispering, "I like that choice. Even if it's a cheesy line you just came up with."

"I like *you.* And it wasn't just a line." Setting my other hand on her waist so I could grip her and pick her up, I scooted her further onto the desk until she was sitting on it fully and I was nudging my hips between her thighs. "Is it bad that I want to take you right here on Thoreau's table?"

"No, but that might be a little more of a workout than it could survive."

I sent her a wolfish grin. "Hell yes, it would."

She laughed and gave my chest a little nudge to get

me to back up. "I know a better place we could go."

"Oh yeah?" I backed away, letting her hop off the table and take my hand before she led me to a closed door. Opening it, she stepped inside, bringing me with her. But I barely cleared the entrance before I halted abruptly, my mouth falling open…again, for probably the twentieth time today.

"Holy shit. Is this…?" I turned to raise my eyebrows at Isobel.

She nodded. "A recreation of van Gogh's bedroom? Yes, it is."

"Wow." I reverently stepped deeper into the room, gaping at the red blanket and white pillows and high footboard on the bed to match the one in the famous van Gogh painting of his bedroom. The chairs, side table, and the window looked exactly as they should. I swear, even the vases on the table and clothes hanging from hooks on the wall were spot-on. The color of the walls, floors, and doors had me shaking my head in awe. It was as if I'd just stepped into the painting itself.

I wandered deeper into the room, pausing in front of one of the van Gogh art prints on the wall, where I let out a low, impressed whistle. "I wonder how much all this cost," I said without thinking.

Isobel hooked her arm through mine and rested her chin on my shoulder as she pointed to the picture. "Much less than this painting right here alone, I imagine. After Dad won this thing in an auction, he had the entire room designed this way to hang it here."

"Wait." I jerked an instinctive step back. "You mean…" Now I was pointing at the framed picture in front of us. "That's an *original* van Gogh?"

Isobel's blue eyes danced with mischief as she grinned. "Yep. One of the less popular ones, of course. It's called *Iron Mill in The Hague*, but it still cost nearly half a million, I believe."

"Half a mill…" I took another step in reverse. "I've

been working in a house with an original van Gogh painting in it, and I had no idea? Holy shit, I just *breathed* on it."

I'd just breathed on something Vincent van Gogh had breathed on.

Isobel laughed. "You're so cute."

I was so out of my depth, that's what I was. If I'd worried I was below her status before, now I was convinced of it. I touched her cheek, my fingers resting against soft, warm flesh, and I wondered how I was ever going to be able to keep such a prize. I didn't deserve this. I didn't deserve her. It couldn't last. I was more certain of that than I was of my next breath. Being with Isobel could only be fleeting.

I should've backed away from her then and embraced my doomed fate. But she was standing here now, smiling at me, accepting me. So, from the words of Richard Bach, via Black Crimson's graffiti art:

The best way to pay for a lovely moment is to enjoy it.

I decided to enjoy this beautiful moment while it lasted. I leaned in and pressed my lips to hers, tender at first until I became hungry and seeking. She wrapped her arms around my neck and arched against me. I backed her toward the bed and toppled her onto the mattress.

Eyes wide, she clutched my shoulders and blinked up at me. "But you're still on the clock."

Since I was the only one in the room who actually cared about that, I knew I was pleasing her when I growled, "Fuck that. I need to be inside you. Now."

Pleasure bloomed on her features. Lips spreading into a grin, she tugged at my clothes, her hands on the zipper of my jeans. I began to unbutton her blouse but didn't have nearly enough skin revealed when the muffled voice of Kit startled us.

"Shaw! Shaw, where are you?"

It sounded as if he was in the next room over with Thoreau's desk, so Isobel and I jerked upright and immediately started buttoning and zipping everything back into place.

"Mom needs some help in the kitchen," the kid hollered. "*Shaw*?"

Isobel and I climbed off the bed, still breathing hard. Since we were as respectable as we were going to get, I called back, "In here."

The door flew open, and Kit bounded inside. "Mom sent me to get you. She needs help with the dishwasher." But he'd already forgotten about me, his gaze on Isobel. "Oh! Hi, Miss Isobel. Whatcha doing in here? Whose room is this?"

As she explained to him who Vincent van Gogh was, her gaze met mine over his head.

Tomorrow, I mouthed. We were so going to finish what we'd started in here on our date night.

Her cheeks brightened and eyes warmed with agreement, but she turned back to Kit, giving him all her attention.

Even though I was uncomfortable as hell with my arousal refusing to die a quick death, I whistled as I made my way toward the kitchen.

Saturday couldn't come soon enough.

chapter TWENTY-FOUR

By the time Saturday arrived, I was nervous.

I'd never been to a fancy restaurant before, and everyone said Urbane was the crème de la crème of eateries in the area. I didn't want to do anything to embarrass Isobel. Shit, I wondered if I should've taken one of those lessons to learn which silverware went with which course.

I was totally going to bomb this.

But at least I was going to look good doing it. Driving Henry Nash's truck and wearing Ezra Nash's suit, no one would be able to tell I was a nobody. A fake.

Henry had set the reservations for seven thirty. Since I got off work at four, I went home to spend a couple hours with Mom before I dressed. She gave a low, impressed whistle as soon as I exited the bedroom, trying to figure out the cuff links.

"My goodness, don't you look handsome?"

I glanced over to where she sat in her worn-out chair, wearing a floral muumuu and watching *Wheel of Fortune* on TV with her walker sitting next to her. An ache rippled through me. How many evenings had we sat in here, eating in our chairs and watching this show together? I felt as if I were abandoning her to go off and try to be something I wasn't.

For a moment, I wanted to call the whole thing off. I didn't belong with Isobel. I was their handyman, their charity case. I belonged here with my mother, making sure she stayed safe and healthy. But then I remembered the excitement on Isobel's face when she'd kissed me goodbye only hours ago.

She had brushed the backs of her knuckles along my jaw and murmured, "See you at seven," and there was no way in hell I could disappoint her.

"Does my tie look straight?" I asked Mom.

"You look perfect," she answered, something bright and satisfied glittering in her eyes before she added, "I'm so proud of you, Shaw. This is the kind of life I always wanted for you."

I paused, not sure exactly what kind of life that was. The one where I felt stuck between two worlds, spending all day in the high life and taking luxury showers, only to come home to my one-room apartment that more often than not stank of the litter box for my neighbor's cat. I felt like a poser.

I think that was all my mom saw, though. The suit I wore and the hair I had combed back. So she assumed I'd turned into some kind of suave, well-to-do man, or something.

"You like this girl, don't you?"

And that was all it took to calm me down. This was about the girl, not the suit.

I nodded. "Yes. Yes, I do."

Mom grinned. "Then bring her by sometime. I want to meet her."

More nerves filled my gut as I imagined Isobel here, seeing the way I lived, meeting my mother who never brushed her hair and rarely showered. I wasn't sure what she'd think of me. Of us. And then there was Mom. I knew she'd never be openly rude to Isobel, but what if she said something about Isobel's scars or money to upset her? I wanted the two to meet and *like* each other. It made me stress and worry something would go wrong.

"I'll see what I can do," I said as I crossed the room to bend down and kiss Mom's paper-thin cheek. "You're staying in tonight, right?" I asked. "I saw the janitor mopping on the main floor, he'll probably do the stairs before the night's over. I don't want you slipping and falling."

Mom tsked and patted my arm. "Don't worry about me. Just go, have fun."

"Okay, then. I love you."

I left with another kiss to her forehead and a glance at the television where a man was spinning the wheel and the crowd was clapping. It was nearly seven by the time I reached the truck. With a half hour to pick up Isobel and make it to Urbane in time for our reservations, I started to Porter Hall, humming under my breath as I nervously tapped my fingers against the steering wheel.

The gate opened as soon as I pulled into the driveway and before I could even push the button to announce myself. Someone had been waiting and watching for me. Hopefully Isobel. The idea that she was anxious for tonight made my blood race and my own anxieties rise. I didn't want to disappoint her.

I almost expected her to open the door and step outside as soon as I rolled to a stop in front of the entrance. But she didn't. I parked and turned off the engine. After alighting, I skirted the bumper, took ten steps up the front steps, hurried between the lane of solar lights that looked like hanging lanterns and stepped under the overhang before I rang the doorbell.

Henry answered, his gaze probing and curious when he let me in. But after a single once-over, he nodded in approval.

"I knew Ezra would find you something nice. You'll

match Izzy perfectly."

I glanced around for her, but she wasn't in the foyer. Hoping she wasn't going to skip out on me, I gulped, my palms growing damper.

"The silly girl wanted to race right out to you," Henry told me on an eye roll. "But I made her wait until you were inside so she could make an entrance."

Snickering, I glanced over. "It's not the prom, you know."

With a scowl, her dad muttered, "Well, it might as well be. She never did make it to her prom."

I started to respond, but he bumped his elbow into mine and pointed up to the second level where the staircase began.

The vision that stood there took my breath away. In a black, ankle-length gown, Isobel began to descend.

"Holy shit," I breathed.

She looked stunning. The dress was nice, with shiny black sequins on the tight bodice, one-inch straps over her shoulders and a silken skirt that flowed out from the cinched waist. But she was the one who made it look good, not the other way around. Her hair was pulled up and her arms were delicate and bare. She did nothing to hide her scars. I loved that.

Her blue eyes met mine, and I could only shake my head, unable to think up the proper words. "You look so…" She'd finally reached us, and I still couldn't say anything sufficient, so I reached out, snagged her waist with one hand and pulled her against me to press my mouth to hers.

"Okay, enough of that," Henry announced, slugging me in the arm, even though he was laughing good-naturedly as he did so. "I had to tug some tricky strings to get this reservation for you."

I dragged my lips from Isobel's but still didn't look at her father. Lifting the single blood-red long-stem rose I'd been holding behind my back since I'd come inside, I said, "This will never be as lovely as you, but at least you can be comforted in the fact I stole it from the best rose garden in the state."

Her mouth fell open before she cracked off a laugh. "You stole one of my own roses to give me."

I wiggled my eyebrows. "And I took off all the thorns too."

Not the least bit offended by my thievery, Isobel reached for one of my hands only to turn it so my palm faced up. When she caught sight of the scratch marks I'd given myself, she shook her head and smiled. "Still can't accomplish it with gloves on, I see."

"Never," I admitted, grinning back.

Henry glanced between us, clearly having no idea what we were talking about. "I swear, you two speak your own language." Then he let out a sad smile. "Annalise and I used to do that."

"Oh, Dad." Isobel turned to hug him. "Don't get sentimental. I didn't bring any tissues."

Her teasing worked. He sniffed out a laugh and motioned us toward the door. "Eh, enough of that. Get out of here already. Have fun. And be safe."

She kissed him on the cheek and opened the front door. I lingered a moment to send her dad a serious nod before murmuring, "Thank you, sir."

He clasped my shoulder. "Thank *you*."

At the truck, Isobel was already reaching for her door handle. I shouted her off it, dashing down the steps until I was at her side and could open the door for her. "You gotta give me my moment here," I said, holding out a hand to help her climb up into the cab of the truck.

With a laugh, she shook her head. "You and my dad, I swear. We're not going to the royal ball, you know."

Well, it certainly felt like it. It felt as if I'd just helped a princess into my truck. To me, we might as well be in some kind of freaking fairy tale.

When I climbed behind the wheel, she was flipping

down the visor to check her lipstick. I winced. "Sorry. I guess I didn't think about how I would mess up your lipstick."

After wiping one corner, she sent me a grin. "Trust me, I didn't mind."

My eyebrows lifted. "So you don't mind if I mess it up again, later on?"

She flipped the visor back up. "Oh, I'm counting on it."

My body stirred with warmth. Suddenly, I was looking forward to what we'd do after dinner much more than I was the actual meal. But the idea of being seen in public beside this fetching lady kept me from suggesting we skip the food and go straight to dessert.

My first experience with valet parking was awkward; I totally forgot to tip the attendant, so Isobel had to. Flushing, I leaned in as I took her elbow to escort her through the front doors to murmur a grateful, "Thank you. I'm used to being the one *getting* tipped, not the other way around."

"You're fine," Isobel started to reassure me, only to slow when she glanced over. Her lips parted with surprise. "You're nervous."

My brow felt damp and my skin was clammy. "Hell yes, I'm nervous," I hissed. "I don't belong in a place like this."

She stopped walking entirely so she could turn to face me fully. My cheeks heated with embarrassment because someone was waiting to hold the door open for us, and it was bringing us undue attention.

Isobel didn't seem to care. She kept her voice low and discreet when she said, "I promise you are more worthy to be here tonight than anyone else." Then she smiled. "And your presence is the only thing keeping me from experiencing my own nerves."

My gaze caught hers. I don't know why I'd totally forgotten to worry about *her*. This was only her second outing in the past six months, and we hadn't even gotten out of the truck the first time we'd left Porter Hall.

Feeling like a dick for not thinking about her, I raised her hand to my lips and kissed her knuckles. "I'll keep you on the level if you can keep me calm."

She gave a dignified nod. "Deal."

So we entered the restaurant, where the maître d' showed us to our table in the back tucked into a darker corner. I assumed he was trying to provide us with something romantic and private, where Isobel and I could talk and focus on nothing but each other.

A waiter arrived to take our drink orders a moment later. He talked directly to me, pretending Isobel wasn't present. I had no idea if she wanted a fancy bottle of champagne or what, so I lifted my gaze across the table, where Isobel said, "Water's fine for me."

So I told the guy, "Just water for both of us."

He nodded to me. "Very well, sir," and took off again.

I frowned after him, not sure why he hadn't even acknowledged her, when a voice from a few tables over floated our way.

"Oh my God, did you see that woman's *face*?"

Blinking, I turned in that direction to find a table of two women, leaning toward each other eagerly as they gossiped.

"I know!" the second one gushed. "Those scars are disgusting. It looks like someone took a meat tenderizer to her."

Stunned by their uncouth behavior, I turned back to Isobel, who sat stiff and straight, her chin tipped up and blue eyes filled with blank acceptance.

"How in God's name can a guy that gorgeous stand being seen with her in public?" the first woman continued.

The other snickered. "She must be super rich. Or incredible in bed."

They shared a laugh. "I don't see how. He'd have to put a bag over her head just to get it up."

Okay, that was it. Enough was enough. I whirled to face the women so fast they jumped, startled, and lifted large-eyed gazes my way.

"Or maybe I'm with her because I find her to be beautiful," I bit out. "Inside *and* out. She makes me laugh and smile. My heart beats faster every time she enters a room. Oh, and she's not an overly loud and rude, opinionated *jerk*. Strange how that kind of shit actually matters to some people, isn't it?"

Mouths falling open, the two women gaped at me as if I'd lost my mind.

"Yeah, we *heard* you," I added, answering their silent suspicions. "Loud and clear. The whole damn restaurant heard you. And frankly, with annoying mouths like yours, I'd be surprised if every man who's ever slept with *you two* didn't need earplugs to get it up."

"Shaw!" Isobel gasped.

I spun to her, snapping, "*What?* They're pissing me off. No one talks about you like that and gets away with it."

Her face flushed and expression turned miserable. I knew she would've rather we'd completely ignored the two women, but I couldn't. I just couldn't.

"Excuse me, sir," the maître d' asked, appearing at our table nervously wringing his hands and glancing around toward the other curious patrons. "Is there a problem here?" he asked politely enough, but the look on his face seemed to say *I* was the problem.

"Yes," I said, the word cutting. "There very much *is* a problem here." Isobel hissed my name again, trying to rein me in, but I was too busy glaring at the headwaiter. "Those two women over there keep insulting us, and it's pissing me off."

The man swallowed and glanced at the women, who looked equal parts guilty and indignant. Then he turned back to me. "I'm so sorry, sir. Would you like us to seat you at another table?"

I lifted my eyebrows at this suggestion. "No," I said. "I liked it here. We were minding our own damn business, not bothering anyone else until *they* started in. Why don't you ask *them* to move? Or better yet, to leave entirely?"

"Oh my God," Isobel moaned under her breath. "Shaw, please stop."

I glanced at her, and my heart wrenched. This was supposed to be her night, her special evening to make up for her prom and every other date she'd missed in the last eight years. I'd wanted it to go perfectly. Nothing bad was supposed to happen.

The maître d' continued fumbling for the right words, because clearly he wasn't going to reprimand the women; he must not have found any offence with *them.*

Swallowing all the rage and injustice I found from the situation, I slowly pulled my cloth napkin from my lap and set it gently on the table in front of me. Then I stood just as deliberately, until I was at my full height, which just so happened to be a good six inches taller than the maître d'.

His eyes widened and he took a step back as if he thought I was going to throttle him. In his defense, I'm sure my gaze blazed with how much I *did* want to throttle him.

But all I said was, "I think we'll just leave." Sending the two loudmouth women one last nasty glare, I added, "We've lost our appetites."

When I turned my attention to Isobel and held my hand down to her, she gracefully took it and rose regally to her feet. I'd never been so proud of anyone in my life. She'd sequestered herself away for eight years because she'd been worried about experiencing moments just like this, and here she was, surviving her worst fear with poised perfection.

With my heart in my throat, I kissed her lips, lingering softly. Then I glanced at the maître d' with narrowed eyes and led her from the restaurant.

Isobel and I remained quiet until the valet returned the truck to us and we were closed inside it. My anger had dissolved and worry gnawed at my gut. I didn't know how to interpret her silence or that blank, expressionless look on her face.

Was she hurt, mad, or maybe just tired of it all? Had I caused the biggest problem by making such a scene?

This not knowing was driving me crazy.

I glanced across the interior of the truck as we pulled onto the road. "Want to go get a pizza instead?"

She shook her head, not meeting my gaze.

"Hamburgers?" I tried. I would take her anywhere, do anything to please her.

"I just want to go home." Except, dammit, that was the last thing I wanted to do for her.

My hopes shriveled. She'd definitely been negatively impacted, and the encounter was still bothering her.

Unable to stop stressing that I'd made things worse, I asked, "Are you mad at me?"

She seared me with a sharp glance. "What?"

"For, you know, escalating the problem?"

With a sniff, she turned back to staring out the front windshield. "Of course not," she mumbled, but there wasn't much fervor behind her words, making me wonder if she was just saying that to shut me up, when really, maybe I *was* the root of her turmoil.

"You didn't believe them, did you?" I kept on, unable to drop it. Not being able to gauge where her mind was killed me. "When they suggested I could only be with you because you're rich?"

Isobel growled in her throat. "Can we please just not talk about it?"

My breathing turned choppy. No, we couldn't not

talk about it. Did she believe them or not? I needed reassurance; I needed to know she and I were still good. I'd been the one to take her out for her first trip into society, and look what had happened. Did she blame me? Did she hate me? Did she ever want to see me again? Why couldn't she just tell me we were still solid?

A second later, I realized how selfish I was being. Isobel had just attempted something she hadn't done in eight years, and it had failed. Of course she wasn't going to be in a good mood. Me trying to push her into saying she didn't hate me wasn't helping anything.

Though my gut rolled with unease, I remained quiet, giving her the silence she'd asked for. Once I delivered her home and parked before her front door, I tried one more time to get her to open up. She hadn't made a move to exit the truck yet; she was just sitting there, staring out the side window. It made me think she did want to say something before we parted.

So I asked, "Are you okay?"

But she sighed as if irritated by the question. "I'm fine."

She wasn't. Clearly, she was anything but fine. I reached for her hand. "Can I come inside with you?"

Pulling her fingers away, she shook her head. "I'd rather be alone right now."

My heart cracked. I felt so helpless, as if everything I did only made matters worse. "I'm sorry," I said, my voice going hoarse.

"Don't," she snapped, scowling at me but only turning halfway toward me. "There's no need for you to apologize. You didn't do anything wrong."

I wanted to be comforted by her words, but everything felt so off. Her misery was beginning to ooze and I couldn't fix it. And then, when I realized why she wasn't facing me fully, I lost it.

"Are you hiding your scars from me?" I accused. "Dammit, Isobel. Don't start that again." I grabbed her arm and tried to steer her around to face me, but she resisted.

"Stop it," she cried, wrenching away. "Just leave me alone. You don't understand this. You couldn't possibly understand."

I understood she was upset. And I understood that ache inside me that needed to soothe her, to make it better. Aside from that, nothing else mattered. I needed the chance to make her better.

Touching her shoulder lightly only to remove my hand when she shrugged me off, I begged, "Then make me understand."

Her breathing picked up. I wasn't sure if she was crying or just getting more upset. In either case, it made me feel worse.

"Tell me how to make this better."

Whirling to face me completely, she hissed, "You can't. You can't make anything better. And I was a fool to ever think a freak like me could mix with the outside world."

"No," I started, not wanting her to feel that way. She'd come so far to lose all the progress she'd made. I could picture her closing herself up for another eight years, and the thought panicked me. "Isobel—"

"Just leave me alone," she cried, throwing open the truck door and hurling herself out into the night.

I jerked open the driver's side door and jumped out, hurrying after her. But I'd no sooner rounded the front of the hood than she threw up a hand, warding me off. The silhouette she made in the solar lights lining the front walk looked like a tragic princess.

"Don't follow me," she commanded. "Just give me some space."

I jarred to a halt, understanding the word *space.* Space and time I could give. Everyone needed a moment to recoup sometimes. Besides, they were both things that passed. It didn't mean she wanted me to stay away forever.

"I'll see you Monday," I called as she opened the front door, letting her know I would give her space, but only for a few days.

She pretended not to hear me, but I knew she had. Cursing under my breath as the front door clamped closed behind her, I shook my head, dejected, and slumped back to the truck.

I wanted to return to Urbane, find the two women who'd caused this, and strangle them both. How could they be so cruel and heartless? Isobel hadn't done anything to bother them, and besides, she'd looked completely stunning to me. So what if she had some nasty scars? They didn't make her who she was. I couldn't believe some people could be so superficial.

Letting my anger smother the worry that she still might be upset with me, I stewed the whole way home. Even the walk from the lot where I parked back to my apartment building didn't help cool my mood. I wanted to plant my fist through a brick wall. I wanted to return to Porter Hall, force my way into Isobel's room and *make* her let me fix everything.

But she'd requested space, so I would give her space.

God, I hated that word. *Space.* It was so vague, and lonely, and miserable.

I shoved open the front door of my building, wondering if she'd even be willing to continue her flower shop dream after this, when a heap of floral clothing at the bottom of the stairwell had me stumbling to a halt before I tripped over it.

At first, I thought someone had dropped their laundry right at the base of the steps, blocking the path. But then a gray head of hair, fleshy arms, and shoes took form from the mound. Realizing that looked like Mom's muumuu she'd been wearing earlier in the evening, I gasped out my fear before rushing forward and falling to my knees beside the limp form.

"Mom?" I croaked, rolling the fallen person toward me until her face fell my way.

My lungs caught on a choked cry when I took in the bloody gash on her forehead.

"Oh God, Oh God. *Mom*?" I pressed my shaking fingers to the pulse point on her neck and nearly wept when I felt a heartbeat. She was unconscious, but at least she was still alive.

Beyond grateful, I pressed my face to hers and just held her against me for the longest second, praying for her heart to keep beating and her lungs to keep pumping air.

Then I went to get help.

chapter TWENTY-FIVE

It was nearly one in the morning by the time they let me into Mom's hospital room to see her. Visiting hours be damned, I think they realized I wasn't going to leave until I could see her in person. And then, once I finally did get shown to her room, there was no way they could pry me away. I was there for good, a permanent fixture plastered to her side.

A large white bandage circled her head. She'd received a concussion but that wasn't the worst of her injuries. I guess whenever she'd fallen, she'd rebroken the not-fully-healed hip from five months before. What was worse, some bone marrow had escaped and gotten into her bloodstream. The doctors had been forced to perform immediate surgery to keep the marrow from reaching her heart.

If I hadn't found her when I had and gotten her to a hospital when I did, she could've died right there on those stairs. If my night had gone well and Isobel hadn't pushed me away, my mother would be dead.

I wasn't sure what to think of that. The world worked in mysterious ways. It left me rattled to the core.

I'd almost lost my mother tonight, and the only reason she was here was because of two nasty women who'd hurt Isobel. It was hard to wrap my brain around that.

Sitting in the chair next to Mom and holding her hand while she slept peacefully after her successful surgery, I thought up every what-if and could-have-been, and none of them ended with a pleasant result. I had no idea why she'd tried to leave the apartment, especially after I asked her to stay in, but that would've led to the best outcome, if she'd just stayed inside.

When I exhausted myself trying to come up with alternate outcomes, I called Justin and Alice. Neither sibling answered their phone, so I left a message for both, letting them know what had happened. I still had no idea how to get hold of the other three, and I didn't even want to talk to Victoria, so I didn't bother trying to find them. I did my duty trying to update them; the rest was on them.

Mom woke about nine the next morning. I'd been dozing, slouching in the most uncomfortable position when I heard my name being croaked. Jumping, I sprang upright and wiped my hands over my face before I realized her eyes were open and she was watching me.

"Mom," I breathed, sitting forward and taking her hand. "You're awake. Are you okay? In pain? Do you need a drink? I'll call a nurse."

I started to reach for the call-nurse button, but Mom waved me silent. "A nurse was just in here taking my vitals." Her voice was weak and tired and her eyes were half-open, filled with exhaustion, but her words were clear and her smile was genuine. "I'm okay," she assured me.

She was far from okay. She was pale, her hip was broken—again—and now we had a concussion to handle. When she coughed, I remembered, oh yeah, and she'd bruised some ribs.

The woman was lucky she hadn't hurt anything

else—she was lucky to be alive—and yet, she was still far from being out of the woods and headed toward recovery.

Unable to stop worrying, I pressed my hand to her brow. When I sucked in a breath over how hot she felt, she waved a hand to dismiss my concerns. "Yes, I have a bit of a fever," she said. "The nurse said she'd be back with some ibuprofen."

I nodded and pushed more water at her. I don't think she was thirsty, but she took a drink to humor me. And then we waited, and waited, and waited. The nurse didn't return until over half an hour later. By then, my mother's cheeks had flushed and a sheen of sweat coated her brow.

"Sorry it took so long to return," she apologized, "but the results from one of Margaret's blood tests came back, and I needed to call the doctor."

I sat up straighter, on full alert. "Is everything okay?"

The nurse wouldn't quite meet my gaze as she focused all her attention on giving Mom her pills. Then she cleared her throat and answered, "It looks as if there could be an infection. The doctor can talk to you more about that when he arrives."

She left soon afterward, and I glanced at my mother, whose head was lulling to the side as she began to fall asleep. I reached out again to touch her brow. I knew there was no way the medicine could work that quickly to fight off her fever, but I swear she felt twice as hot as she had the last time I'd checked. It worried me.

She tutted softly and murmured my name as if trying to reassure me, and then she was out, sleeping fitfully between the occasional coughing.

By noon, I realized there was no way she'd make it home before the next day, and there was no way I would be able to tear myself away from her side, so I called Porter Hall.

Henry himself answered the phone. I'd been expecting Constance or maybe Mrs. Pan, but when I heard his voice, I was a little disappointed Isobel hadn't answered instead.

After explaining to him what had happened and telling him I wasn't sure when I'd be back to work, he was extremely understanding. And yet I still kept apologizing.

"Don't worry about it, Shaw. Your mother needs you. I totally understand. Take as much time as you need."

I nodded gratefully and mumbled a gruff, "Thank you."

My mind turned to Isobel. As it had many times throughout the night while I'd been sitting there, worrying about my mother. Her dad hadn't mentioned her. I wasn't sure if he knew about the outcome of our date, or if he was politely not mentioning it because I had other concerns, but I wanted to hear how she was doing.

Actually, I wanted to hear her voice and talk to her for my own selfish needs. I wanted to tell her what I'd been through and heap all my worries on her, gush how scared shitless for my mother's life I was. But I was afraid if I asked to talk to her and I heard her voice, the ache to see her would grow so strong I'd beg her to come sit with me at the hospital. I needed her, greedily wanted her with me, supporting me through this. I needed her hand wrapped around mine and her soothing rose scent in my nose.

But she was dealing with her own problems, and I didn't want to ask her to leave home if it was too much to ask.

So I simply said, "You'll let Isobel know?"

Her dad answered, "Yes. Yes, of course." And I felt marginally better, hoping maybe—if she was improved from the night before—she'd come to me on her own.

After I hung up, I stared bleakly at my mother's face

while she slept. Her tossing and turning grew worse. Her coughing turned to hacking. And the doctor, who finally showed, shook his head as if to say, *This isn't good. This isn't good at all.*

More blood tests were taken, more painkillers administered, and Mom didn't improve.

I stayed in the hospital by her side for three days straight, only leaving to find food in the cafeteria or to use the bathroom, where I splashed water onto my face as the only way to wash.

By the time Gloria appeared in the doorway of the hospital room on Tuesday, I was sure my hair was a nasty matted greaseball and my clothes—or rather Ezra's clothes—were about to wrinkle right off me.

I blinked at her from bloodshot, exhausted eyes and shook my head. "Gloria? What're you doing here?" How had she even learned where I was?

She swept into the room, her hazel eyes full of worry as she shifted her gaze between me and my sleeping mother. "I went to your apartment, but no one answered the door. A neighbor finally told me about an ambulance they saw the other night, loading your mom onto a stretcher. My God, Shaw." She sat in the chair next to mine and took Mom's pale hand as if genuinely worried about her. "What happened? And why are you wearing a suit?"

It didn't matter that she wasn't my favorite person on earth; she really did seem to adore my mother, so I ignored the suit question and explained everything Mom had been through. I even set my hand on her shoulder when she turned teary-eyed.

"She could've died," Gloria choked out.

I swallowed painfully and nodded. "She's a fighter, though." I turned back to Mom. "She'll fight it off."

"Of course she will. She has something very precious to fight *for*."

When I realized she was referring to me, I sent her

an exhausted glance, not in the mood to deal with any kind of advance from her.

But she merely sighed. "Oh, Shaw." She squeezed my arm. "You look awful. How long have you been here with her?"

I shook my head, not answering, but I was sure I looked bad. My muscles were sore from sleeping and sitting all day in the hard chair at Mom's bedside, and my stomach hurt from eating nothing but vending machine food.

"Go home," Gloria urged gently. "Take a shower, steal a nap, get some real food into your system. I'll sit here with her for a couple hours."

I started to shake my head no, but of course Mom chose that moment to wake from her nap. Gloria I could have easily denied, but when my mother urged me to go home for a while as well, I couldn't tell *her* no. So I left, reluctantly.

I was only gone a few hours. I cleaned up and fixed myself some food but no way could I sleep. Not while my mother was still in the hospital, fighting an infection.

When I returned, Gloria was actually in a rush to leave.

"She slept most of the time," she said, rising to her feet and grabbing her purse as soon as I entered the room.

I paused, blinking at her. Mom was coughing in her sleep, but there didn't seem to be any other reason why she'd chase someone away the way Gloria seemed so eager to leave. But she hurried by me, not even making eye contact as she mumbled a harried farewell, saying she had somewhere to be, and disappeared out the door. She hadn't even given me a chance to thank her for sitting with my mom.

I stared after her, not upset about her being gone but pondering why she'd been so eager to go.

Curious. Very curious.

Then, with a sigh, I turned back to Mom and settled into my chair beside her.

Another two days passed. Gloria never returned, and Isobel didn't appear. I thought about her though. More than once, I was tempted to call to see how she was doing, to tell her how I was doing. But after the way we'd left off on Saturday, I was uncertain how to proceed from there. I missed her, though. I missed her with an ache that struck at the oddest moments. Whenever I felt my lowest, I wanted her there to help me through. Whenever Mom had a good moment, I wanted her there to celebrate with me. Whenever Mom was asleep and I was bored, I wanted her there to talk about books or her flower shop plans, or anything. I just…I wanted her there.

Thursday evening arrived before anyone else non-medical appeared in the doorway of Mom's hospital room. My oldest sister, Alice, peered into the room before she took in Mom's sleeping form and gasped.

"Lord," she breathed, coming closer to gaze down at our mother with wide, surprised eyes. "She really is bad off, isn't she?"

"She's better than she was," I said, not sure why I was trying to comfort Alice. I wanted to be mad at her for staying away for five days. Where the hell had she been? Why had it taken her so long to check in? Did our mother mean that little to her?

But she looked genuinely concerned as she sat next to me, and besides, she was the only sibling to show at all. So I decided I was glad to share some of the worry with her. I filled her in on all the progress Mom had made. She nodded and asked questions, then offered to help.

I nodded, grateful for the support. "I've been away from work for four days." Plus, I needed to see Isobel. "Do you think you could sit with Mom tomorrow?"

Alice nodded mutely, and everything felt better.

It felt better until Friday morning, anyway, when I stopped at the gate to Porter Hall and pressed the button, requesting entrance.

They opened for me immediately, and I drove up the lane between the pear trees, eager to see Isobel, anxious to hold her in my arms and bury my face in her hair.

When Henry opened the side door and folded his arms across his chest, waiting for me as I parked, I blinked, confused. He didn't typically stay home on Fridays. What was even more concerning was the stony expression on his face.

Something was wrong.

"What's going on?" I asked, popping out of the truck and hurrying to meet him.

"Mr. Hollander," he greeted, his voice hard and unyielding, his eyes the same. "Your services here are no longer required. Please vacate the premises and never come back. If you do, we'll treat it as trespassing and have you arrested."

chapter TWENTY-SIX

My mouth fell open.

Shock and confusion mixed with anger. But seriously, what the fuck? I'd just survived a week from hell, almost lost my mother, and still might lose her if she didn't recover. Why would he do this to me?

Offering no explanation, he held out his hand. "The keys to the truck, if you please."

I blinked, not quite able to process what he was saying. After a second of making no sense of his words at all, I shook my head, even as I dug the keys from my pocket. As I dropped them into his waiting palm, I said, "I don't understand. What happened? Is this because I missed four days?"

"Of course not." Henry stepped closer, his eyes narrowed. "I thought I made it explicitly clear to you *not* to hurt her."

I squinted, even more confused. "You mean Isobel?"

He drew in a sharp, livid breath as if offended I would dare to say her name.

"I *didn't* hurt her," was all I could think to say. "I would never."

"Oh really?" he challenged, lifting his eyebrows. "Then explain her rose garden to me."

With no idea what he meant by that, I blew past him, marching into the house and toward her garden.

"Hey," he boomed, hurrying to catch up. I began to walk faster. He latched a hand around my upper arm just as I shoved open the French doors leading into the conservatory. But I didn't need to take another step. All the heads of her roses had been chopped off and lay scattered on the ground like dead soldiers who'd lost a war.

I stood there, frozen, gawking. Air rushed from my lungs. "Who…" I gasped for breath and whirled toward Henry. "Who did this?"

I would kill the bastard. I'd grab him—or her—by the neck and smash his head into a wall for touching Isobel's precious roses. How could anyone be so cruel?

"Who do you think?" Henry said quietly. "Isobel did it herself."

I blinked, not understanding. But the look in his eyes narrowed until I knew it had to be true. His expression was too bleak, too defeated.

Shaking my head, I turned my attention back to the roses. "No. No way. She wouldn't."

"I caught her in the act, scissors in hand."

"But…" My head wouldn't stop moving back and forth, denying it. "Why?" I croaked. "Why would she do this?"

"You tell me." His voice was low and full of venom.

I glared at him. "If you think I caused this, that I did something to make her upset enough to do this? You're fucking insane. I'd never cause her this much despair."

Needing to see Isobel, to learn what was wrong, I started toward the library. But Henry caught my arm, his fingers digging deep into my bicep.

I growled at him. "I'm going to find Isobel." And then I was going to kill whoever had hurt her.

"No. You're leaving. Right now."

I barked out a harsh laugh. Yeah right. The woman I loved was suffering. No one was going to keep me from seeing her.

"Get out of my way." I didn't want to hurt the old man, but he was beginning to piss me off.

"Constance," Henry called, "call the police."

Shocked, I glanced over to find Constance, Lewis, Mrs. Pan and even Kit standing there, gaping at me. Mrs. Pan was crying softly into a tissue, Kit was hiding behind her as if scared of *me*, and Constance held a phone in one trembling hand. Lewis stepped forward, murmuring my name gently as if to call me off.

I just stared at them, confused. "What the fuck is going on?" I demanded, only to turn back to Henry. "Do you really have no idea why she's so upset? None at all?"

He finally wavered, looking sad instead of mad. "I wish I did."

"Then give me ten minutes with her," I pleaded, "and I'll find out. I swear. This isn't about me. It can't be."

But he stubbornly shook his head no. "She doesn't want to see you."

Shards of my breaking heart stabbed into me from the inside. "She said that?"

"Not in so many words," Henry allowed as if not certain himself, but then he straightened and said, "But the meaning was clear. So you are no longer welcome at Porter Hall."

I ground my teeth. "You realize how messed up this is, right? You think I did something wrong, but you don't know what. You think I hurt Isobel, but you don't know how. So you're just…you're sending me away forever? Just like that? Without any proof or explanation?"

"I made myself very clear the first day you came here, Hollander."

"And I'm making myself very clear right now!" I shouted right back, spreading my arms wide. "I didn't hurt her. When could I have? I've been stuck at the hospital with my dying mother. For God's sake, don't…" My chest heaved as I tried to steady my breathing. The only thing that had been keeping me together these past few days was the thought of seeing Isobel again, of her being there for me. And now…now they were telling me that wasn't going to happen?

"Don't do this to me," I begged. "Just let me see her. I can fix everything. I know I can."

When he shook his head, Lewis hurried over to help him contain me in case I resisted. I stared at both men, then I glanced at the women, and I wanted to howl at the injustice of it. Why were they keeping me from her?

Shaking my head, I turned away and left the house. I started toward the truck before I remembered it was no longer mine to drive.

Stewing, I walked back to the hospital. None of this made sense, and it was even more maddening that no one felt inclined to seek answers. I alternated between anger and heartbreak.

I could only guess what had happened to Isobel, but none of the reasons I came up with added up to why she'd never want to see me again.

Determined to find out, I snuck back onto the grounds of Porter Hall at 5 a.m. on Saturday morning to catch her on the lake before she began her run. I wasn't sure if she'd run at five or seven. She'd only adjusted the time to seven after I'd started running with her, so I had a feeling she'd move it back to her normal pre-Shaw time now that I was supposedly gone from her life. But she didn't show up at either five *or* seven, and I hated being away from Mom for any longer than that. So I returned to the hospital.

My mother didn't improve, and yet it was impossible for me to focus all my concern on her. I wanted to hate Isobel for taking that away from me, except I was too worried about her to feel such a nasty emotion.

The next day, I was back at five. It was a Sunday. I didn't know if she ran on Sunday mornings, but I went anyway.

She never showed up.

Alice grew pissed at me. I'd taken off two days in a row and disappeared from 3:30 a.m. to 8:30 a.m. But I couldn't help it. I left again on Monday, needing to see Isobel.

Something in my life needed to go right. Sooner or later, I was going to get my answer as to why Henry had fired me.

My heart leapt at seven on Monday when I finally saw Isobel walking up the path toward the lake, wearing her jogging gear. Seven. She'd kept our running time. For some reason, that gave me hope. I stepped from the shadow of a tree I'd been waiting under and murmured her name.

She slowed to a stop, her stance turning weary. "What're you doing here?"

It broke me to see her on guard. It confused me, and then it pissed me off. I hadn't done anything wrong enough to deserve this.

"I need to talk to you."

She turned right back around and started back down the trail toward the house. "Well, I don't want to talk to you."

"Why?" I started after her. "I'm so confused, Isobel. I have no idea what happened. Are you okay? Why did your dad kick me off the property and tell me never to come back? Why did you vandalize all your roses? Please, just tell me what's going on here."

"Don't," she warned. "Stop pretending to care. Your act won't work on me any longer. It was a good performance; you were very convincing. But it's over now."

"Performance? What the hell are you *talking* about? I don't understand any of this."

She spun around to march up to me and glare into

my eyes. "If you don't already know, then you don't *deserve* to understand. Now get off my father's property. No one wants you here."

I only shook my head. "You don't mean that," I said, desperate for it to be true. "You can't mean that. We love each other. We—"

She slapped me. Hard. Right across the face. Then her finger shook as she pointed at my nose. "Don't you ever say that to me again."

Spinning away, she marched off.

I pressed my hand to my stinging face and gaped after her, shocked and growing more upset by the second.

"But *why*?" I yelled. "You can't do this to me. You can't make yourself become my everything and then turn around and shove me out the door. God…*dammit,* Isobel."

I charged after her, grabbing her arm, and forced her around to face me.

She immediately began to struggle. "Get your hands off me."

"Tell me why," I growled. "Was it because of what those two girls at the restaurant said? You're worried it was true, that I'm only with you because of your money? Was it because I didn't talk to you directly over the phone when my mom got hurt? Why? Just fucking *tell* me."

"Let me *go*." She started to struggle more; her eyes became frantic. I didn't think she was scared, though. How the hell could she be scared when it was just *me* holding her? I'd never hurt her. I loved her.

But her struggling became intense; I feared she'd hurt herself if I didn't release her.

"I said let me go," she screamed at the top of her lungs.

I didn't want to. I needed answers. But I let her go, because shit, she looked scared of me.

It made no sense. I was so confused.

What the hell was happening?

"Why?" I whispered, defeated. Tears clogged my lashes. She was wrecking me. And I didn't even know why. That was the worst part. The not-knowing.

She looked into my eyes, and I swear she felt the same pain I did. But all she did was whirl around and run inside her house.

I stayed outside, just standing there. It was the perfect opportunity for the clouds to open, for rain to pour down on me and drench my soul. I would've remained there, soaked and miserable, waiting for her to return, to tell me this was all just a cruel, nasty joke, or at least explain what was going on. But the morning remained uncommonly bright and cheerful. And Isobel didn't return.

I remained, though, the pieces of my ruined heart scattered around my feet.

Eventually, a police car arrived. That's when Henry stepped outside. I watched him talk to the officer before pointing my way, but I didn't move, just stared at them, bleak and broken.

The officer approached me, pulling his handcuffs from his duty belt. I didn't fight, or argue, or protest as he hooked me up. I just looked to Henry and asked, "Why?"

He actually appeared sad, as if he might feel bad for me. Then he slowly shook his head. "I don't know."

The police officer began to lead me to his patrol car. I glanced at Henry over my shoulder. "Would you, though?" I called. "If you ever found out, would you tell me?"

I think he gave a barely discernible nod. That was all the reassurance I needed. I was sure I could still get her back. I just had to find out what I'd done wrong. It couldn't be that bad. I loved her, worshiped the ground she walked on. How could I have done anything so wrong that it couldn't be fixed?

I didn't think about my mother until they began to book me in. She was still in the hospital. Alice couldn't sit with her forever. Who would stay with her if I ended up not being able to get out of here?

I'd trespassed on private ground. Nothing else. What was the maximum penalty for such a petty crime?

I never found out because they released me while I was being booked in. I never actually saw the inside of a cell. One correctional worker called out to the other who was taking my fingerprints, asking, "Is that Hollander?"

"Yeah," came the reply as the guy kept most of his attention on rolling my pinky across an ink pad.

"Well, stop booking him in. His charges have already been dropped. He's free to go."

I didn't know if it was Henry or maybe even Isobel who'd had me released, but I guessed it didn't matter. They'd both made it explicitly clear I wasn't welcome back.

So…I'd write a letter. That was what I'd do. I'd mail it to her, pour my heart into every word, and beg her to tell me what was going on.

I was already composing it in my head as I returned to the hospital to check on Mom.

When I returned to her room, though, she wasn't there. Her bed was empty, and only Alice sat in the chair beside it, crying into her hands.

My heart stopped. "Wha…?"

Alice looked up. "Shaw." She jumped to her feet. "Where the hell have you been?" But before she waited for an answer, she charged toward me and pulled me into a desperate hug.

I hugged her back, even though I couldn't take my gaze away from the empty hospital bed.

"Where's Mom? What happened?" I hadn't been gone that long. Half a day. She'd been fine last night when I'd sat with her. We'd watched *Wheel of Fortune* together and laughed over some of the words we'd come up with to try to solve the puzzles. She'd been smiling, and her face had some color back in it.

She'd been fine.

"They found a blood clot." Alice hiccupped and pushed some tears off her cheek. "A bad one. It was getting too close to her heart, so she went back into surgery."

"Surgery," I repeated, my skin prickling and then chilling with the strangest sensation. Relief and yet fear flooded me. "So she's still alive?"

"Hollander?" a man in blue scrubs asked, glancing hesitantly into the room.

"Here." Alice and I pulled apart to face him. "Is our mom okay?"

He blinked once, then said, "I'm sorry. No. She didn't make it." He went on to explain more. But I didn't hear a thing after *she didn't make it.*

It didn't seem real.

My mother was dead..

chapter TWENTY-SEVEN

Three days passed.

They were a complete blur as if they flew by at warp speed, and yet each hour, minute and second ticked along too slowly for me to handle. Time was so messed up.

I was messed up.

It was hot, dry, and sunny when we buried Mom. Amazingly, all five of her children made it to the service. I don't know how Alice found them, but they filed into the cemetery just in time for the final farewell to begin. I glanced at them but said nothing. I wanted to be mad that they waited too late to show, except I couldn't summon the emotion.

I was numb.

Mom was gone. My purpose these last six months was done.

What the hell was I supposed to do now?

I'd worked so hard to save her, to make her life better. I was a complete failure.

Jesus, I was going to miss her.

How could my mother be gone? Forever?

After the ceremony, Alice invited the other four to

my place. "We need to go through Mom's things and get all her affairs in order, then decide what we're going to do with everything."

The others nodded. I shook my head. "Do we have to do that *today*?"

"When else will we be together?" Justin asked, sounding way too logical, way too unaffected. I kind of wanted to smash my fist into his jaw. "It's a good idea to get it over with now."

"Does she still have anything left from the bakery?" Victoria asked. "I've been thinking about opening my own shop."

I glared, transferring my anger from my older brother to her. "Are you fucking kidding me? You're opening a new shop with the money you stole from *Mom*?"

Blinking in surprise, she reared back as if I might throttle her, which I actually considered, even though I would never physically touch her. I'd just dream about it.

"You're the reason she went out of business in the first place and had to sell her house and move in with *me*, where she ended up *falling* down the stairs and *dying*."

"Hey, hey!" Bryce and Justin grabbed me and pulled me back, away from Victoria. "Calm your shit down, little brother."

Me? My shit had every right to be turbulent.

I pointed toward Victoria. "How dare she? How dare she steal from our mother and then start talking about what she wants to take before Mom is even cold in the ground."

"Oh, like *you* really deserve anything," Becky sneered. "It was *your* apartment building that killed her."

My heart wrenched, and a spike of guilt dug deep into my soul. That fact had already been haunting me for over a week. I'd known it was dangerous for her to navigate those steps. She'd already fallen on them once, and I hadn't found a new place for us to live.

Becky was right. It *was* my fault.

"Fine." I faced away from all of them so I didn't have to see five of my siblings glare at me as if I'd used my bare hands to murder Mom. "Go through the apartment, take whatever you want. I don't care."

I didn't need any of her things to remember her. I just wanted her back.

I didn't know what was worse: all my siblings browsing through my mother's boxes full of things, remarking on all the old stuff they remembered from their childhood, oftentimes observing how tacky and gaudy it was, or all the neighbors who stopped by with food, telling me how sorry they were for my loss. I wanted to scream at every single one of them, ask why they hadn't noticed Mom lying broken and hurt at the bottom of the stairs. Why hadn't anyone heard her fall and helped her? And why did I feel guiltier with each casserole because I'd been gone and not there for her myself?

When a knock came on the door, at nearly seven in the evening, I about snapped. My refrigerator couldn't hold any more pity food, and my patience couldn't stand another "*I'm so sorry.*" I just wanted to be left alone.

No, actually, I wanted Isobel. I hadn't been able to stop thinking about her. Not while I'd been picking out a casket, or flower arrangements, or watching my mother being lowered into the ground. I'd ached, just wanting her near, her hand to hold or body to hug, her rose scent calming my grief.

I kept wondering if she'd show up to be there for me. I was always looking for her. It was pathetic. She'd pushed me out, let a police officer arrest me to keep me away, and here, she was still the only thing I wanted.

So when I opened the door, and there she was, I

nearly wept from the relief. Just seeing her made everything better. And yet worse.

It physically hurt to look at her. I'd shared so much with her, given her a piece of my soul, pressed my chest directly against her heartbeat, tasted her on my tongue, buried myself deeper in her than I'd ever been in anyone. And I could've sworn she'd given the same back to me. Yet she'd proven me wrong by shoving me from her life.

When I'd needed her most, she hadn't been there.

Seeing her now stirred all that up, and still, I was ready to forget everything just for the chance to touch her one more time.

"You came," I breathed out the word like a prayer of thanksgiving.

Lifting my fist to my mouth even as I stepped toward her, I needed to feel her against me. But then I realized someone was with her.

Her brother.

Ezra glared at me, his eyes narrowed with icy disdain. I returned my attention to Isobel, finally focusing on her face. She didn't look very sympathetic for my loss. Her jaw was hard and eyes were a cold, frosted blue.

Lifting her chin, she said, "I just came to get my mother's mirror back."

At first, I was sure I'd misheard her. She couldn't do that, certainly not today of all days. No one was that heartless. That evil.

She continued to stare at me, though, as if she fully expected me to go fetch the mirror for her. I stared back, positive this was all a mistake. I couldn't have been this wrong about her. Yes, she'd been icy and standoffish at the beginning, but she'd only been trying to protect her own pain. She'd never been intentionally cruel.

But to mess with me on the day I buried my mother…

Who did that?

When I glanced toward her brother and asked, "Is

she fucking serious?" he scowled back.

"Just go get the mirror, and we'll be gone again."

Get the mirror, huh? Oh, I would get the mirror. I'd get her goddamn precious mirror and break it right in front of her. Shatter it on the floor between us the same way she was shattering me.

Spinning away stonily, I left the door hanging open and retreated to my book bag I had sitting on the floor by the sofa sleeper. I still had clothes packed inside, ready to change into after running with her. The muscles in my chest clenched even tighter. I'd never run with her again.

After unzipping the front pocket, I pulled the mirror free, only for the grief to hit me all over again. My knees gave and I almost went to the floor. Such a small, old, scratched mirror, and giving it back was akin to dispensing with my humanity.

What the hell had I done to warrant her losing so much faith and understanding in me?

The anger drained, and defeat reigned.

I returned to the doorway where brother and sister remained, waiting to be reunited with their family heirloom. When I calmly held it out to her between two fingers, she hesitated. There must've been some look on my face that conveyed how much she'd just killed me, but it didn't give her much of a pause. She snagged the mirror and tucked it into her purse.

Then she glanced past my shoulder and into my apartment when Becky and Bryce burst out laughing over something I had no interest in. I kept watching her face as it wrinkled with disdain.

"Sorry for interrupting your *party*," she sneered.

As she and her brother turned away to leave, I crossed my arms over my chest and pressed my back to the doorjamb, watching them go. "If you want to call my scavenger siblings going through all my mom's shit *hours* after burying her to see what they can claim a party, then you're more heartless than I ever imagined."

Isobel slowed to a stop. My blood surged. I hated her in that moment, and yet the idea of her turning around to argue with me made something in me come back to life.

Turn around, that sick and twisted part of me silently begged. *Please, God, just turn back around and face me.*

She turned, and her face was drained of color.

My breath heaved through my lungs.

I wanted to strangle her.

I wanted to kiss her.

I wanted to bury my face in her hair and weep.

"Burying her?" she repeated softly.

"What?" I growled, keeping my back to the doorjamb and arms crossed as tightly over my chest as I could wind them…to keep from going to her, falling onto my knees in front of her and begging her to love me again. "Like you didn't know?"

"I…" A strange sound left her lungs. "I didn't. When…when…?"

"Monday," I answered, narrowing my eyes and trying to figure out if she really hadn't known about Mom. "She died on Monday, while I was being arrested."

She set her hand against her heart and swallowed visibly. "I… Oh, God. I'm so sorry." The words rasped from her hoarsely. Then she turned to her brother, looking lost, seeking guidance.

He took her elbow, looking not so hostile either. "We should go."

Isobel began to shake her head; her chin trembled, her eyes filled with moisture. "But—"

"Izzy, let's *go*."

Ezra turned her toward the stairwell, but just as she started to move that way, something made her stumble back into her brother.

I peered past her to find Gloria arriving at the top of the steps, holding a casserole dish. And though seeing another one of those today was horrifying all on its own, I couldn't see why it'd affect Isobel as strongly as it did.

Until Gloria saw her back.

My mother's friend and the bane of my existence screeched to a halt. Her eyes went wide with recognition, then with horror, before she gasped, "Oh, no," and turned right back around, hurrying down the stairs away from us.

I stepped out of my apartment, alerted to something big happening.

"What was that?" I demanded.

Isobel glanced back at me, her face white, as if she'd just seen a ghost.

I pointed to where Gloria had been standing. "Did you know her?"

Isobel gulped but said nothing. Tears still swam in her eyes and her chin continued to tremble. It was enough to make me want to pull her into my arms and hug all her pain away, except her continued silent treatment pissed me off.

"She *recognized* you," I insisted, stepping closer. Ezra put up a hand to ward me off, but I ignored him, my focus on his sister, whose blue-blue eyes were full of pain and confusion. I shook my head, harboring plenty of my own pain and confusion. "How the hell do you know Gloria?"

There was no reason at all for her to ever have met Gloria, but there was no denying they'd definitely recognized each other.

Isobel blinked. Then she straightened. "Wait, what?" She shook her head, turned toward where Gloria had been standing, only to whirl back to me. "*That* was Gloria?"

I nodded, my confusion growing. "Yes. Who did you think it was?"

"I…I…" She shook her head before blurting, "She said she was your girlfriend."

chapter
TWENTY-EIGHT

My lips parted. "My…what?"

Isobel's eyes were large and horrified. "She...she…"

"When the hell did you meet Gloria?"

"At the hospital," she rushed her answer. "I came to visit. She was there with your mom. She said…she said..."

I shook my head, then pushed Ezra aside so I could see her better. "You came to the hospital?" My voice cracked and eyes misted. "Really?" My lips trembled, wanting to smile, except…except everything was still so wrong.

Isobel bobbed her head up and down. "I wanted to come the first day, but you didn't ask me to. I wasn't sure if you wanted—"

"Of course I wanted you there," I hissed before clenching my teeth. "But I didn't know if I should ask. You said you wanted space, and you acted as if you never wanted to leave your house again. It felt selfish to ask you to come."

"I would have," she said, wiping tears from her cheeks. "I wanted to, and when I finally did, *she* was there. She was there with your mother, and you hadn't asked me to come at all."

"I didn't ask her to either," I insisted. "I didn't even *tell* her what happened. She just found out and showed up. She and my mom were close. I didn't feel as if I could send her away, not when my mom wanted her there. And then she offered to sit with Mom while I went home and washed up. I needed a moment to recoup—just a few hours—I swear, I was only gone a few hours."

How could Isobel have come to be with me during the few hours I'd been gone?

"When I saw her, a stranger I'd never met before sitting with your mother while I hadn't even been invited..." Her entire expression crumpled as she admitted, "It hurt. It shattered me."

I drew in a breath and shook my head. "Isobel."

But she lifted a finger, asking me to let her keep talking. "And then, when I asked who she was, she said she was your girlfriend, and...and..."

"And you just *believed* her?" I asked, disappointed and upset. I'd suffered twice as much as I should have these past few days because she'd taken the word of a complete stranger over everything I'd ever said to her? I wanted to rage at her for doing that to me.

Tears trickled down her cheeks. "She was *there*," she insisted, "sitting with your mother as if she belonged. And she already knew who I was. She didn't have to ask. She took one look at my scars and said, 'You must be the daughter of that rich man he's been working for.' She told me you'd only been kind and complimentary to me because you didn't want to get fired. She made it sound like you'd just been playing me the whole time because of your job and the situation you were in. And I...I..."

Sighing, I closed my eyes and pinched the bridge of my nose. "I'm going to kill her," I said to myself. Gloria was dead to me.

"How did she know who I was?" Isobel demanded, her voice breaking. "How did she know about my scars?"

"I told my mother," I admitted, feeling small. "I told my mother about you, how you didn't like to leave your house after you'd been hurt in a fire." Then I shrugged helplessly. "And Gloria is her friend." I didn't admit that Gloria had been there *when* I'd told Mom about Isobel. It felt worse to admit that, and besides, it didn't matter that much. Gloria had found out because of me, and she'd used the information against Isobel to hurt her.

Shaking my head, I focused on the woman before me. "I still don't understand why you didn't at least confront me about this. She's done this kind of thing before. She's lied to keep other women away from me. If I'd ever thought you two would meet, I would've warned you not to believe a thing she ever said. I would've been able to fix all this. But you didn't even tell me about it. I *begged* you to tell me what happened, and you refused! Jesus Christ, Isobel, why didn't you just tell me? Or…or get her name. Or—"

"I *did* go back to get her name," she said softly. More tears trailed down her cheek. "I left that hospital room, ready to confront you and demand the truth, but I got halfway down the hall before I realized I at least needed to know her name if I was going to talk to you about her. So I turned back."

I wanted to wipe her tears away and pull her into my arms, and yet I wanted to push her back and yell about how much she'd broken me. So unnecessarily broken me.

Pulled in two directions, I narrowed my eyes. "So what did she tell you her name was?"

Isobel shook her head, and another tear slipped down her cheek. "She didn't. When I reached the doorway, your mom had just woken. She saw...saw *Gloria* and smiled at her, then reached for her hand. Then…then she thanked her for being there and told her she was such a good daughter, and she couldn't wait until *you* married her and made her a daughter in truth."

I clenched my teeth and spiked my fingers into my hair. My own mother had unknowingly backed Gloria's lie. The misery of it took my breath.

"They're…they're friends," was all I could think to say before I shook my head, lost and defeated. "Mom is always…" Realizing I'd just spoken of her in the present tense, I paused, waited for the spear of pain to pass, and then said, "She was always saying shit like that, trying to force the two of us together, but nothing—and I mean, *nothing*—ever came of it. I am not and have never been with Gloria in any way."

Isobel nodded, believing me, before she buried her face into her hands and wept. "I'm sorry."

Rage and pain swamped me. I should've been meaner to Gloria years ago and forced her out of my life for good. I should've…I don't know. But it felt as if I could've stopped this from happening. If only I'd done little things here and there differently, I could've prevented this.

Wiping at her cheeks, Isobel drew in a breath and met my gaze, her devastation clear and brutally exposed. "I…I'm so sorry, Shaw. I should've talked to you about it, I know that. But I just couldn't. We'd only known each other a couple months. It was still so fresh and new and…and there wasn't any solid proof behind anything you'd ever said to me. All I had was your word to go on whether your feelings were true or not. You always seemed to back away whenever we started to talk about a future between the two of us. And after the hospital visit, I felt like a fool, a stupid, idiotic fool. I assumed I'd just been so desperate and lonely that I'd been willing to believe the first guy who acted interested. It suddenly seemed crazy that you might've actually loved me back. I never did anything to deserve someone who seemed as perfect as you were."

"Love isn't about deserving," I hissed, shaking my

head. "Because who really *deserves* love? We're all miserable, imperfect idiots who probably need swift kicks in the ass more than anything. No, love is about connection and feelings, and I *had* that with you. I had *all* that with you. I never had it with anyone else."

Isobel sent me a sad, watery smile. "I had the same connection and feelings for you."

I didn't know what to say to that, what to do about any of this.

I wanted to forgive her and pull her into my arms to ease some of the grief plaguing me, yet I couldn't.

I wanted to hate her for what I'd been through the last few days, and yet I couldn't do that either.

Behind me, more laughter trickled from my apartment. Becky loudly started to recount a memory of a time she'd gotten into trouble with Mom. It was more than I could take. I ran my hands through my hair before gripping it with both hands.

"Shaw?" Isobel's wobbly voice haunted me. She reached out her hand.

I took a step away, and she quickly withdrew her fingers.

I swear, watching the agony cross her features after my rejection hurt me as much as it hurt her.

Closing my eyes, I gritted out, "I just need some time. I can't deal with everything all at once."

"Of course," she rushed out. "Yes, of course."

When I opened my eyes, she'd whirled away and was dashing down the stairs.

An image of my mother crumpled and broken at the bottom of those very steps seized me, and instinctively I started after her, worried about her tripping in her haste. Falling. Dying. But Ezra set a hand on my chest.

If he'd been forceful or angry, I would've fought past him. I would've punched him in the eye and caught up with his sister before she left the building. But the guy only looked sad and sympathetic.

"I think you're right about the time thing. Why don't you give it a day?" he suggested. "Take care of everything with your mom, deal with…" He waved a hand toward the opened door of my apartment where my siblings were still inside, spilling out memories. "Izzy needs a day too, to let the reality of what she did soak in. *Then* go see her."

I heard the door at the bottom of the stairs open and bang shut, letting me know she had made it off the steps safely, so I nodded and let her go.

chapter TWENTY-NINE

One day actually spanned into two. My five siblings cleaned out pretty much everything that once belonged to Mom. The only things left were her walker, some clothes no one would ever want, and a bunch of broken bakery remains. I *did* find a chipped cup she used to love to drink from, so I kept that, but everything else, I boxed up and hauled down to the dumpster.

Every time I passed the base of the stairwell where I'd found her, my throat would go dry and my chest would twist with pain. I really needed to move out of this hellhole.

I had no idea what I was going to do with the rest of my life. I hadn't received any word that Henry had rescinded any of the loans or bills he'd paid off for my mom, but I hadn't seen any proof of the opposite either. If I ended up owing him, at least I was free to find a job somewhere that actually paid me so I could attempt to pay him back. I wasn't tied to taking care of Mom anymore, so I was free to do anything now, though that thought made me feel even crappier. Any hardship would've been worth keeping her alive longer.

Besides, without her, I had no purpose. I honestly felt lost, like a wadded-up piece of newspaper drifting in the breeze. It was only a matter of time before someone caught me and threw me into the trash where I belonged.

On Saturday, I fully planned to sit on the couch and drown myself in my misery for the entire day, but I ended up with two visitors. I wasn't particularly happy to see either, but they both surprised me.

Gloria showed up first, just before noon.

I didn't want to answer the door. I didn't feel like being kind or polite to anyone and there was nothing left here for my siblings to take. The only reason I dragged myself from the couch was because I thought it might be Isobel, though I wasn't too sure I wanted to see her either. I still didn't have the energy to deal with the kind of talk we needed to have, and my head wasn't yet in the right place to make decisions about us. But the draw of maybe seeing her again had me opening the door anyway, even as my gut tensed with anxiety.

At first, I didn't recognize the person in front of me. It took me another minute to realize she was even a woman. Her head was shaved, not just short but completely bald, and her clothes were sagging loose, hanging off her in a bland beige heap, kind of like sackcloth. No makeup lined her lips or eyes. It took her saying my name and me recognizing her voice to realize who she was.

My eyes widened. "Gloria?"

After drawing in a deep breath, she smoothed her hands over her stomach and said, "I know what I did was wrong. But I'm sorry, so see…" She spread her arms to show me her new look. "I did all this to show you the depth of my woe. Now you know I'm not lying when I say how very sorry I am."

I blinked at her, stared two seconds longer, then said, "You shaved your own head to get me to forgive you?"

She nodded and bit her lip. "Did it work?"

I snorted. "No. That's the stupidest thing I ever heard of anyone doing," and I slammed the door in her face.

If only that had run her off.

If only.

She smacked her palms against the door, cursing my name through the wood. Then she yelled, "I thought if I became hideous like *her*, you'd finally see me."

Those words hit a trigger. Detonating, I flung open the door and marched out into the hall to loom ominously over her. And she knew she'd said the wrong thing. Her mouth opened to backtrack, but I pointed at her, silencing her.

"Oh, I saw you," I told her in a deadly calm voice. "I saw you all these years; I just didn't *like* you."

When her eyes filled with horror and her mouth gaped, I shifted closer, making her retreat a fearful step in reverse. "But you didn't care what *I* wanted, did you? You never cared what I wanted. If you had, you might not have been such a malicious lying bitch when Isobel walked into that hospital room. You might've realized how much I loved her and *needed* her that day. But no, you only thought about yourself, and you chased her away to fill your own purpose, which destroyed me. You wrecked my life."

"But I thought you—"

"No!" I roared. "You didn't think about me at all. You thought about you, how *you* could step in and pick up the pieces of my poor, pitiful broken heart, then fit me back together into some mold you thought I could fill so I could give you the happily ever after *you've* always wanted. But I can't. I'm not the man you keep trying to make me, and I don't *want* to be."

Her bottom lip trembled. It only angered me more. I pointed toward the stairwell.

"Get out and never come back. If I ever see you again, I will hurt you in ways you never even knew were possible." I'd hurt her the way she'd caused me to hurt.

Even though she'd just backed away from me, revealing her fear, she lifted her chin in challenge. "You don't mean that. You'd never hurt me."

Oh, yes, I would. Maybe not physically, but if I *were* ever to hurt any woman, it would've been her.

"Get out!" I shouted so loud I caused a couple doors to open down the hall and neighbors to peer out curiously. I stepped toward Gloria, lifting my hands as if to strangle her. "Get out."

She yelped in fear.

My fingers shook from the force of my rage. "Get off of my floor."

Gloria skidded a few more feet in reverse.

"Get out of my building." I started to follow her, the intent clear in my eyes. I wasn't sure what I actually would've done if I caught her, but it was a good thing she retreated, turning away from me and hauling ass toward the stairwell.

"Get out of my *life*!" I hollered after her.

As soon as the top of her bald head disappeared from view, I added, "And I hope your hair never grows back."

Less than ten minutes after I slammed my way back into my apartment, another knock came on my door. I was still too hyped up on anger and adrenaline to realize the knock had been far too polite to be Gloria. But I couldn't think who else it would be, so I stormed forward and threw the door open, ready to tell her how much she disgusted me.

When I came face to face with Henry instead, I faltered, stumbling off balance before I could steady myself. He didn't seem to notice the fluster he caused. His head had been bowed humbly.

When he lifted his face, he looked regretful. "Shaw," he murmured, nodding respectfully. "Ezra told me what happened. I'm sorry to hear about Margaret."

I nodded and let out an unsteady breath. "Thank

you, sir."

I wanted to ask about Isobel, but I wasn't sure how.

When he held up a hand where my truck keys dangled, silently returning them to me, I wrinkled my eyebrows, confused.

"Go on," he insisted. "Take them. They were never mine to remove from you, anyway. Isobel's the one who bought the truck for you."

My gaze flashed to him, pure shock reverberating through me.

He smiled sadly. "She didn't want you to know she'd bought you a truck; that's why we made it look like a work truck from me. She was pissed when I took the keys back. So, here. It's yours, free and clear. No strings attached."

Slowly I reached out, taking the keys, even though I wasn't certain yet whether I was agreeing to keep them or not.

"And…" Henry shuffled uneasily. "If you can forgive me for the way I reacted without finding out the truth first, then our deal is complete. With everything you've done at the house, you've more than paid me back for the loans I paid off. Besides, with Margaret gone…well, you just don't owe me anything else. Our agreement is concluded, and your life is your own again."

I nodded, not sure what to say.

But he shook his head. "The main reason I came here, though, was to thank you."

My eyebrows lifted. "Thank me?"

"Yes, Shaw, thank you." He blew out an unsteady breath. "Since I lost my wife and what seemed like my daughter in that fire, I'd felt as if I'd lost myself, too. I thought if only I could be a better person, if I did enough charitable deeds, if I paid my penance for whatever I did wrong to lose them in the first place, I could at least get Izzy back. Year after year, I handed out loans that ended up never paying back, hoping someday, fate would turn back and karma would shine on me again. And then you came into my office."

He gave me a strange smile. "I never really thought it'd change much to bring you into my home and force you around her, but it did. You were the miracle I'd been waiting for. *You* brought my daughter back."

I started to shake my head, unable to accept that kind of credit, but he gripped my shoulder and nodded. "You did. I'm not sure how you did it, but she's a different person now, not exactly the teenage girl I lost all those years ago, but a lovely, amazing adult version of her. And no matter what happens from here on out, I wanted you to know I'm grateful for those few weeks you gave me of her true, genuine smile. I'd never seen her happier than she was with you."

Agony and bittersweet memories of Isobel's smile sluiced through me. I nearly double over from the waves.

Henry kept watching me as if wanting me to say I was over my pain and anger and I was ready to forgive her and move on, but I shook my head. I wasn't sure what I felt. I was still so lost and confused.

"She really hurt me," I admitted.

He nodded, not denying it. "I know. She messed up. Just like we're all prone to do. Her mistake wasn't intended to hurt you, though, it just ended up that way. She loved you the whole time and loves you now. Plus, she's sorry for what she did, and I believe she's fully learned her lesson."

Of course her father would say that and side with her, but his words affected me, anyway. I knew she'd never had any evil intent. I'd always known that. And no one was perfect. But…

Dammit. I didn't know what the *but* was. It seemed like there should be one, except I couldn't think up what it would be. I either pulled myself together and forgave her, or…or what? *Never* forgave her? Never saw her again? Never kissed her again? Lived the rest of my life without her?

All because of one mistake that had hurt my feelings?

A mistake I was sure she'd never repeat.

When I met her father's gaze, he nodded, realizing what conclusion I'd come to. A small smile lit his face. "I'll see you soon," was all he said before he turned away and left me to come to terms with what I'd decided.

It took me another day before I showed up at the front gate of Porter Hall and pressed the button, seeking entrance.

When the gate slowly slid open, I swear, it felt as if I was being admitted into heaven.

I drove up the lane and parked on the circle drive in front of the door where Henry stepped outside to greet me.

Patting my back when I reached him, he nudged me toward the house. "She's in the library."

I tripped away from him before I could catch my footing. Spotting Constance, Lewis and Mrs. Pan peering around a corner at me, I waved when they shot me grins and signs of encouragement. When I noticed the cook and groundskeeper were holding hands, I picked up my pace, jogging through the house until I'd made my way to the library. Happily every afters *could* be reached, and I was going to grab mine with both hands.

When I stepped inside and saw her sitting on the sofa, staring at the bookshelves we'd made together, my breath caught in my throat.

My legs suddenly went shaky.

So I hobbled the last few feet forward and sat next to her on the couch. She didn't acknowledge me but she knew I was there. I licked my lips and glanced around at the library, remembering all the work we'd put into it, all the hours we'd spent together, getting to know each other, falling for each other. And I was freshly amazed by how good of a job we'd done. We made an excellent team. We could make an excellent team for a long time to come if we were willing to try.

And it just so happened I was.

"It's strange to think this room looked totally different only a few months ago. Feels like years ago."

Isobel nodded slowly. "It does," she agreed quietly.

Reaching out, I took her hand without looking at her. Her fingers wrapped around mine before she squeezed lightly. I squeezed back.

Finally, she said, "What're you doing here?"

"I'm here because you're here."

"But..." She shook her head. "How can you ever forgive me?"

I shrugged. "How can I not? I love you. Love forgives. It works through problems. And it stays."

"Oh God." She began to sob, her shoulders shaking, chest heaving, and tears pouring. "I love you, too."

I pulled her into my arms. She curled onto my lap and cried into my shoulder, gripping me as if she'd never let me go again. I hoped she didn't.

"I missed you," I admitted into her hair.

She sniffed and nodded. "I missed you too." Hiding her face as if ashamed to face me, she added, "I don't deserve this. You...you shouldn't forgive me. You have every right to hate me. I—"

"Shh." I stroked her hair. "I could never hate you. Besides, you did nothing wrong."

"I believed her. Then I refused to get the truth from you. If only—"

"If only," I cut in. "Jesus, there are a million *if onlys* I could've done to prevent any of this from happening in the first place. It's enough to drive me insane. But none of that matters because it's over and done, in the past now. We found our way back together and that's all that counts."

"But you had to deal with your mom's death alone. You had to...you had no one."

"Do I have you now?" I asked. "Will you help me through it now?"

She pulled back to look up at my face. Tears clogged her long lashes. "Of course."

I smiled. "Good. That's what I want too. We'll deal with the rest as it comes."

"I love you," she breathed.

And the world was back to where it should be.

EPILOGUE

The bell over the door of Rosewood dinged, alerting me to the entrance of another customer. I smiled even as I lifted my face to greet the new arrival, only for my grin to stretch wider when I recognized him.

"Hey, it's Cinderella."

Ezra's eyes narrowed as he strolled inside. "That's still the lamest comeback ever."

I shrugged. "Hey, if the shoe fits…" Then I pointed and started laughing at my own corny pun.

His glare was dry as dust. "You are so not amusing. I'm seriously thinking about sending my sister to a psychiatrist for falling for an idiot like you."

"What can I say? Love doesn't care about brain capacity." Then I sent him a wink. "Which means there's still hope for you too, buddy."

He sighed. "Just tell me where my sister is."

"I'm right here." Isobel emerged from the door behind the counter that led into her workroom. "I could hear you two bickering all the way from the back."

Nearly three months had passed since my mother's funeral. It'd been enough time for all of Isobel's roses to grow back and for her to build up the nerve to try reentering society again to open her business. What I hadn't counted on was for her to suggest we turn Rosewood into a flower slash custom woodworking shop. Now, along with selling flowers, we built shelves and tables and other assorted woodworks customers requested.

We'd also cleaned out the rooms above the shop and turned it into an apartment where we were currently living together. Henry had grumbled about Isobel moving out, but honestly, we loved it. It might've been a step down for her—er, make that about fifty steps down—but it was pretty much happily ever after for the two of us together. I went to bed deliriously happy each night and woke up just as pleased, with Isobel secure in my arms. And from the grin she sent me every time our gazes met, I'd say she was just as content.

As soon as I saved enough money, I was buying her a ring and asking her to marry me.

"So, what's going on?" Isobel asked as she stopped beside me and rested her cheek on my shoulder. I wrapped an arm around her waist, enjoying her warmth and proximity.

Ezra sighed as if dissatisfied with life, then he moodily picked a leaf off a nearby rose plant that was for sale. "Nothing," he mumbled. "I just needed to see my little sister and de-stress."

Isobel glanced worriedly at me before turning back to him. "The wicked witch…again?"

He rolled his eyes. "Always."

"What'd she do this time?"

"What *didn't* she do would be a better question." He took a moment to watch me and Isobel together, his gaze lingering on my hand that stroked lazily up and down her arm. Then he blinked and focused on our faces. "You remember that Halloween party I wanted to throw for all my employees? The one that's *this* weekend?"

Isobel and I nodded. He'd only mentioned it every time we talked to him for the past month.

"Yeah. Well, she called both the caterer and band,

and canceled them. Just this morning."

"What?" Isobel set a hand on her chest. "Oh my God, why would she do that?"

"Because she's evil," he enunciated. "Pure, unadulterated evil. It took me two hours to find a DJ and another caterer to replace them at the last minute. The party's in three days. *Three* days! It cost me four times their regular rates to do a last-minute job like this."

"Wow. That's pretty cold," I admitted.

"Cold!" he exploded. "It's downright heartless. I can't put up with her much longer. If I have to keep working with her, I'm just going to…" He shook his head and seemed to deflate. "I don't even know. I want to throw my hands up and call it quits, have Dad sell out our portion of the company, but then I think of all the employees stuck there with her, and I can't leave them to handle it alone. I almost think they need me there more than anyone else to keep battling her on their behalf."

I lifted my brows at such a dramatic proclamation. Then I glanced at Isobel to see if I was the only one who thought he was being a little bit too intense. When I found her glancing back with her eyebrows raised, we both burst into laughter.

Ezra huffed and glared at us. "What?" he demanded.

"They *need* you?" Isobel repeated before snickering. "Wow, bro. We didn't realize you were such a superhero. Should we buy you a cape and tights to go with that complex?"

"Oh, shut up," he mumbled moodily, tugging at his tie. "If you worked there, you'd understand."

Feeling pity for the guy, since he was clearly at the end of his rope, I patted his arm. "Don't give up yet, man. I have a good feeling about this. If you stick it out just a little longer, I think you'll realize it was worth the effort." Because it usually was. I only had to glance toward Isobel to reaffirm that.

"I hope you're right," he said, even though he eyed

me as if he totally disagreed.

Isobel opened her mouth to put in her opinion, but the bell above Rosewood dinged again, admitting a new customer.

Even though we'd only been open a month, the guy who entered was a regular. He always ordered three white roses and an apology note for us to deliver to his girlfriend, who worked down the street at the coffee shop.

The three of us hanging out at the counter watched him meander through the woodworking portion of the store first, checking out a quilt rack, then a wooden chessboard table. I have no idea why he always browsed that area before moving to the flowers when he bought the same thing every time he came in. I guessed some habits were hard to break.

"I think that customer's for you, Hollander," Ezra said quietly, motioning for me to approach the man and do my job.

But Isobel shook her head. "Nah. He's here for some flowers."

Her brother lifted his eyebrows. "Oh, you think, huh? Looks like he's interested in the woodworking side to me."

She blinked at him before sniffing. "He's *here* for the flowers."

Ezra narrowed his eyes. "I bet he's not."

"Oh, you are on," Isobel hissed. "What're the stakes?"

Ezra shrugged. "A grand?" he suggested, looking completely sure of himself.

I opened my mouth to warn him not to be so cocky, only to get Isobel's elbow thrust in my side, shutting me up.

Then she wrinkled her nose at her brother. "Oh, no, no, no. It can't be a monetary amount. That's no fun. It has to be something humiliating or—ooh! I got it. If I win, I get to decide what costume you're going to wear to your company's Halloween party."

Ezra sniffed. "Yeah, right. No dice."

"Wow, you must really think you're going to lose," she taunted.

His eyes narrowed. "Fine. You're on. And if I win, you have to work out here in the front—with all the customers—for a week straight."

What Ezra didn't know was that Isobel came out of the back quite frequently. At least once a day. And there was always a customer around when she did it. She was doing so well about not letting her scars hold her back any longer, she didn't need her brother to prod her into the open.

But I kept my trap shut because I already knew my girl was going to win this bet. And she did too. She sent me a glance and we shared a brief knowing look before she turned back to Ezra. "Deal."

He looked smug as he held out a hand for her to shake. But then Isobel looked pretty damn smug too.

Grinning, she turned to me. "So…what embarrassing outfit should we make him wear to the party?"

I smirked, catching Ezra's eye. "Oh, I know the perfect costume for him."

Cinderella's face blanched when he realized exactly what I was thinking. "No," he flat-out begged. "Please, God. No.

Which, to Isobel and me, meant *oh hell, yes.* This was going to be fun.

Next in the Fairy Tale Quartet

KISSING THE BOSS

A Cinderella Story

BEHIND
MONSTER AMONG THE ROSES

INSPIRATION
for Porter Hall, Residence of Entrepreneur Henry Nash:

At the time of writing this story, a very real place called Chestnut Hall Estates was on the market for sale in Georgia for a cool $48 million.
http://www.priceypads.com/chestnut-hall-48000000/# This 17,000 square feet of living space boasted of sitting on 18 acres of land, but it was the collection of artifacts that came with the house that made it so pricey. Some of the statues came from a garden in Versailles. It contained a chandelier from the Civil War era, which brought about the idea of the chandelier in my fictitious Porter Hall coming from a mansion in France that was confiscated from the Gestapo in World War II. Also in Chestnut Hall, there was a bronze eagle from Benito Mussolini. So I stuck that statue in my Porter Hall as well. Shaw helped Constance move it across the hallway to preserve the carpet.

INSPIRATION
for Isobel's Rose Garden:

All I knew when I started writing was that I wanted her rose garden to be connected to the main house and I would love it to look like a gazebo-shaped greenhouse. When I came across this conservatory on Tanglewood Conservatories of Denton, Maryland from an online search, I knew it was Isobel's garden. They converted an old carriage house into a glasshouse. At the time I wrote this, the inspiration for Isobel's garden was #7 in their conservatories portfolio.
http://tanglewoodconservatories.com/our-portfolio/modern

INSPIRATION
for the Rock Cave Pool House:

When I did a search of pool houses so I could describe the one at Porter Hall, I hadn't originally intended to make it a rock cave until I came across this one:
http://ricorock.com/project/residential-custom-rock-work-virginia/ From that point on, the Porter Hall pool house could be nothing else. Note: I'm not sure if there is actually a bedroom in the real rock cave pool house. I'm guessing no.

THE TABLE
Henry David Thoreau's writing desk:

The writing table mentioned in the story is an actual thing. It really is green and looks as if it could fall apart any moment. In the story, Isobel told Shaw her father bought it from the Pratchett Museum, which is a fictitious place. As far as I know, the Concord Museum currently has possession of the table. http://www.concordmuseum.org/assets/4.thoreau_desk.jpg

THE PAINTING

Iron Mill in The Hague by Vincent van Gogh:

This painting is a real thing. http://vggallery.com/misc/auctions.htm It appears the painting was last up for auction in 2007 and was sold for a steal, only 321,600 pounds in London. And if you've never seen the painting of van Gogh's bedroom, here's a replica to help you envision what the room looked like: https://news.artnet.com/app/news-upload/2016/02/van-gogh-bedroom-01-1200x471.jpg

NAMES IN THE STORY:

You can probably tell most of the names were adapted from the Disney version of *Beauty and the Beast.* Belle became Isobel, Gaston equals Gloria, Lumiere turned into Lewis. Mrs. Potts became Mrs. Pan, Cogsworth to Constance, and I originally had Chip becoming Charlie, but I liked how Kip rhymed with Chip. Except Kip was so close to Kit, and Kit Harrington is my absolute favorite actor on the show *Game of Thrones,* so that is how Kit got his name.

Shaw…who knows where Shaw came from! I just liked it. I have this strange compulsion to write enough heroes that I cover every letter in the alphabet. And I noticed I hadn't yet written a hero whose name started with S, so to me, this meant his name had to start with an S! He could've very easily been Sam or Sebastian or Scully, but for some reason, I went with Shaw.

I *can* tell you where the name Hollander came from, though. At some point, I was going to have Shaw and Isobel have a conversation where Shaw talked about his great-grandfather, Gene, who survived the Holocaust. I wanted his surname to be authentic, so I searched for names of Holocaust survivors, until I found a Eugene

Hollander who wrote the book *From the Hell of the Holocaust: A Survivor's Story*. I ended up not writing that actual conversation in the book, but that is how I arrived at the name Shaw Hollander, nonetheless! It's strange how my mind works, isn't it?

ROSES:

I had to do a little research about roses because, like Shaw, I knew nothing. My goal was to name a really rare rose for Isobel to grow, and that's how I came across the name of the "Midnight Supreme Rose Bush" online. The seeds were for sale, and they were supposed to grow black roses with blue tips. That sounded pretty rare—and cool—to me, so I put them into the story…only to find out with a tad more research that black roses with blue tips were a fraud, because they didn't even exist! Gasp, I know! The nerve of them to fool me like that. I then stumbled across this color wheel guide for roses: http://www.rosefile.com/RosePages/ColorsOfTheRose.html so I could learn what possible colors roses really could be. Still feeling deceived, I did a little more research to learn if you could even grow roses from seeds (I know that was a silly worry! I mean, how would any rose get here if at least one didn't originally come from some seed?), and that's where I learned about something called stratification to get a rose seed to take root. I did cheat a little on that part, though. Rose seeds really need to be in their cold/wet stratification treatment for four to sixteen weeks, and I don't think Isobel's rose seeds stratified that long before the baby roses bloomed. I'm such a cheater. Anywho…instead of taking out the fake "Midnight Supreme Rose Bush," I decided to make it Shaw's goof as well, which steered the story in the direction it ended up going!

BURN SURVIVORS:

I wasn't accurate on everything Isobel went through. Aside from hearing problems, she probably would have suffered from vision problems too, and some scarred lungs as well as larynx issues, which would probably change her voice. There might also be the possibility of complications bearing children in the future due to all the chest x-rays and medications she would've had to take. If you want to read some accurate accounts of amazing real people who not only survived burn wounds but went on to do great things helping others, here's a good place to go: https://www.phoenix-society.org/stories. You can learn about the man trapped in a burning nightclub under piles of people, who had to dig his way out, only to get hit on the head by a metal beam and yet still managed to find the exit through the smoke and flames. Or the soldier in Iraq who was conscious the whole time his hands were being burned after his convoy drove over a land mine. He went on to be a runner, just like Isobel. But mostly, you'll learn the support a burn survivor can receive is vast and wonderful, and no one has to go through the years of seclusion that Isobel did. You can always find someone willing to help you if you seek it.

THE FAIRY TALE:

I wanted to learn a couple of the most original versions of *Beauty and the Beast* before writing the book, but it was impossible to pin down where the story originated! The best answer is eighteenth-century France. Some people say the earliest version came from Charles Perrault (who died in 1703), while some say Gabrielle-Suzanne Barbot de Villeneuve wrote it in 1740. In one version, Beauty was the youngest of six children. In another version, she was the youngest of three. But in most versions, the Beast caught someone stealing a rose, so I knew that had to stay.

I believe the 1946 movie adaptation came up with Avenant, a villain who wanted to kill the Beast, instead of Beauty's sisters being the evil culprits. Disney turned Avenant into Gaston, and that's where I came up with Gloria. It seemed crazy for my Gloria to attempt to physically kill my Beast (Isobel), but I thought she could definitely kill Isobel's spirit, so that's what she did.

I liked how the 1978 book *Beauty* by Robin McKinley and the Disney version made Beauty bookish, so I kept that. Plus, I wanted to keep the main theme that a person needed to express their heart and mind to become worth loving, so I used that too.

There is also a mirror involved in the original fairy tale that helps bring Beauty and the Beast back together at the end, so I found a way for a mirror—without all the cool magical stuff involved—to bring them back together at the end of my tale as well. And that's how Shaw and Isobel's story became Shaw and Isobel's story!

Made in the USA
San Bernardino, CA
03 February 2018